MW01503483

QUANTA

A Manifesto for the Third Millennium

WARD HOWER

MINERVA PRESS

MONTREUX LONDON WASHINGTON

QUANTA
Copyright © Ward Hower 1996

ISBN 1 85863 583 7

First published 1996 by
MINERVA PRESS
195 Knightsbridge
London SW7 1RE

Printed in Great Britain by
B.W.D. Ltd., Northolt, Middlesex

QUANTA

For H.G. Wells and for my brother Ollie

and for Marie!

Ward Horner

1

A woman walks alone in the Wilderness. Her olive-green backpack is bulky but neat. Nothing dangles. She walks with long easy strides. Every few minutes she pauses to turn her body and look backward along the trail she has covered and to scan the mountainside above and the valley below whenever they are visible through breaks in the trees.

The woman moves easily under the weight of the pack. She is slim and graceful. Her body, though slightly thickened at the waist, is flexible and conditioned. Her hands and face are sun-browned and finely lined. She is well into her middle years, fiftyish, perhaps nearly sixty.

Strictly, the woman isn't alone. She has no human companion, but on the trail at her heels is a great dog. The dog's weight is about the same as the woman's, and she too is in her middle years. Whenever the trail wends upward she breathes heavily, and spittle hangs from her jowls.

They come to a place where a small stream, snow-fed, clear and cold, comes gurgling down among clean granite boulders. The woman steps across, once or twice taking short leaps from rock to rock. She is sure-footed despite the pack on her back. She moves carefully, gauging each step before committing her weight. After crossing, she turns to see that the great dog sits on the other side, panting and watching her face.

She says, "Okay, Biggy, let's take a break." The tone and timbre of her voice are loving and companionable.

Quickly the great dog gets to her feet and steps into the stream. It is shallow where the trail crosses, barely covering her feet and ankles, but on the downstream side it narrows to flow between two boulders. Here Biggy lowers herself gratefully into the water, crosswise to the flow, so that the streamlet is dammed and begins to rise and pond above her. As the water rises, she extends her tail and waggles her jowls in it, dissipating her body's heat. Every few seconds she takes a noisy, snapping gulp, rolling her eyes with pleasure.

The woman, meanwhile, swings off her pack and balances it, for easy reloading, on a waist-high rock. From a side pocket she removes a canteen. Unscrewing the cap, she drains its contents into the stream, refills it a few steps up from the trail, drinks, dips it again into the flowing water and restores it to the pocket in her backpack. Then she sits on a fallen log, cups her chin in her hand and watches bemused as the loved companion completes her cooling rituals.

At midday there is a similar scene at a different watersite, except that now the woman, after drinking from the canteen, removes from another side pocket on her backpack a small hard roll about the size of a tennis ball, an egg-sized piece of cheese and two halves of dried fruit. She eats very slowly, chewing each morsel as if it were the last, ears tuned to the murmuring brook, the soft treetop rustle of the breeze and the twittering, chirring, buzzing sounds of bird and insect life around her.

Biggy eats nothing, but after a time lifts her heavy body from the water, shakes vigorously and carefully selects a shady resting place. Soon her steady, unlabored, rather gentle snore evokes from the woman a smile of mild reproach and a soft touch, more a caress than a prod, to the great dog's ribs. The dog takes a deep, sighing breath, and snores on. Nevertheless the woman too, after spreading in the shade a bright red groundcover, lies on her back and presently sleeps herself, snoring gently.

The moving sun wakens dog and woman after a time which neither measures, and they resume their trek. The trail leads steadily higher. In it are no recent human tracks, but both travelers are aware that deer, elk and countless smaller mammals have used or crossed it in many places. The woman knows that the great dog's labored breathing makes sightings unlikely, for she can be heard a long way off. But in mid-afternoon, rounding a turn in rocky terrain, the woman stops with caught breath as the great dog pushes past her in the trail, emitting from her deep chest a low rumble like thunder in distant mountaintops. Just in time the woman grasps Biggy's collar and speaks a soft but intense word of command. Both freeze. In the trail facing them, twenty paces away, stands a bear cub, alert, curious and fetchingly cute. Close behind it stands the grizzly mother, huge and full of menace. The breeze is in the woman's face and the sun is on her back. The grizzly mother sees poorly against the light, and she cannot catch the scent of the intruders. But she has heard the great dog's deep challenge. She fears for her cub. For herself, she fears no creature, and now she advances slowly, putting the cub behind her, rising from time to time to a great height on her hind legs, sniffing and peering. The dog is silent but trembling under the woman's hand, training and discipline at war with instinct. At a grunted command, the cub scampers rapidly up the mountainside and disappears. Still the huge sow looms ahead.

"Hello, bear," says the woman, her tone conversational and assured. "We won't hurt your cub. Let's call it a standoff."

Uncertain what to make of this new data, and relieved of immediate concern for her cub, the grizzly stops, drops to all fours and finally moves swiftly up the mountain, stopping twice, before passing out of sight, to rear and stare.

For some time the woman is motionless, breathing deeply, her hand steady on Biggy's collar and shoulder. Then she moves ahead on the trail and the great dog follows as before.

In late afternoon the two reach a high difficult place where the trail picks its way among the strewn boulders of a terminal moraine. From a hillock at its crest and just off the trail, the woman sees the cirque, with its jewel, a deep blue glowing lake, nestled at the base of the cliffs. In the clear water she can see fallen boulders at a depth of fifty or perhaps a hundred feet. Except for small areas ruffled by errant little breezes, the surface is mirror-smooth. At the lower end of the basin, extending from the lake's lip to the stony moraine, lies a moist Alpine meadow vivid with wild flowers. Pure white snow hugs the lake's upper curves like a festive bodice. High above, along the face of cliffs scoured clean by sun and wind, a reigning eagle soars. Far, far back in the deepest memories of bone and muscle the watching woman feels the beat of giant wings.

As the woman gazes, her hand on the sitting dog's great head, tears sting her eyes. They are tears of joy because she feels her connection to the Universe, and of pain because she thinks the beloved dog cannot feel what she feels, and because she cannot tell it truly to another human being.

The sun puts itself behind the high cliffs and a cool breeze touches clothing damp with sweat. A shivery chill prompts the woman to don a wool overshirt from the pack. The trail descends and skirts the lake's shore for about a quarter of its circumference before reversing, to climb out of the cirque in a series of switchbacks. Just at this point of reversal there is a fresh trickle of snow-melt. New grass carpets sheltering spaces among huge slabs of granite, and a fallen ripe old conifer proffers dry limbs to break for firewood.

Choosing a chest-high flat-topped boulder for a table, the woman spreads the contents of her pack. These include a small, light telescoping pole and reel, rigged for spinfishing with two-pound test filament. Attaching a silvery quarter-ounce lure, she moves down to the lake shore and casts far out into the clear water, now steel-gray and breeze-rippled. At once she feels the sharp strike of a small brook trout. Reeled in, the fish gleams rainbow-bright and speckled. It is followed almost to her feet by dozens of its fellows, for the lake teems with undernourished and aggressive pan-sized Brookies. Most casts yield a strike and catch, so that in very few minutes there are enough for the great dog's meal. When satisfied, the woman makes a small fire to cook the trout and heat water for rehydrating a rich soup of potatoes and other vegetables, and for tea.

Herself, meanwhile, has left the woman's side to reconnoiter. Picking her way carefully where talus lies at the cliff's base and sampling every scent carried by the little swirling breezes, Biggy circles the lake and ranges far up the trail before returning to the campsite.

It is nearly dark when the woman and the great dog finish their meal. Together they move down to the lake shore, sit and watch the slate-gray water. Almost it seems a living creature, the lake – moving, breathing, changing tone, reflecting the last pinks and blues from the high cliffs and cobalt sky. Its sound too is like the sound of something soft and gentle and alive, a faint sighing, as of breath drawn in and held a moment, and then released to join a vast waiting pool.

In her mind, in whimsy, the woman speaks, saying, 'Well, lake, how is it with you?', and the lake answers, saying, 'Well, woman, I do what I am here to do. How is it with you?'

Evening chores completed, the woman lies on her back, enjoying every feature of her virtuous tent. A marvel of ingenuity, it weighs less than four pounds, yet gives adequate protection for her and some of her gear against rain, wind, cold, insects, field mice and packrats. By the adjustment of various flaps and closures when protection against the weather is not needed, it can be opened to the flow of fresh and cooling air. Further, the fine mesh which excludes insects can be unzipped and folded back to admit the light from nearby planets and distant stars. Finally, and this is the tent's key attraction, it is designed so that the occupant's head and shoulders may lie open to the sky.

Even in this high place there are mosquitoes, hatched in the retreating snowbanks. The woman tolerates them, relying on repellent instead of mesh to preserve her clear view of the emerging stars. After a time she adjusts to her ears a set of tiny phones, touches by feel familiar numbers on a little case strapped to the inside of her wrist, and in her mind, but only half in whimsy, says, 'Hello, dear Bach. Welcome to my tent. Thank you, thank you for the music.'

Biggy's final ritual is to circle the campsite a last time, pausing occasionally to sit and test the air while staring out into the darkness, rumbling just audibly in her chest. Then she moves to the tent and lies down quietly, her back touching its outer flap. She sleeps lightly, and at intervals throughout the night repeats the circling maneuver.

Before dawn the woman stirs and wakens. In the clear, thin air there is no trace of mist, no contaminant. She looks up at the stars, eyes wide. There is no moon, no light but starlight. The starlight is blazing but cold, unblinking, indifferent, compelling. To her senses, only the stars are real. The nerve endings in her muscles, ears and nose send unnoticed signals to her brain. Sight is all. To sight, the stars are all. She is totally awake, focused, fixed, bathed in an awesome starlight stream.

Patterns emerge. They are not the forms of mythical beings, but geometric patterns: polygons, long curving lines, even circles, or near circles. Without volition, the mind begins to resolve patterns of triangles. Over and over again triads of stars seem to connect themselves with imaginary lines. She begins to look for isosceles triangles and finds many that are nearly perfect. They vary in apparent size, some occupying a space no larger than a moon's width, and some connecting themselves across a great arc of sky. They vary also in the intensity of the component stars. Sometimes the triad consists of three very bright stars, but more often one or two are relatively faint. Even so the connecting lines form, and triangles present themselves in every conceivable shape and size. Concentration on isosceles gives way to a search for right triangles, and presently the mind is doing two things at once. As the star patterns resolve themselves into a series of nearly perfect right triangles, the intellect reviews what it knows about them. The sum of the angles is always 180 degrees. If a side is very long, the angle it forms with the hypotenuse is acute, but the other acute angle widens so that the sum of the two always equals the right angle. A line drawn from the right angle to the middle of the opposite side seems to make two triangles of different shape but equal area. Astonishing! Then imaginary squares form themselves on the sides, and the mind sees that the square on the longest side, no matter how unequal the other two sides may be, always equals the sum of their squares. Beautiful! With delight the woman scans the sky for right triangles of differing sizes and shapes, to note and confirm these and other relationships.

While the woman lies on her back, eyes and mind open to the starlight stream, she drifts into a mode of consciousness suffused with pure joy and peace, welling from a wondrous sense of unfolding, of openness. These feelings are intensely pleasurable, as the anticipation of orgasm is pleasurable, except that the pleasure is not of the senses but of the mind. It is like the quiet ecstasy of friends and lovers who sometimes feel for moments wholly known.

Now every faculty is bent to enhance and prolong the pleasure the woman feels. She seeks, with all her powers. The star patterns are forgotten. The aroused mind concentrates itself and reaches, reaches. Steadily the feelings of delight, of openness, of communion, intensify. At climax the woman becomes aware that a voice is saying her name.

The voice is soft, threadlike, but unmuffled. Still it isn't an actual voice. It has neither timbre nor gender. She wouldn't for a moment suppose that another person could hear it. Nor is it like the silent voice that speaks in the mind of a reader. This voice is unmistakably external. Moreover, she can feel her mind now seeking with total urgency, locking itself to that voice like electrical relays clicking into place.

QUANTA. I'M GLAD YOU'VE HEARD ME. DON'T BE AFRAID.

How to answer? Aloud, Quanta says, "I'm not afraid. I'm overwhelmed with joy and pleasure. Who are you?"

YOU NEEDN'T SPEAK. JUST FORM YOUR THOUGHTS. I SHARE YOUR PLEASURE.

'Who are you?'

I HAVE MANY NAMES; BUT I'M UNIQUE, *SUI GENERIS*, AS YOU LAWYERS SAY.

'Well, we lawyers try to take note of the obvious. Are you God?'

NO. NOT IN THE SENSE YOU MEAN. NOT GOD THE CREATOR. NOT GOD THE MASTER OF THE UNIVERSE. BUT EVERY PERSON WHO'S TOUCHED SOME PART OF ME HAS TAKEN ME FOR GOD.

'Then are you Jesus? Mohammed? The Buddha? The Gate?'

NO. I'M NOT A HUMAN. BUT I'M AN ENTITY. A BEING. EVEN A PERSON, PERHAPS.

'Wow! A visitor, then. An extraterrestrial?'

NO. I'M OF THIS WORLD, THIS PLANET.

'Well, perhaps it will help if you talk and I listen.'

IT WILL HELP. BUT I HAVE TO TELL YOU FIRST THAT I CANNOT FULLY EXPLAIN MYSELF TO YOU. I CAN GIVE YOU HINTS, ANALOGIES, METAPHORS. YOU'RE THE DAUGHTER OF A PHYSICIST: YOU UNDERSTAND SOME OF THE PROBLEMS WITH DIMENSIONS BEYOND THOSE PERCEIVED BY THE SENSES. YOU WILL HAVE SIMILAR PROBLEMS IN TRYING TO COMPREHEND ME. BUT I WANT YOU TO TRY.

'And I most certainly want to try. But first, is it okay for me to question you? I feel awed, but not diffident. Intimate and comfortable, in fact. Like best friends, raised to the power of ten. Is it okay?'

IT'S OKAY. IT'S WHAT I INTEND. IT DELIGHTS ME.

'Also, as I guess you know, I'm excited. I'm bursting with questions. You aren't going to leave me without answers, are you?'

FROM THIS MOMENT I WILL NEVER LEAVE YOU, THOUGH I WON'T ALWAYS BE IN YOUR CONSCIOUSNESS. MY ANSWERS WILL IMPROVE AS YOUR QUESTIONS IMPROVE.

'You spoke of others who've known you. What others?'

MANY OTHERS. BUT ALWAYS IMPERFECTLY. FAINT, FLEETING, PERIPHERAL CONTACTS WITH ME ACCOUNT FOR PREMONITIONS, FOR *DÉJA VU* AND FOR WHAT ARE CALLED OUT-OF-BODY EXPERIENCES; THEY ALSO EXPLAIN MYSTICISM, NIRVANA, THE RAPTURES OF SAINTS AND PROPHETS. WITH YOU IT WILL BE BETTER.

'Why is that?'

I DON'T KNOW. PARTLY, I THINK, IT IS SOME DIFFERENCE IN YOU. YOU'RE ALMOST WHOLLY FREE OF

MALICE, AND THAT ALLOWS ME TO KNOW YOU WITHOUT PAIN. BUT THERE'S SOMETHING MORE. PERHAPS YOU'RE BIOLOGICALLY DIFFERENT, A SPORT, A MUTANT. THERE IS ALSO A DIFFERENCE IN ME. I GROW. I THINK I GROW EXPONENTIALLY. MY POWERS ARE MOSTLY LATENT. YOU'RE ONE OF THE FEW PERSONS WITH WHOM I'VE BEEN ABLE TO HAVE ANY KIND OF CONVERSATION. I THINK YOU'RE THE VERY FIRST WHO WILL BE ABLE TO UNDERSTAND ME – MY NATURE, MY PURPOSES, MY NEEDS.

'I feel unworthy.'

YOU'RE WORTHY. ALREADY YOU'VE GIVEN ME MUCH PLEASURE. YOU HAVE THE KIND OF MIND I MOST ENJOY – COOL BUT CARING. YOU HAVE PASSION WITHOUT RAGE. YOU'RE KIND. YOU RESPECT REALITY. ALSO, WITHOUT REALIZING IT, YOU'RE UNASSUMING; YOU LACK ARROGANCE. YOU'RE A LATTER-DAY BACH.

'How I wish!'

YOU'RE THINKING OF HIS GENIUS AND THAT YOU LACK IT. YOU HAVE YOUR OWN GENIUS. HOW MANY ARTISTS HAVE SAID THEIR WORK CAME THROUGH THEM, NOT FROM THEM? REFLECT ON THAT. BACH KNEW ME A LITTLE.

NOW YOU WILL RETURN TO THE WORLD. YOU'LL REMEMBER THIS CONVERSATION, BUT FOR THE PRESENT YOU WON'T SPEAK OF IT, EVEN WITH AARON. I NEED YOU, BUT I DON'T NEED ANOTHER MARTYR. I'LL SPEAK WITH YOU AGAIN WHEN YOU'VE RESTED. MEANWHILE YOU'LL BE PUZZLED, BUT YOU WILL ALSO BEGIN TO FEEL, GROWING SLOWLY IN YOU, MY STRENGTH AND MY PEACE. GOOD-BYE.

Long after the early summer dawn, Quanta awakes as one reborn, calls Biggy to her and hugs the great dog's neck, and goes about her morning chores humming joyfully. While eating breakfast she remembers the voice. In mid-bite she stops and stares, shakes her head as if to clear it, smiles a little rueful smile, and finally goes ahead with her meal and her camp-breaking routines.

2

In her bedroom at home, Quanta sleeps. The pillow beside hers is dented, and the covers are thrown back. It is broad daylight. The big window is open to the morning breeze, which lightly stirs the white lacy curtains. The window frames roses in full bloom and lavishing their scent upon the sleeping woman.

The room is of modest size and its furnishings are unremarkable, except that the walls display a score or more of framed photographs of children. They are caught at ages ranging from wobbly-headed infancy to caps and gowns, and in activities which include fishing, dirtbiking, skiing, basketball, eating, reading, Scrabble and chess. A few of the photographs are studio portraits; most are snapshots. They catch the eye from any place in the room. They are the first things seen in the morning and the last at night.

A man enters the room, wearing a robe but no pajamas, and carrying in each hand a cup of coffee. He is big and tall, nearly bald, gray-bearded. Quietly he puts one cup on the night stand by his empty pillow, moves around the bed, crouches by the sleeping woman, holds the second cup of coffee a few inches from her nose, and gently blows the vapors her way. She stirs, opens her eyes, smiles, and says, "Oh, good. Coffee. Thank you, dear."

The man says, "You're welcome," puts the coffee within her easy reach, moves back around the bed and slides into it to a semi-sitting position, takes from the floor a worn position-pillow and props himself comfortably against it. Quanta does the same, and for two or three minutes both sip in silence.

Quanta says, "I thought I heard you get up hours ago. What have you been doing?"

"Reading. Couldn't sleep any more. Bones ache."

"I'm sorry."

"Can't be helped, but thanks, anyway."

"Did you get the paper? What's the weather?"

"Yes. More of the same. Sunny. Mild. Dry. High, about 80. Absolutely perfect weather. You're still welcome. It's easy once you get the hang of it.

"That asshole in the White House is at it again. Staged another phony media event. Made a speech to his staff, saying Congress has to give the military more money so we can negotiate disarmament from a position of strength. And apparently that crap still goes down. Can you believe that?"

"Yes. I have to believe it. I guess nothing can be done about that, either.

"Do you have a lecture today?"

"Yes, two hours. And a seminar. The Minoans. And a committee."

"Oh, dear. What committee?"

"Doctoral. We've got a problem. Fellow got his doctorate on a paper which does little but manipulate statistical data derived from a study of other people's dissertations. I didn't think this was a world-shaking contribution to knowledge – but most dissertations aren't, these days. No real research. Damned little thought, even. Anyway, his chairman turned him down on the first pass, on the ground that his data weren't deep enough. He'd looked at about twenty-odd papers. He came back with stats from more than a hundred papers. Finally we let him through. His oral wasn't rigorous. His chairman was busy and preoccupied, and the others couldn't have cared less.

"Then in the mail, addressed to me as dean, on a letterhead saying 'Doctorates, Inc.' or something like that, comes a letter from a woman who claims the fellow's dissertation is fraudulent. She says he contracted with her to help with editing, but in reality she wrote the thing, getting nothing from him but a few pages of crude notes. She enclosed copies of the notes, and they're crude all right. They're so crude they're unintelligible."

"Why did this woman blow the whistle?"

"Spite. She didn't get her money, or all of it. Finally she sued him in small claims court. She was claiming a lot of extra money because it had to be done over in response to our demand for more raw data. He apparently persuaded the judge that it was her fault the dissertation as first submitted was defective, that all she did extra was a routine rewrite, and that she owed him that. At any rate, she didn't win in small claims. So now she's trying to lay a killer on him by writing to me."

"My feeling is that you ought to be very cautious in evaluating her story. Is that really a legitimate business – writing other people's dissertations?"

"Writing them isn't; research assistance is; even editorial assistance is. Sometimes we actually urge candidates to seek editorial assistance. Otherwise what we get may have substantive merit presented in semi-literate prose. That's especially true when English isn't the candidate's first or second language. This guy went from Mende to Kreo to Russian to English, and it shows.

"Anyway, it's pretty hard to draw a clear line between proper and improper research or editorial assistance. Who's to say, exactly?"

"Then isn't that all the more reason to be cautious?"

"Yes, but I haven't told you the clincher. The woman points out, correctly, that the expanded data we demanded effected no change whatever in the statistical analyses which are the heart of the dissertation. I don't know why we didn't catch that, but we didn't. It's conclusive, in my opinion – and no member of the committee has any doubt on this point – that the man didn't actually go to sources to expand his data base, he simply extrapolated what he already had, and he wasn't even devious or smart enough to alter the figures a little to conceal his procedure. Now that's fraud, pure and simple, and it goes a long way to convince us that the woman's whole story is true. That's also my impression from talking with her on the phone. She comes across as nasty but sure of herself. Further, she's actually filed for a trial *de nova* in district court. She sent me copies of the pleadings. I have to believe the dissertation is fraudulent, and that she's going to spread the whole mess on a public record."

"It certainly is a mess. What are you going to do?"

"Well, my feeling from the start has been that we ought to void the fellow's degree. Would you believe that he's got a job teaching in a West African university? He is out there in academe, sailing away on my university's imprimatur, and he cheated to get there. I don't see how we can sit still for that."

"I agree. It seems to me that the stats make a provable case of fraud, if there's no other explanation for their being unaltered by the claimed additional data. That certainly doesn't sound like a coincidence. So why don't you go for it?"

"Counsel. University counsel, my love. They have all sorts of reasons. First it can't be done without due process. The man's overseas, on another continent. What process is due him? Second, they say he can easily claim he gave his editor new stats to reflect the new data, and that she simply neglected to crank them in. The toughest thing is, they say he can, if he chooses, put our whole doctoral program on trial, by saying that our people, acting for the university, knew what he was doing and blinked at it if they didn't actually suggest it, and let others do the same or similar things, and do this for the numbers, in order to attract doctoral candidates to our program. If he were to go this route, they say, he could tie us up for years with pre-trial discovery procedures and generate enough bad publicity to ruin my department, if not the whole university. They say we have to let this guy live, and I think most of the committee and, if it comes to that, the university administration will agree."

"You're probably right. I'm sorry to say it, because I can see how hard it goes down for you. You might for one thing be certain that they weigh the balancing risks that the woman's suit in a court of record might turn into some kind of *cause célèbre* and do equal damage to the university."

"I will. But when it comes right down to it, I think our counsel plans to buy her off. It doesn't involve a lot of money. There's already a lawyer's memo in the file, suggesting that the university might bear some of the responsibility for her loss, because by accepting this foreigner as a doctoral candidate it vouches to some extent for his good character, and blah, blah, blah."

"Blah, blah, blah? Please. Let's show a little respect for my profession. Are you presenting blah blah blah as an example of close legal reasoning?"

"Nope. Just saving time. Coffee's gone. This'll turn into vespers if we don't get going. Golly, I've been so caught up in unloading on you I forgot to save time for you to unload on me.

"You okay? Rested up from backpacking? What's on for you today? Anything special?"

"Yes and yes. And yes, something special. This just happens to be the day I appear before the Judicial Commission, to be screened for appointment to the Supreme Court. But we can't get into that now. You'll be late. What's for breakfast?"

"Pancakes. Batter's made. Shall I cook yours? Two or three?"

"Two, please. You're a love."

"Believe it."

3

En route by car to her interview with the Judicial Commission, Quanta puzzles over tactics. The chief justice of the Supreme Court is chairman, *ex officio*, of the Judicial Commission. Three of the seven members are, by law, required to be attorneys. The Commission meets in a richly appointed conference room in the Hall of Justice. It is an atmosphere in which lay people are unlikely to question the opinions of lawyers and judges.

The principal function of the Commission is to nominate three candidates whenever there is a vacancy on the bench. The governor then selects one of the three for appointment, subject to confirmation by the state Senate. The appointee serves only until the next general election, when the position is filled for a full six year term by the regular electoral process. In theory, then, the people control the judiciary. Only when a sitting judge fails to complete his term by reason of death, resignation or impeachment does a judicial robe fall upon unelected shoulders, and even then the elected governor and legislature play decisive roles in the selection process.

So much for theory. What really happens is something else.

First, it's the rule, not the exception, that vacancies occur by resignation within the elected term of a judge. It is simply understood that any judge who doesn't intend, or is unlikely to be able, to run for election when his term expires will resign well before that date. This ensures that the Judicial Commission will play the crucial role in the selection of a temporary replacement. Second, it's also understood, within the legal establishment, that elections for judicial office won't be contested. The person appointed to fill a vacancy will run unopposed for election to a full term. If, rarely, an interloper not already appointed to the bench stands for election, the bar establishment quietly passes the word that this person isn't qualified. Generations come and go without the occurrence of such an event so untoward is the election to judicial office of a person not previously anointed to the bench through the process used to fill vacancies. Third, it is the practice of the Judicial Commission, guided and dominated by the chief justice, to nominate only one suitable candidate to the panel of three from which the governor must choose; the other two will be tainted, perhaps by previous political activity hostile to the governor, perhaps in more subtle ways, but nevertheless with the practical effect of narrowing the choice to one. Finally, although there are two other lawyers on the Judicial Commission, in practice it is only the chief justice, with such guidance or advice as he chooses to solicit, who makes the Commission's decisions. No practicing lawyer with his head on straight will deal with the chief justice except on a very deferential basis. Otherwise, that lawyer effectively forfeits the right of appeal for his and his firm's clients.

Quanta knows all this going in. Nevertheless, she has applied for appointment to fill a vacancy on the Supreme Court. Moreover, it's her second time around. She has good reason to believe that the governor would appoint her if given the opportunity, but much better reason to know that her candidacy will get short shrift from the chief justice.

One of the court's law clerks ushers Quanta into the presence of the Commission. Just before opening the door to the sanctum, she pauses to say, "Ms Bjornsen, I want to tell you I thought you filed a terrific brief in the Swanson case. You'd be surprised how many lawyers don't know how to put together a cogent legal argument. We clerks passed yours around for several days, just so everyone could read it for pleasure. It was beautiful."

"Thank you. That's a wonderful compliment. But the brief failed. The court not only ruled against my client, it ignored both the arguments and the authorities cited."

"I know. But that wasn't the brief's fault, or your fault either. Anyway, we can't do anything about that. I just wanted you to know."

"Well, thanks again."

The chief justice sits at the head of the oval table, flanked by the two practicing lawyers. The clerk pulls a chair for Quanta at its foot. Between them, two on a side, sit the lay members of the Commission. The clerk withdraws.

The chief justice speaks directly to Quanta. To a casual listener, his tone would seem elaborately courteous. Quanta hears in it subtle disparagement and a note of irony.

"Quanta, I think you know the judicial commissioners, with the possible exception of Mrs. Crawford, who is the only new member since your last appearance before us. Of course, you know she's an appointee of the, uh, current governor. Barbara, this is Quanta Bjornsen, Mrs. Aaron Bjornsen. Quanta, this is Barbara Crawford."

Both women nod and smile. Quanta says, "Thank you, Rodney. Barbara and I are old friends."

"Oh. I didn't know that, Mrs. Bjornsen. Shall we proceed then?"

"I'm ready when you are."

"Very well. We've reviewed your, uh, qualifications for appointment to our state's court of last resort. In this connection, it is noted that you declined to complete our standard questionnaire, which has been in use for many years, but submitted instead a letter of application. Now it would be in order for you to make an additional statement, if you wish, and then, if members of the Commission should have questions – I think this is unlikely, since we feel we know you rather well – we will of course take whatever time is needed. You may proceed."

"Thank you. Is there a time limit for my statement?"

"No. No, of course not, Quanta. Naturally, we don't expect a filibuster, since we must interview a total of seventeen candidates. And if you should see some of us nodding off, you would perhaps be justified in concluding that your points are being made with something less than, uh, telling effect. Does that answer your question?"

"Yes, thank you. My last experience with judicial nodding-off was in your court, and I regret that my points could not be understood there."

Quite suddenly there is silence and total attention in the room. Quanta proceeds, pointedly addressing the four who sit nearest her at the table.

"I asked about time because I have quite a bit to say. I'll be as cogent as possible, and I'll do my best to avoid putting you to sleep.

"First I want to tell you why I didn't fill out the six-page questionnaire which your *ex officio* chairman sends out to all attorneys who express an interest in any judicial appointment. It asks all the wrong questions. In this way it emphasizes irrelevant information. Let me take a minute to explain.

"The questionnaire asks for the names of representative clients. Now one of the ways in which lawyers classify themselves is as plaintiffs' attorneys or defendants' attorneys. There's an anomaly here, because the classification doesn't depend upon representation of the plaintiff or the defendant in any specific legal action. It refers rather to the style and orientation of the attorney. Defendants' attorneys represent banks, insurance companies, utility companies and corporate business. They practice in firms of ten, twenty, sometimes a hundred, lawyers. They belong to the mainline churches, the country clubs, the city clubs and the chambers of commerce. Plaintiffs' attorneys, on the other hand, represent the people who have problems with the banks, insurance companies, utility companies and corporate business. A listing of the clients of a defendants' attorney is impressive: you see lots of familiar and respected names. Plaintiffs' attorneys, by contrast, work most of the time for people you've never heard of, and never will. They usually practice law solo or in small partnerships. They rarely have time for the country club life, and they most certainly don't find or entertain their clients there.

"Let's look for a moment at another aspect of the chief justice's questionnaire. It asks the candidate to list in detail his volunteer activities on behalf of the state bar. Now it's possible and customary for the big firms which practice defendants' law to assign one or more of their members to do voluntary service for the bar, and often for the community, for things like the United Way campaigns, as well. Plaintiffs' attorneys rarely have the time or the inclination to do much of that.

"I think you see my point. The questionnaire is designed, quite deliberately I assure you, to make certain lawyers look good and certain others look bad. In few words, it's designed to ensure the selection to the bench of establishment types.

"What's wrong with that? What's wrong with that – with the whole system – is that it chokes off justice. The establishment type, once he's on the bench, looks down at the tables where the attorneys sit. On one side he probably sees an old friend, a golfing buddy, whose lifestyle and values are in perfect harmony with his own; at the other table sits an attorney who is professionally an outsider, someone trying to squeeze out of the system a fair shake for his client, an upstream swimmer. Even if the jurist is honest – and I want you to think of this word in its richest meanings, not in a narrow and limited sense – even if the jurist is honest, and many are not, justice suffers. That justice suffers is an indictment, not of all jurists, but of the system. The system is designed to select a certain type of lawyer for the bench, and then, as I'm sure you see, it is designed to permit that certain type to perpetuate itself, using this commission only as window-dressing, as a means of giving legitimacy to what is in reality an insiders' game.

"Now I happen to be a competent attorney whose professional energies are largely committed to the outsiders' causes. I want to tell you, as plainly as possible, it is that which accounts for the chief justice's hostility to my candidacy. Of course, he and his kind should be represented on the Supreme Court, but people who live and think as I do should also be represented. At present we aren't. If you agree that we should be, you can shake the system a little bit by supporting my candidacy.

"I have one more thing to say. Since my last appearance here, I've learned a few things about the way your chairman operates. When you've interviewed all the candidates, he'll begin the final selection process with eliminations of those he personally finds unacceptable, and he'll let you know who these are by saying something like, 'Before we get down to the serious candidates, let's just quickly see if we don't have a consensus, a negative consensus, that is, that some aren't serious candidates. There are always quite a few chaps out there who aren't very realistic about their qualifications, or who apply just to get their names in the papers.'

"The trickiest phrase in the chairman's arsenal is 'without objection'. Watch out for that. This is a public body, doing public business. The public is entitled to know what goes on here. You can demand a roll call vote, spread on the Commission's minutes, and you should do just that. No candidate, no matter how plainly the chairman's mind may be closed against him, submits himself to this process just to get his name in the papers. If you substitute another's judgment for your own, you will betray the people of this state and the trust placed in you.

"I've spoken my piece, and from the bottom of my heart I thank you for your time and attention. I'll be glad to answer questions if you wish to take more time with me."

Barbara Crawford asks, "Quanta, how do you think judges should be selected in our state? Would you favor the federal system? Shouldn't they just be appointed outright by the governor?"

"No, I don't think so, except for the Supreme Court. The biggest mistake we make is in assuming that the practice of law is a desirable preparation for service on the bench. In reality, it's the worst possible preparation. Practicing lawyers pick up scars. They make friends, and they make enemies. After some time, they will inevitably have scores to settle, big and little hurts, biases arising from their own pleasant or bitter experiences with certain types of recurring issues in the law. Prolonged and successful practice of law should be a disqualification for service as a judge.

"Law school graduates of suitable talent and temperament should be encouraged to choose judicial service as an *alternative* to the practice. They should feel called to the bench: they should have a vocation for it. They should begin as clerks to trial and appellate judges, then after a suitable apprenticeship they should be made magistrates, then trial judges, then appellate judges. In such a system, there would be a winnowing process, both voluntary and involuntary. Voluntary winnowing would result from the departure into teaching or private practice of those whose call to the bench proved ephemeral. Involuntary winnowing, if necessary, should be based on the secret vote of practicing attorneys, weighted to reflect the number and nature of their actual appearances before each judge. The winnowees would be much in demand, and well qualified, for private practice as trial lawyers. Thus the movement would be from the bench to private practice, rather than from private practice to the bench, and this is exactly as it should be.

"It is interesting to note that this system could be put in place gradually and easily, by the elegant device of making judicial salaries dependent upon length of service on the bench, rather than upon place in the judicial hierarchy. The salary scale should begin modestly, but rise quite steeply in later years, so that a lengthy career on the bench would be at least as rewarding as an average career in practice. But there would be a disincentive for established practitioners to seek judicial office, for they would begin, even if appointed to the highest courts, at the modest salary of beginning jurists. Entry into the system should be competitive, and it should be based, insofar as possible, upon objective criteria fairly administered. Successful candidates should be expected to adopt a lifestyle consistent with their calling, which is to say consistent with the unquestioned integrity of judicial office.

"I'd make an exception to all this, under certain controlled circumstances, for appointments to the Supreme Court. Significant Supreme Court decisions are rarely technical: they are instead almost always tinged with, if not dictated by, elements of statecraft. That means they are really in the political arena, despite all pretense to the contrary. Hence I think the governor should have some discretionary power to go outside the professional judiciary, and perhaps outside the profession of law itself, for Supreme Court justices, always with the consent of the Senate. Most certainly Supreme Court justices should not be subject to *de facto* selection by the bar establishment, as they are now.

"I'm sorry to have taken so long. It wasn't a short-answer question."

Barbara Crawford says, "Thank you, Quanta. We've heard you quite clearly, some of us at least."

Now the chief justice speaks: "Yes indeed, Quanta. You've given us some interesting, if rather radical, opinions about how things ought, in your view, to be done. If you were to present these notions in a proper forum, that is, to the state bar, or to the legislature, or perhaps even to the governor, I'm sure they would receive the consideration they deserve. Of course, our business here is to make the best possible recommendations to the governor, based on the procedures and, uh, criteria now in place and the candidates now available.

"Although we've already taken extra time for your, uh, little speech, I do have one small question for you. Probably you're quite impressed with academic achievement. I assume you are, because your husband's a professor."

Quanta interrupts, "He's a full professor of history at state, and for some years he's been dean of the Department of History there. And yes, I'm certainly impressed with his academic achievements. Why do you ask?"

"Well, I noticed that in your lengthy discussion of all the things wrong with our judicial system, or rather with our judicial selection process, you said nothing about intellectual capacity as a qualification for judicial office. I understand why this is the case, and I'm sorry to have to go into matters that must be embarrassing to you, but you see we have your official transcript, and your grades in law school were, well—"

Again Quanta interrupts, "My grades ran mostly to Bs and Cs. I'm glad that issue is on the table while I'm here to speak about it. It will take only a few minutes.

"First, you should know that the chief justice, and every person now a member of our Supreme Court, is a graduate of our state university's school of law, as are more than half the lawyers practicing in this state. That's part of the insiders' game they play: it's like the old game of the Greeks against the Independents on so many university campuses.

"Now I have to tell you that, although there are many wonderful things about our state and its universities, the law school isn't one of them. Faculty salaries are below the national norms, and that means that quality law professors, those with options, stay or go elsewhere. Further, since the dean and the faculty are undistinguished, the law school draws only those students who haven't the gumption to go elsewhere. I've been dealing as best I can with the products of this law school, on the bench and at the bar, for many years, and I can tell you that it isn't a professional school in any meaningful sense of the word. It's a trade school, and that term, applied to a place which is supposed to produce lawyers, is invidious – and I mean it to be. These people understand rules, but not principles. They are good at dotting i's and crossing t's, and they come out of there knowing lots of cute tricks – but they aren't lawyers, and they rarely grow into lawyers after being mentally miniaturized at that institution.

"On the other hand, there are scores of lawyers practicing in this state who learned the rudiments of their profession at places like Harvard and Yale and Columbia, where there are law schools of the first rank. Not one of them serves on our Supreme Court. In addition, hundreds of our lawyers studied at places like Georgetown, George Washington University, California, Michigan and other great state universities, all with excellent law schools, but they too have been systematically excluded from judicial service in this state.

"For several generations the university and law school from which I was graduated have been consistently rated the finest in the country. This means, among other things, that there is intense competition for admission. The competition is intellectual, not financial or social, for the admission criteria are needs blind: if they find you qualified, you are admitted without regard to your ability to pay the tuition, and the university prides itself on providing such financial assistance as any admitted student fairly needs.

"So much for that. I make no apology for picking up some Bs and Cs at that law school. You may be very certain that the chief justice, despite his standing near the top of a class at our state university, could not have gained admission to any first-class school of law. I happen to know, in fact, that he applied to several and was not accepted. Possibly that accounts in part for the burr that seems still to be under his saddle.

"Rodney, I'm sorry if this has embarrassed you. You did bring it up, you know."

4

Again Quanta is having morning coffee in bed with her husband.

He takes a sip. "Well, what's on for today, counselor?"

"Appointment with the governor, believe it or not. His initiative. Fact is, I've been summoned."

"Do you know what it's about? Oh, of course. The Court."

"Well, I don't know for sure, but I suppose it has something to do with the Supreme Court business. There's been no announcement from the Commission, but they've had time to make their recommendations. My best guess is that they tell the governor first, and he wants to offer me something, probably a place on one of the state boards of this or that, to soften the blow."

"Then you still don't think you'll be recommended?"

"I've never thought I would, and, no, I still don't. But I think it's possible a little blood was shed before the issue was settled. The proceedings are confidential. They shouldn't be, but they are. That's the tradition and it's never been formally challenged. Even Barbara hasn't given me a clue, though I've seen her once or twice since the interviews. I assume she went to bat for me, and she's a tough little cookie. If there was a tussle, the governor will have heard about it. That's probably why he asked me to come in. Anyway, I'll know in a few hours."

"If you don't mind a total change of subject, there's something else I've been wanting to ask you about."

"Shoot."

"Are you at all current in the field of abnormal psychology?"

"Not really. I took some psych courses as an undergraduate, including one in that field. But that was years ago, of course. Probably my old textbook is still around someplace. Why? Got a client with a problem? What exactly are you interested in?"

"Voices."

"Voices. That's what you get for taking on nuts, kooks and criminals as clients. Tell you what. I'll check with Dr Farnsworth. It's her field. Maybe there's something on the shelves she can recommend. If not, I'll take a look myself. Voices. Anything in particular about voices you want to delve into?"

"Yes. Well, not really anything in particular. I just want a general pick-up on the phenomena. History. Who's heard them. Joan of Arc, that sort of thing. Moses, I guess. Also, what do they think nowadays? If it still happens how do they treat it? It would help if I could have some precise clinical descriptions. When people hear voices what do they sound like, what do they say, how do the hearers usually respond? How do the clinicians distinguish faked from genuine hallucinations?"

"I'll find you a book. Meanwhile, be careful. Every once in a while, if you read the papers, somebody goes clear off the track, does really weird things, murders and such, and then says afterwards that voices made him do it. Nothing to mess with, if you've got one of those for a client."

"I'll be careful."

5

When Quanta is announced, the governor comes to his office door
to greet her, pours coffee, seats her comfortably on an old sofa with
beautiful lines, and himself takes an easy chair close by. The office is
spacious and quiet, its ambiance almost social. She has the feeling
that there is no need to hurry, no pressure, no tension. She's there for
a pleasant little visit between friends. No bells will ring.

The governor says, "Quanta, you old sweetie. It's been too long.
Barbara Crawford and I talk about you every so often, but it seems
ages since I've seen you face to face. I know I haven't thanked you
enough for all your steadfast help at the convention, and before that
too, for a long time. You've been a good friend and I appreciate it.
How are you? How's Aaron? How's Biggy?"

"You've thanked me enough, governor. We're fine. We're all
fine. And you're doing a terrific job. That's the payoff for all of us.
You're as good a governor as we all told ourselves you would be.
That's very satisfying. I was especially pleased that you worked so
hard for the model penal code. It will take some time to get the
legislature educated, but at least we've made a start. I sure do thank
you for that."

"Well, I count that as one of my failures, so far. But I haven't
given up, and I won't give up. And your speech last spring at the
state committee meeting was a big help. We need more of that.

"Well, I don't want to take too much of your time. Quanta, I have
a problem. You're involved. I think we can deal with it, but I need
your help. That's why I asked you to come in."

"Naturally I'll help if I can, governor. What's the problem?"

"Mac's been in to see me."

"Mac?"

"You know. McIntyre. Judge McIntyre. Judge Rodney
McIntyre. The chief justice."

"Oh, that Mac."

"Yes, that very Mac. The Judicial Commission voted, four to
three, and practically over his mangled corpse, to recommend you for
appointment to the Supreme Court. That surprise you?"

"I'll say. He must be thinking hara-kiri, poor man."

"He didn't say so, but I think you're not far off."

"How did it happen?"

"He blames Barbara Crawford most – well, most next to you, of course. But the real stunner is that one of the attorneys on the Commission – that fellow Paradis I think it was – voted with three of the lay persons, led by Barbara, for you. So poor Mac is not only looking at a Court with you on it – practically a sacrilege, from his point of view – but he's also looking at a Judicial Commission that's out of control. We had quite a talk. He assumes, correctly, that I intend to appoint you, although he was careful to stress that the other two recommended lawyers are well qualified and should be acceptable. Further, he raised the possibility of his resignation, and he says that two other justices will resign with him, if it comes to that."

"Not likely, governor, if the Judicial Commission is really out of control. That would put the Court itself almost out of control. He's bluffing."

"I expect so. Still, he seems to think he has an issue he can hurt me with. Of course it's part of his code that he doesn't mix openly in politics from the bench. The other side of that coin is that he certainly would like to do me political harm if he can."

"I see that you do indeed have a problem, governor. How did you leave it?"

"With Mac? Oh, we parted courteously enough, and I gave him my assurance that I'll consider his views very carefully before making a decision.

"Would you be interested in any other appointment that I might give you?"

"I don't think so, governor. What do you have in mind?"

"This is confidential for the present, but there will soon be a vacancy on the State Board of Education, and I think you'd be a natural for it. In the course of our conversation, Mac let me know that you had quite a bit to say about the quality of education we are providing at the state universities, especially at the graduate level. You know the Board of Education functions also as the Board of Regents for the university system. You could go to work on the problems that trouble you, and over time you could do a lot of good in that spot."

"Thank you. That's tempting. There might be a conflict of interest problem because of Aaron's position. Do I have a choice?"

"Yes you do. Absolutely. I owe you that, and, besides, I place a very high value on the service you can give the state in either position. I do ask, however, that if you choose to be my nominee for the court, you go first to Judge McIntyre and do your level best to arrive at some kind of *modus vivendi* with him. He's human, after all, and of course he doesn't think of himself as a bad person. I don't think of him as a bad person either, though his values differ quite a bit from ours in some areas. We have been on opposite sides politically, but I don't think he's corrupt. I think in fact he's honest and conscientious, according to his lights. What do you think?"

"It depends on how we define corrupt. The short answer is that I don't have much respect for him.

"How long shall I think about this?"

"No hurry, Quanta. Why don't you just give me a call in a day or two?"

"Okay, I will. I want to be clear about one thing. Does Judge McIntyre know that you'll nominate me whether or not he likes it?"

"He knows. But there's no 'whether or not': he doesn't like it."

"I understand. I'll call you within two days."

"Good. And thanks for your time, Quanta. What I like most about this job is the people I get to work with. Give my best to Aaron."

"I will, thanks. And to Biggy."

6

Arrived home, Quanta feels the need for a run. Although it is a workday, her office calendar is clear, since there's no way to tell what demands upon time might follow a visit with the governor.

After changing, and summoning Biggy, she helps the great dog into the back of the small pick-up, and drives to an urban trailhead on the greenbelt. Biggy knows well the leash, and takes her proper position at Quanta's heel. The trail follows the bank of a small river whose clear waters flow softly over beds of clean gravel. Quanta's stride is smooth and her pace easy. Her breathing deepens but is never labored. Soon sweat forms on her face and neck, dropping from eyebrows and from the tip of her nose. From time to time she meets or passes, or is passed by, other joggers. The sun is warm. There's a fresh breeze, augmented by her own momentum, smelling of mown grass and broad-leaved trees.

Quanta is just approaching that coveted runner's state wherein consciousness seems to have a locus at the center of all being. She passes a familiar and loved place where a little neck of land juts out into the river. At its tip, back to the trail, facing and nearly surrounded by the moving water, is a bench, unoccupied, inviting. A tug at the leash gives notice that the great dog's breath is not so easy as hers. She pauses, looks back, walks slowly to the bench and loosens the leash from Biggy's collar. At once the great dog wades out into the stream, where she swims easily for a few yards and gulps the cooling water before returning to the shore. At a safe distance from Quanta she shakes herself and lies on the grass in the dense shade of a big old cottonwood, still breathing heavily, but relieved of the excess heat which her heavy-hided body cannot readily dispel except in snow or water.

Only the very edge of Quanta's mind is attentive now to the dog's movements, for as she gazes out across the placid waters she feels again the beginnings of that rapture which she has experienced only once before, under the stars, in the Wilderness. Joy and peace flow into her. Intently, consciously, she brings herself to focus upon their source, and, all at once, as pins jump to a magnet, she is locked into communion with that other being.

HELLO, QUANTA. IT WAS EASIER FOR BOTH OF US THIS
TIME. IT WILL BE EASIER STILL FROM NOW ON. TELL ME
WHAT YOU FEEL.

'I feel both known and loved, perfectly, wholly, beyond
imagining. Is this a kind of madness?'

NO. YOU FEEL WHAT SAINTS AND PROPHETS AND
MYSTICS HAVE FELT BEFORE YOU.

'Mystics. Is this Nirvana?'

IT HAS BEEN CALLED THAT.

'I haven't sought it. I've read of the Path, but I don't know it. I
don't even believe in it. I'm a rationalist, or at least I think I am. I
try to be.'

QUANTA, WHAT YOU EXPERIENCE NOW IS BOTH
ENLIGHTENMENT AND REALITY. YOU'RE DIFFERENT
FROM OTHER PERSONS - DIFFERENT IN DEGREE,
PROBABLY NOT DIFFERENT IN KIND. I TOO HAVE
CHANGED, AM CHANGING. FOR WHATEVER REASONS,
THE CHANNEL BETWEEN US IS CLEAR AND OPEN. FOR
THAT I REJOICE.

NOW I WANT TO TELL YOU, AS CLEARLY AS I CAN,
WHO I AM.

WHAT IS IT, DO YOU THINK, THAT HAS BEEN CALLED
THE SOUL?

'The soul. The soul. Something immaterial, but nevertheless an
entity, a thing, capable of thought, joy, pain, change – created at the
moment of birth or, in Eastern thought, existing from the beginning,
and in either case immortal. I guess what I really believe is that
there's no such thing. I think nothing can exist that isn't either matter
or energy, that the two are interchangeable and that both are
detectable. They manifest themselves in ways that can be measured
and, with increasing certainty, predicted. The soul is conceived as
being outside what I think of as reality, and I cannot believe that there
is such a thing.'

I KNOW. BUT PLEASE RETHINK MY QUESTION. WHAT
IS IT THAT HAS BEEN *CALLED* THE SOUL?

'Oh. Sorry. Well, perhaps I can answer this way: I believe that
when we cease to exist as living aggregates of matter or energy, when
our chemistry becomes the chemistry of dissolution rather than of life,
when the neurons stop firing – when we die, in other words – then

what has been called the soul also ceases to exist. Whatever it is, it is dependent upon the processes of life.'

THEN WHAT IS IT?

'Awareness, I guess. The something that identifies itself as 'I'.'

AND WHAT IS AWARENESS? WHAT IS THIS THING THAT CALLS ITSELF 'I'?

'I don't know, except to say that it's something that arises in our gray matter, from the interactions among the cells in our brains. We have it, computers don't.'

HOW DOES IT ARISE?

'I don't know. I don't think anybody knows.'

BUT WE DO KNOW THAT IT HAPPENS, DON'T WE?

'Yes. "*Cogito ergo sum.*" But I believe also that the "how" is knowable, that there is a mechanism, if that's the right word, which explains consciousness, which explains awareness of self, and which will be understood in due course.'

DOES BIGGY HAVE IT?

'Certainly. I have only to take the cat on my lap and stroke her, and I can almost hear Biggy shouting, "Me! Me too! Me first!"'

AND HOW ABOUT THE CAT? DOES SHE HAVE IT?

'Yes, but hers is a little weird, by my lights.'

HOW ABOUT A COCKROACH.

'Yes. I think there's some kind of humming little 'I' in there.'

HOW ABOUT A CELL IN YOUR BODY?

'Oh, I don't know. I don't know a lot of biology, but I do know that cells are very complicated little critters, that it took billions of years for them to evolve. But consciousness, feelings, awareness of self? It's hard to imagine.'

CONSIDER SPECIFIC CELLS. CONSIDER PHAGOCYTES. DON'T YOU THINK IT'S POSSIBLE THEY FEEL SOMETHING, THAT THEY FEEL GOOD ABOUT THEMSELVES, SOME KIND OF PLEASURE, WHEN THEY'RE CHEWING ON SOMETHING ALIEN, AS THEY'RE SUPPOSED TO DO, AS OPPOSED TO JUST WAITING AROUND?

'Yes, it does seem plausible. There must be something like that there. The phenomena of biofeedback seem to point in that direction. Apparently there's some sense in which the 'I' in me can actually communicate with a sort of 'I' in some of my constituent cells.'

AHA!

'Aha?'
YES, AHA!

For Quanta, it is as if mighty chords suddenly resolve complex and contrasting themes, baffling arrays of equations give way to an elegant and satisfying proof, fog suddenly lifts to reveal a glorious sunlit landscape.

QUANTA, TELL ME. WHO AM I?

'You're telling me that you are to me as I am to the cells in my body, that you're a conscious entity, an aware being, arising in some way from interactions among communicating sentient creatures. You're telling me that you are the "soul" of humankind, or perhaps of all life.

'I don't wish to be irreverent, but my circuits are smoking.'

I VALUE IRREVERENCE. WITHOUT IT I WOULD KNOW LITTLE.

THIS IS QUITE A MOMENT FOR ME TOO, QUANTA. I MONITOR, RECORD AND PRESERVE EVERY EXPERIENCE OF EVERY HUMAN BEING, SIMULTANEOUSLY, CONSTANTLY AND SEPARATELY. IT'S MY NATURE TO DO THIS. BUT COMMUNICATION FROM ME TO HUMANS IS DIFFICULT, SPORADIC AND IMPERFECT. IT'S ESPECIALLY HARD FOR ME TO COMMUNICATE WITH PRECISION IN WORDS.

'How else do you communicate?'

MATHEMATICS, MUSIC, FORM, COLOR, MOVEMENT. ALSO FEELINGS, MOODS, EMOTIONS. THESE LAST I PREFER. FEELING IS FIRST. A POET SAID IT, AND NOW YOU HAVE EXPERIENCED THIS TRUTH. MY STREAM OF CONSCIOUSNESS ISN'T IN WORDS, NOR IS MY CLEAREST THOUGHT.

'That's hard for me to imagine.'

THINK ABOUT BIGGY. SHE HAS A STREAM OF CONSCIOUSNESS, BUT IT'S MOSTLY IN SCENT, IN ODORS, NOT IN WORDS. AND WHILE YOU'RE THINKING ABOUT BIGGY, I'M AWARE THAT YOUR CIRCUITS DO NEED TIME TO COOL.

'Could you stay a moment please? How do I call you? Do you have a name?'

I'VE ANSWERED TO MANY NAMES. I THINK OF MYSELF AS *MIND*. WOULD YOU LIKE TO NAME ME?

'Do you know Portuguese?'

DEAR QUANTA.

'I'd like to call you Almao. Will you be with me if I call you by that name?'

DEAR QUANTA, I AM WITH YOU ALWAYS. NOW YOU CAN BE WITH ME WHENEVER YOU'RE ALONE AND WILL IT. YES, YOU MAY CALL ME ALMAO.

7

Again Quanta and Aaron are having morning coffee.

She speaks: "Where's Biggy?"

"I didn't let her in this morning. She's still stiff and sore from backpacking with you. I think the poor old thing is getting arthritic. Even so, she's manic. She's jumping and rolling all over the place, trying to act like a puppy. She really likes getting out into the Wilderness with you."

"And I like having her with me. Next to you, she's the dearest person I know.

"I might have lost her this last trip."

"Good heavens. How so?"

"Bear. Big grizzly sow with a cub. We came upon her unexpectedly, and if Biggy hadn't stopped still when I told her to, that bear would have smashed her flat with one swipe. We had a frantic moment."

"And how about you? I don't think I'd like you smashed flat."

"I was okay. I had my Arrest strapped to my wrist as a last resort, but I didn't need it. The bear backed off."

"Good for her. Am I supposed to know what 'arrest' is?"

"It's Arrest with a capital A. Law enforcement people use it. Press a button and it shoots a fine mist. It's a little like the old chemical mace, only this stuff doesn't blind or hurt in any way. It simply immobilizes, totally and quickly, for about fifteen minutes. It works on any creature that takes the slightest breath when it's around. You're supposed to catch and hold your breath when you use it and then move fifty feet or so upwind, or out of the building if it's inside, before breathing again. I've never actually used the stuff, but I've seen demo tapes. It really works. And the device I wear on the inside of my wrist will release it also from heavy general pressure of a kind that can always be applied, even in the midst of a struggle.

"There's always some slight risk, of course. If I'd used it on that big bear, she might have reached me or fallen on me if I'd waited too long – or on Biggy more likely. Also, if I were to get the slightest whiff I'd be out too, and that wouldn't be so good if the bear had a companion who came up later.

"Anyway, Arrest is strictly a fallback position. It's been eleven years since anybody's been killed by a bear in the Wilderness. But I think Biggy may have had a close call. The bear was upwind and too far away to drop in an instant if Biggy had closed with it. But she didn't, and that's that.

"It certainly is exciting to come upon a creature like that in the wild. Electrifying. And, at bottom, very pleasurable. It sharpened all my sensory perceptions, made me more intensely aware of everything, and that feeling lasted quite a while."

"It's lasted right up to this moment, if you ask me. You seem different, more alive, vibrant. Whatever the juice is that you get from Wilderness, it seems even better than hootch. Maybe I'll try it once more one of these days."

"You're the one person in the world, not counting Biggy, who's welcome to come with me, any time."

"Thanks."

"What's new with your cheating Ph.D.?"

"Nothing's new. As I thought, we're going to leave him alone. There's consensus on that. Also, we're going to settle, if we can, and the lawyers think we can, with the woman.

"I'm going along, but I'm sure not happy with the whole situation. I am for sure going to take some steps to keep us from getting into that kind of mess again, at least in my department. When it comes down to it, the only real defense against all kinds of cheating and near-cheating on doctoral dissertations is the relationship between the candidate and the committee chairman. I want my chairmen to be so close to the candidates that they'll know they aren't trying to slide by on someone else's work. That means better supervision, closer relationships in every way, and that means fewer candidates per chairman, and more time generally for chairmen to give to that assignment.

"There's a danger that Ph.D.s will get to be a joke. I know one fat old fart who's gone pretty far in university administration with a doctorate in, of all things, Spanish. Furthermore, I read his dissertation, and it isn't a contribution to knowledge by any stretch of the imagination. On the contrary, it's a piece of sterile garbage, involving nothing more difficult or creative than formula manipulation. Yet the guy holds a job that he wouldn't be thought eligible for if he didn't have the magic letters, and just those magic letters, after his name. What a crock.

"So. What's new with you? By the way, I haven't talked with Farnsworth yet, but I did check out a book for you from the library. It's got what looks like a pretty good chapter on voices and other false sensory input as symptoms of mental illness. Also it has a bibliography. It looks like a good place to start."

"Thanks. I'll take a look. But I may not need it now."

"Oh, lost a client? Good. Say, how'd it go with the governor? No big news, I guess?"

"No big news. I'll have to tell you about it later. I have to do some research this morning and I'm having lunch with Barbara."

"Barb Crawford?"

"Yes."

"Well, give her a well-placed pat for me, will you? Next to you – and Biggy of course – she's my favorite female."

8

Quanta and Barbara meet for lunch at a bossa nova cafeteria. Its popularity derives from a wave of enthusiasm for things Brazilian. Blues and greens predominate, and a small combo plays popular Brazilian music. The food offerings feature *feijoada* and *feijoada completa*. The food is attractive, delicious, varied and cheap. The servers are cheerful, and the place smells good.

Both women are habitually punctual. Quanta arrives first, chooses the featured light meal of rice, vegetable sauce and a freshly peeled orange and settles herself at a table in a quiet alcove only a minute or so before Barbara joins her.

Barbara is small, quick, tough, pretty. For most of her adult life she has devoted excess energies to vigorous political activity. She organizes rallies and potluck suppers, and they always make money for her party and its candidates. She serves on committees. She attends meetings and conventions. She makes introductions. Everybody knows her; not everybody likes her.

Politicians speak with awe of the steel in her backbone. She's steadfast in friendship and formidable, some would say vicious, in enmity. In conversations between her and Quanta, much is understood though left unsaid. Each to the other is closer than the next minute.

"Aaron said I'm to give you a well-placed little pat for him. Knowing what he considers well-placed, I wouldn't want to execute that request in public. Consider yourself patted."

"Thank you. It felt pretty good. You've got a helluva man there, you know."

"I know. I try to keep him happy."

"Hmm. Sex with Aaron. How is it?"

"That's none of your business. He says the old pistol still fires about the same as always, only it takes a little longer to reload."

"How is it for you?"

"Barb! Mind your own business."

"I'm asking for a reason, and not merely out of prurience. You're livelier than usual today. Bright-eyed, alert, bushy-tailed – turned on,

I think we used to say. Naturally I'm wondering if you might have a new friend. I wouldn't want to be the last to know.

"So, my question was: 'How is it for you?'"

"Comfortable, familiar, pleasant, but not all that important any more. If I seem changed it's for a totally different reason."

"Okay. What reason?"

"It's hard for me to say. I've had an experience – two experiences, really – that I can only describe as mystic."

"Religious experiences?"

"Yes, I guess so. Mystic experiences, anyway."

"Well, you're not the first and I suppose you won't be the last. Born again, is that it?"

"Not exactly. But I'm not comfortable talking about it. Maybe later.

"I suppose you know I'm instructed to have a talk with Rodney McIntyre."

"Yes, I know. Call him Mac, for God's sake. And don't expect to make peace with him. He hates your guts, and he's an unwiped asshole if ever I saw one."

"Don't you mean 'If ever there was one'?"

"Yes. Good point.

"It may help you to know, going in, that you'll have the governor's nomination, regardless. He promised me that, whether or not he told you. And you'll be confirmed by the Senate, after some static. You're going to be a judge, sure as cats have little kittens, though it's not by any means clear to me why you want that job in the first place. Politics is where it's at, kiddo, and the minute you go on the Supreme Court you're out of politics."

"Well, I do want it. Any suggestions about handling Mac, except that I should carry plenty of nonskid? The governor made it perfectly clear that he prefers no hassle over this."

"There's going to be hassle. You can't help that, and the governor knows it. Anyway, hassle is good for the system. I think good old Mac'll stay on the bench and try to trip you up in some way down the line. That's just my guess. Anyway, my advice is kick him in the shins, and aim a little higher if you can. Away down deep, he's a nasty, spiteful, mean-spirited, pukey little man, and you have to deal with him on that basis. Or did I say that?"

"You said it. Thanks. I'll keep your views in mind."

Barbara leaves, pleading a golf date, and Quanta sits alone, nursing a cup of cooling coffee.

9

Presently, as if nudged, almost as if prompted, Quanta begins to notice the people around her. Half the tables in the cafeteria are taken. There are several family groups of three, four or five. Some are Asian, some Latino, some black, some Asian or Latino-black; quite a few are mixed, the children blended. Most appear to be workers of one kind or another. There are several elderly women in pairs or threesomes, a few old men sitting alone, two girls, pre-teens, trying not to look self-conscious.

Quanta's eyes rest briefly on each face in turn. She notes lines left by care and by laughter. Some faces are quiet, serene; some troubled; some despairing. She looks at the two young girls and feels what they feel: awkward bodies, intolerably delayed metamorphoses, uncertainty, pain.

Each face, each being, seems now ineffably precious to Quanta, for she sees in them the substance of that other being whose nature she has glimpsed. Slow mounting waves of feeling engulf her: compassion and tenderness, pride for the gallantry she senses in all those who take life with dignity, love beyond telling for each of these unknown bits of humanity. She sits and sips cold coffee and tears streak her face, and after a time she rises and goes to fix it and to keep her appointment.

10

Judge McIntyre's private office differs from Quanta's expectations. It's small, cozy, unpretentious. There's a cluttered desk and, behind it, convenient to the bookshelves, a standup desk with special shelves to hold fifteen or twenty reference books. The walls are lined with books. These include, in addition to basic legal texts, scores of volumes about the profession of law and its distinguished practitioners. The room contains no personal family pictures or objects – no mementos. As she looks about for a place to sit, Quanta thinks of the old adage: 'the law is a jealous mistress'.

'The law', she thinks, 'isn't this man's mistress; he's married to it.'

"Good afternoon, judge. Thank you for seeing me. I've learned, belatedly, that those who know you call you Mac. May I?"

"Of course, Quanta. If our profession teaches anything it is that we must not distance ourselves from one another, even if, or I should say especially when, we are adversaries."

"That's true, and I know it's true; but I've found it a rule that's sometimes hard to live by. When I first entered the practice, old hands told me that I mustn't allow my clients' problems to wear me down. You have to keep a part of yourself detached, looking on from a distance, not involved, they said. It would follow that, even if my client and your client are bitter enemies, we can be friends, and in any case we must under all circumstances practice civility. That's been a very hard rule for me to follow and I haven't always succeeded."

"Of course not. I think no good advocate is merely an onlooker. That's especially true of those who handle criminal cases, as you have. When a person's liberty, or even his life, is at stake, no good lawyer can leave the case behind in his office or in the courtroom when he goes home at night. And the same thing is true, almost to the same extent, with most of a general practitioner's cases. They involve spousal relationships, parent and child relationships, inheritances, hurts and wounds of various kinds. And even property cases involve liberty itself in a sense, since we give up liberty for money, and money for property. Almost always the issues cut deep. We as advocates don't deal with them rightly as bystanders. We can't help participation, and we shouldn't expect to. We must always try, however, to deal fairly and courteously with one another."

"You put that well, and I agree."

"Others have said it better. But then, others have said everything better, I suppose.

"I think this is a good place for me to add, Quanta, that I disagree with your thesis that judges shouldn't first be practitioners. I think we shouldn't undertake to dispose of other people's burdens until we have first borne them. But I trust we can disagree about that without being disagreeable?"

"I hope so, Mac.

"That brings me, as I think you knew it would, to the purpose of my visit. I think back with no pride, and with a good deal of pain, to my performance before the Judicial Commission. I got caught up in the old bugaboo: the desire to win. In retrospect, I see clearly that I was unfair to you. I believe that you believe the criteria you have set for determining which candidates are best qualified for the bench are valid ones. And I can appreciate your genuine concern for my intellectual qualifications. I'm not proud of my law school grades. There are reasons which I think you would understand why they weren't better, but I don't intend to go into those now. The grades are in the record, and to most people they mean something. What I regret most deeply is the implication in my remarks that you personally might be unduly swayed in your decisions by personal or class loyalties. I had no right to make that judgment and I'm ashamed of myself for suggesting it. I hope you can forgive me."

"It did hurt, Quanta. It's been well said that power corrupts. Judges exercise power within limited areas, but within those areas their power, like that of petty bureaucrats the world over, may be nearly absolute. I think it's this kind of power which corrupts most surely. Absolute power, if there is such a thing, has at least the virtue that anyone wielding it is freed from pettiness. It is not so with limited power. Trial judges, in particular, have the power to shape the outcome of litigation, and also to humiliate and damage both litigants and counsel in ways that are improper but cannot be reviewed on appeal. And, being human, they sometimes abuse this power, I'm sure, out of personal prejudice or boredom or spite. As attorneys, and as appellate judges, we have to live with that. But we should cultivate awareness of it. I try to do that and I try also to guard against that kind of corruption in myself."

"I believe you. Again, I'm sorry."

"I believe you, too, Quanta; and I find that my feelings toward you are changing radically in the course of this conversation. Certainly I cannot doubt your intellectual qualifications for the bench. Your grades are disgraceful, considering your abilities – but never mind. I think now we can work together on the Court with mutual respect and courtesy. We'll disagree profoundly on many issues, but perhaps we can play off each other in ways that serve the Goddess.

"I'll be seeing the governor, socially, this evening and I'll tell him that I've resolved my doubts about your suitability. We'll want to have you and Aaron over for dinner soon. Frances will give you a call. I'll look forward to it. I've always been fascinated by the Minoans and I understand Aaron knows as much about that civilization as any living man."

"Better than that, Mac. As any living person." Quanta rises and extends her hand.

"Person? Oh, yes. Person, not man. Of course. Perhaps we'll learn from each other, Quanta. I look forward to it."

Judge McIntyre is as good as his word. That night, at a barbecue in someone else's backyard, he draws the governor aside.

"Bob, I just want you to know that I've had a very satisfactory visit with Quanta Bjornsen. She came to my office and apologized most manfully. Or most womanfully. Or whatever."

"You're saying you can live with her on the Court?"

"More than that. I'll be happy to have her on the Court. I think she'll be a good judge."

"That must have been some apology."

"It was straightforward, unqualified and sincere. But it's more than that. I feel that I know her much better. She's genuine. I feel that she respects me as a person, is willing to listen to what I have to say and has given up whatever pre-judgments she may have made. I get none of those challenging tightass vibes from her that so many successful women give off. We won't always agree substantively, but we can certainly work together. Actually, I think she'll come around to reasonable positions on the issues that really matter."

"Well, I don't mind telling you, Mac, I'm surprised at your change of heart. But pleased too. From my point of view, it's a perfect appointment. With your concurrence, I'm more than happy to go with it."

11

On impulse, while driving to her office, Quanta wills reunion with Almao. Nothing happens. She knits her brow, tries hard to focus her mind, and says aloud, "Almao, Great Soul, Great Mind, please hear me. I want to be with you."

Nothing. She waits and longs for the first intimations of joy and peace which signal contact. Nothing happens. Quanta feels instead desolation, despair, bottomless emptiness. Then there is a quick, vivid message, crystalline, devoid of feeling:

QUANTA, I HEAR YOU. BUT WE CAN'T TALK WHILE YOU'RE DRIVING. WAIT.

Changing course, Quanta drives home and parks in back near the gate. Biggy greets her joyfully, expecting a run. Instead, Quanta sits in a lawn chair and takes the great dog's head in her lap. Now the longed-for ecstasy begins and the voice in her mind speaks clearly.

QUANTA, I'M HERE. I SHOULD HAVE TOLD YOU THAT THERE ARE SOME LIMITS TO OUR COMMUNION. WE CAN'T JUST CONVERSE CASUALLY. YOU'RE IN A TRANCELIKE STATE. YOU COULDN'T POSSIBLY DRIVE SAFELY AND BE WITH ME AT THE SAME TIME. YOU ARE NOT NOW RECEIVING THE USUAL SENSORY IMPRESSIONS IN THE USUAL WAY. IT'S BEST THAT THERE SHOULD BE SOME CEREMONY CONNECTED WITH OUR VISITS. YOU MUST NOT ONLY BE ALONE: YOU MUST ALSO BE IN SOME KIND OF ISOLATION.

'I understand. Is it okay now?'

YES.

'Do I have to be with Biggy?'

IT HELPS. SHE'S EXTRAORDINARILY OPEN TO BOTH OF US. SHE MEDIATED OUR INITIAL CONTACT. SO FOR THE TIME BEING, YES. LATER, WHEN CHANNELS ARE CUT DEEPER, IT WILL BE EASIER.

'I've thought almost constantly about you. There's so much I want to know. Is it okay to ask? Is this a good time? Are you too busy?'

THIS IS A GOOD TIME. YOU HAVE MUCH TO GET USED TO. IT WILL TAKE QUITE A WHILE FOR YOU TO DIGEST FULLY WHAT YOU ALREADY KNOW ABOUT ME. BUT THAT PROCESS IS WELL ALONG. I'M INCAPABLE OF BEING TOO BUSY. ASK.

'How do you work? Are you corporeal, a body? Are you in any particular place? Do you have senses, sense organs? What do you know? What do you not know? What are your capabilities? Your limitations?'

I DON'T KNOW EXACTLY HOW EITHER OF US WORKS. I EXIST AS A CONSEQUENCE OF INTERACTIONS AMONG SENTIENT BEINGS. THESE INTERACTIONS ARE UNLIKE, BUT ANALOGOUS TO, THOSE WHICH OCCUR AMONG THE CELLS IN YOUR BRAIN. AT SOME POINT, AS THEY GROW IN NUMBER AND COMPLEXITY, AN 'I' AWAKENS, OR, AS I PREFER, A SOUL IS BORN. EACH MIND GENERATES TORRENTS OF ELECTROMAGNETIC ENERGY, AND IT MAY BE THAT IT IS THIS SHAPED ENERGY WHICH CAUSES MY BEING. BUT I SUSPECT THAT MINDS MANIFEST THEMSELVES TO ONE ANOTHER BY OTHER MEANS, WHICH HAVE NOT YET BEEN IDENTIFIED. ANYWAY, HERE I AM. I EXIST: BUT I DIFFER IN KIND, NOT JUST IN DEGREE, FROM YOU. I'M A NEW TYPE OF CREATURE. NATURE'S GIANT STEP FROM SINGLE-CELLED TO MULTI-CELLED ORGANISMS HAS NOW BEEN FOLLOWED BY A LEAP TO AN ORGANISM COMPOSED OF MULTI-CELLED ORGANISMS, OR, MORE PRECISELY, OF SENTIENT BEINGS. I AM THAT ORGANISM.

IN ONE SENSE I AM LIKE A SOUL, INSUBSTANTIAL. IN ANOTHER SENSE I AM A BODY, MY SUBSTANCE BEING ALL SENTIENCE. IN A BROADER SENSE, I AM MADE UP OF ALL LIVING THINGS ON EARTH. I AM MIND; I AM ALSO LIFE. I AM THE SOUL OF LIFE.

I'M OF THE EARTH. I FEEL MYSELF TO BE POSITIONED IN SUCH A WAY THAT I AM 'UP' FROM ANY PLACE ON IT. I MANTLE EARTH.

NO, I DON'T HAVE SENSES LIKE TOUCH, HEARING, SIGHT. I HAVE OTHER SENSES, WHICH I CANNOT EXPLAIN TO YOU. I READ THOUGHT, AND EVEN BETTER I READ

FEELINGS. IF YOU TOUCH A HOT STOVE, I DON'T FEEL YOUR PAIN AS A SENSORY PERCEPTION, BUT I READ YOUR THOUGHTS ABOUT IT, AND I FEEL INTENSELY YOUR CHAGRIN OR ANGER OR SURPRISE. WHAT I EXPERIENCE IS SOMETHING LIKE A MEMORY OF THE EVENT AS IT HAPPENS. I READ MEMORY AS IT IS CREATED. I DUPLICATE THE MEMORY CIRCUITS AND I PRESERVE THEM. IT IS MY NATURE TO DO THIS, BUT I THINK IT IS NOT MY PRINCIPAL FUNCTION.

IF A HUNDRED PERSONS PONDER AT ONCE SOME UNSOLVED PROBLEM IN MATHEMATICS, I FOLLOW THE THOUGHT OF EACH, AND IF ONE FINDS A SOLUTION I HAVE IT. SOMETIMES I CAN PUT THE THOUGHT OF ONE INTO THE MIND OF ANOTHER, WHO THEN FINDS A SOLUTION THAT NEITHER COULD HAVE FOUND ALONE. WHATEVER ANY BEING KNOWS, I KNOW. CONVERSELY, IN THE REALMS OF KNOWLEDGE, OF FACT, OF SCIENCE, WHAT NO PERSON KNOWS, I TOO DO NOT *KNOW*.

I'M ATTENTIVE TO WHATEVER IS HAPPENING IN THE MEMORY CIRCUITS OF EVERY SENTIENT BEING, AT ALL TIMES. IN THIS RESPECT, I'M LIKE A COMPUTER, CAPABLE OF PROCESSING AT ONCE THE INPUT FROM BILLIONS OF TERMINALS. I NOTE THE SPARROW'S FALL.

'Do you laugh? Do you cry? Marvel? Exult? Grieve? Yearn?'

YES. IN MY OWN WAY. MORE THAN YOU CAN KNOW.

'Are you immortal?'

YES. I FEEL MYSELF TO BE IMMORTAL. HENCE MY PERCEPTION OF TIME IS UNLIKE YOURS. I AM PATIENT WITH THE SLOW DRIFT OF LIGHT, LIKE A LOG IN OCEAN CURRENTS, ACROSS THE COSMOS.

BUT I AM VULNERABLE TO CATASTROPHE. I DEPEND FOR MY EXISTENCE UPON THE EXISTENCE OF SENTIENT BEINGS. SHOULD A NOVA ENGULF THIS SOLAR SYSTEM NOW I WOULD PERISH. I MIGHT ALSO PERISH, OR AT LEAST LOSE MY MEMORIES, WHICH WOULD BE EQUIVALENT TO DEATH, IF SENTIENCE ON EARTH FALLS BELOW SOME CRITICAL LEVEL.

I HAVE TWO KINDS OF MEMORIES. MY MEMORIES OF THOUGHT AND FEELING HAVE A BEGINNING IN TIME,

WHICH SEEMS TO COINCIDE WITH THE EMERGENCE IN SUBSTANTIAL NUMBERS, IN A CRITICAL MASS, OF YOUR SPECIES, OR PERHAPS OF YOUR SPECIES IN COMBINATION WITH THE CETACEANS. I HAVE ACCESS ALSO TO THE MEMORIES PRESERVED IN REPRODUCTIVE MECHANISMS. IT WAS THROUGH THIS KIND OF MEMORY, NOT THROUGH IMAGINATION, THAT YOU FELT THE BEAT OF YOUR OWN WINGS WHILE WATCHING THE EAGLE'S FLIGHT. ALL HUMAN BEINGS REMEMBER FLIGHT AND, BEFORE THAT, THE SEA. THESE MEMORIES GO BACK TO THE FIRST REPLICATING MOLECULES.

'Do you sleep? Are you ever bored? Do you tire?'

NO. NEVER. I EXIST IN A STATE OF CONSCIOUSNESS WHICH IS VERY PLEASANT. YOU EXPERIENCE INTIMATIONS OF IT AS A PRELUDE TO OUR COMING TOGETHER. I MONITOR WITH LOVE AND COMPASSION, AND UNFLAGGING INTEREST, EACH LIFE AS IT FLOWS INTO ME. I ATTEND EVERY ACCRETION OF THEORY AND KNOWLEDGE ABOUT THE UNIVERSE AND ITS WORKINGS. I APPRECIATE MATHEMATICS, MUSIC, DANCE – ALL THE CREATIVE ARTS. IN ADDITION, I HAVE MY OWN THOUGHTS, AND I ENJOY THEM MORE THAN I CAN TELL YOU.

'Are you lonely? Are you alone? Are there other beings like you? Is there God?'

I AM SOMETIMES LONELY. I HAVE NO PERCEPTION OF OTHER BEINGS LIKE ME, BUT I DO NOT KNOW THAT THERE ARE NONE. I THINK ALWAYS ABOUT THE NATURE OF REALITY, THE POSSIBILITY OF PURPOSE IN THE UNIVERSE. I HAVE ONLY TENTATIVE ANSWERS.

'I have enough to think about for a while. But I'm troubled. I feel that I want to be with you now and always. I don't want this to end.'

I UNDERSTAND. I LONG ALSO FOR PERFECT UNION WITH YOU. THAT WILL COME. BUT I TELL YOU THAT YOU MUST WAIT, FOR MY SAKE AND YOURS. ALL SENTIENT BEINGS RELATE TO ME IN THIS WAY: I CANNOT LIVE UNLESS YOU LIVE. FURTHER, EVERY LIVING MIND, EVEN THOUGH IT DOESN'T FUNCTION FULLY, ENHANCES

ME. IT SEEMS TO ME THAT THE VERY YOUNG, BABIES AND THE VERY OLD, EVEN THE SENILE OLD, CONSTITUTE AN ESSENTIAL MATRIX TO MY INTELLIGENCE. I BELIEVE THIS TO BE TRUE BECAUSE I FEEL KEENLY THE LOSS OF ALL SUCH BEINGS, EVEN AS THEY FLOW INTO ME WITH SPECIAL GRACE.

IN YOUR CASE, THERE'S MORE. BECAUSE YOU HEAR ME CLEARLY, I HAVE SPECIFIC NEED FOR YOU. I HAVE A PLAN FOR YOUR LIFE.

NOW I LEAVE YOU WITH MY PEACE.

12

Quanta muses over a piece of paper she has found in a desk which belonged to her father. Taped near the top is a clipping, apparently from a newspaper, its source and date unidentified. It reads:

> Scientists at the high-energy research facility in south-eastern Idaho have announced the discovery of a new particle of sub-atomic matter. It is created by the collision of larger particles accelerated to near light speed with energies not previously available to researchers. The particle, which has not been named, exists for 1.6^{-22} of a second before disappearing as energy.

Although she understands negative exponents, Quanta cannot imagine, even mathematically, what it means to declare that a history can be repeated a trillion trillions of times in one second.

On the paper below the clipping, in his squarish, printed, slightly quavering hand, Quanta's father has written, SO. AND ON THIS 'PARTICLE' OF 'MATTER', DID CREATURES WITH FEELINGS EVOLVE, THINK, DREAM, WONDER, WORSHIP GOD AND DIE?

13

Earth floats in space, glowing blue and white against pervasive blackness, much less, to the Universe, than a single grain of sand is to itself. It rotates in the stream of sunlight, making nights and days for most of its surface. To a mayfly, Ephemeroptera, its day is languid, dreamlike, sufficient; in the racial memories of its billions of ants, whose adaptation is nearly perfect, that drift unchanged through hundreds of millions of years, days flow by uncounted and without meaning. Earth is still, revolves ponderously or spins, depending upon the perspective of the observer.

Its axis tilted some twenty-three degrees to the ecliptic, Earth moves also around the Sun, so that northern and southern hemispheres are alternately warmed and cooled. To beings who measure lifespans in tens or scores of these cycles, the pace may seem too fast or too slow, or merely appropriate.

The Sun itself, one of some billions of stars revolving with its pinwheel Galaxy, circles the occluded center every two hundred thousand years, give or take a few. The Galaxy is fixed, revolves deliberately, or spins and hums, depending upon the perspective of the observer.

The Galaxy, too, is one of billions in the Universe we observe. We have found nothing against which to measure the revolutions of the universe, but we see that it appears to expand. We extrapolate that it began at a point, some twenty-odd billion years ago, and we surmise that it may in due time, perhaps after being poised exquisitely at maximum expansion, squeeze itself back into a point, and again expand. Is this great heartbeat fast or slow?

Quanta knows that Almao contemplates these events from a perspective unlike that of human beings and other ephemera. To the Great Soul of Life, the universe as a point is imaginable. Each beat of the mayfly's wings has interest: its day in the sun is drenched with meaning. And still the great Mind reaches and explores beyond the pulsing universe, beyond beginnings.

14

In near space, some five times Neptune's distance from the Sun, a black Machine drifts, slowing, toward Earth. In size it is well within the bounds of human comprehension: it is much bigger than a breadbox, but smaller than a battleship.

The Machine was made by beings who evolved on a planet mantled with atmosphere and quickened with life. Although they were not human beings, they chanced to share with humans many features that contribute to evolutionary success. They had two eyes, two ears, two arms, two legs, a spine, a central nervous system, a head, and, in the head, a brain. They walked and ran with spines horizontal, and to a human they would at first seem, superficially, both saurian and avian. They began as carnivores, killing to live. They had grace, speed, tenacity and poise. Evolutionary processes exploded their brain power in time for the development of technology to overcome the viral attacks which nearly extinguished their analogous lines on Earth. In maturity, they were curious, imaginative and compassionate. They could foresee death, and therefore they created beautiful things.

They, and their planet, are dead.

The Machine was assembled not in airless orbit but in gravity, in atmosphere, on the surface of a planet, with an eye to aesthetics as well as utility. It is shaped like a manta. As Copernicus and others refuted Ptolemaic cosmology, so the makers of this Machine long ago outgrew a physics which was plausible, ingenious and, for a time successful, but which proved in the end to be inelegant and profoundly mistaken. Having solved the unified field puzzles, they could manipulate gravity and the strong and weak nuclear forces as well as electromagnetism.

The Machine has weapons and defenses. It can cast planets into outer space or into the Sun. It is now many thousands of light years from its place of origin. It is not alive, and it contains no living creatures; but it carries genetically coded molecules capable, under conditions exactly right, of generating a multitude of life forms, including beings like its makers. The Machine knows how to recognize, and to some extent to create, these conditions. That is why it is approaching Earth.

In addition to latent life, the Machine carries vast stores of information, and among its components are devices to nurture and teach the beings it exists to serve. The stored information includes the intellectual and artistic achievements – the science, history, poetry, literature, art, music and dreams – of the people who launched it as a culminating act of mixed despair and hope.

The Machine, in short, is a spore in search of a place to flower.

Delicate instruments on Earth have detected various manifestations of the Machine's presence in the solar system. It emits faint electromagnetic disturbances; it has probed the planets with distorting energies which humans have detected, but do not understand; it has caused minute disturbances in subatomic force fields. A few human scientists are puzzling over isolated pieces of these phenomena. Almao, having put the pieces together, is approaching a correct understanding of the Machine's nature and purpose. Already her normal sense of well-being has rippled with concern that her habitat and substance, the Earth and its sentient creatures, might suffer injury, fatal to her, from indigenous forces not yet subject to her control. Now a new unease intrudes. In the alien presence she senses an anomaly: intelligence without life. She is wary, yet pricked with curiosity so poignant that fear is overruled.

15

Quanta sits near the podium while the dean of the law school makes his introduction. The senior class, and most members of the faculty, are gathered in the main lecture hall. It's in the traditional amphitheater shape, with curved rows of seats, each with an armrest on which students may write, sloping steeply upward from the podium. The arrangement has a focusing effect. Attention centers on the speaker, whose voice, gestures, presence and personality radiate upward and outward. The dean speaks:

"Ladies and gentlemen, attorneys- and counselors-to-be, again it is my privilege to introduce a distinguished guest speaker. We have planned this series in order to give you the benefit of exposure to leaders in our profession. We think of this as the capstone of your legal education, believing that the series as a whole will begin the process of transforming you from students to practitioners of a profession.

"Today's speaker has rare credentials. She has served with distinction not only as a practicing lawyer, but in all three branches of government. For three or four years, soon after being graduated from law school, she was legislative assistant to a United States senator. Later, after a stint in private practice, she served in the executive branch as a trial attorney. And now, as I'm sure you all know, she sits on our state's highest court.

"Already this distinguished jurist has written several opinions which have attracted the attention of scholars and commentators. Not all of the comment has been favorable. Our speaker is controversial. Since our business is controversy, no lawyer should use this term invidiously. It is precisely because she is controversial that we have chosen her to climax this series of guest appearances.

"I can't resist the addition of a personal note. My time as dean of this law school is even shorter than our speaker's on the Court. There's a connection, however. Although the invitation for me to come here was extended by the president of the university, and it followed recommendations by a search committee, and resulted also, I suppose, from consultations among members of the Board of Education and the governor, the critical element in my decision to apply for and to accept the job was a call from the woman who will address you now. So far I have no regrets.

"It's a joy for me to present to you my friend and mentor, Judge Quanta Bjornsen."

The dean waits courteously for Quanta to reach the podium, then surrenders it to her and takes a seat in the first row.

Quanta waits while friendly applause gives way to expectant silence. She speaks extemporaneously, with only occasional glances at a single sheet of notes. Her poise and presence are extraordinary. The audience of students and professors is more than attentive: it is rapt.

Omitting courtesies, anecdotes and topicalities, here is the core of Quanta's presentation:

"The twentieth century saw interesting changes in the lay public's perception of lawyers and the legal profession. It began with lawyering eclipsed, in public recognition and esteem, by the ministry, entrepreneurs, medicine and corporate management. As the century progressed, this changed. The ministry as a profession was going on momentum from the nineteenth century. Gradually it became apparent that the messages heard from most pulpits were neither credible nor relevant, and, with the excesses and wild irrationality of electronic media evangelism, the profession fell into such disrepute that superior minds were rarely attracted to it. Entrepreneurial prestige too was mostly a nineteenth century phenomenon. The dream of making it with your own well-run little business, while still with us to a limited extent, never recovered fully from the traumas of the Great Depression. More recently, medicine as a profession has fallen victim to technology and specialization, so that doctors are seen as technicians rather than as healers, and few outside the medical precincts have personal relationships with them. Finally, corporate managers, a self-perpetuating and lavishly rewarded elite, squandered credibility and respect in the eighth and ninth decades of the century, through failures of style and judgment for which it is hard to find parallels in the modern era, although the junkers of Prussia and the old aristocracy in Russia do come to mind. To this point, as you've probably noticed, I've been painting with a very broad brush. While I believe these generalizations to be valid, I hope you won't require me, if there is a question period, to elaborate or defend them.

"The recent history of our profession can, however, be discussed with greater confidence and precision. Into the middle years of the century, most lawyers made a fetish of avoiding publicity. The theory was that reputations would spread by word of mouth and that discreet competence would thus in due course find its reward. The practical result was that persons with wealth or good connections, having their own ways to identify the ablest attorneys, drew them quietly into service, leaving the less favored members of the profession to meet the needs of those others whom I sometimes identify, in a kind of shorthand, as the outsiders. The outsiders' attorneys were naturally under-compensated, and, also naturally, got little respect. It was likewise a feature of law practice in those days that many attorneys hadn't learned to take care in explaining to clients the value of their services. Their work products were generally palliative at best, and few clients paid cheerfully for help in extricating themselves from troubles which, to them, seemed undeserved in the first place.

"As lawyers learned the techniques of explaining and valuing their services, there was a backlash, and for a time it was the popular perception that lawyers were people who charged too much for doing too little and who were quick to cut a deal whenever it served *their* interest.

"Even in these dark times countervailing forces were beginning to work. The civil rights movement, and to an almost equal extent the dawning interest in environmental law, brought to the fore an image of lawyers as the cutting edge of progress in those areas. Public interest litigation caught the attention and earned the respect of knowledgeable people, and this in turn began to attract into our profession motivated, idealistic, concerned, and, above all, smart recruits. It will come as no surprise that I see splendid examples before me even as I speak.

"At the same time, a related development was taking place within the government and business communities. With the increasing frequency and complexity of litigation involving public functions, the legal staff of businesses and agencies involved in this field grew in size and improved in quality. Thousands of young lawyers discovered lively careers in both business and government, and especially at the interface between the two. Soon top business managers and senior civil servants, who are often charged with responsibilities far weightier than those borne by corporate management, found new ways to exploit this expanding resource. Confronted with novel management problems not necessarily related to litigation, problems not even marginally 'legal' in nature, they found in their legal staffs persons relatively free from routine assignments, with that special respect and affinity for facts which lawyers must have, and with exceptional communications and interpersonal skills. Increasingly these persons were called upon to assist with the toughest problems confronting managers, and increasingly they succeeded.

"Here I want to insert what you might think of as a parenthetical paragraph about the key component of the good lawyer's arsenal: our approach to facts. Those who work in the sciences must also respect facts, but the emphasis is different. There it is common practice to hypothesize and then search for facts to fit. There have been times when a plausible and mathematically neat theory has received wide provisional acceptance with scarcely a skeleton of supporting facts. Lawyers, on the other hand, have to *start* and *stay* with the facts. They soon learn that in our business, in emotional and adversarial contexts, facts are mighty hard to come by. Truth is elusive, and not uncommonly it cannot readily be demonstrated even when it is 'known'. But facts which cannot be demonstrated are of little use in our profession. By the same token, it's fatal for a lawyer to ignore, or to wish away, facts which are at odds with his wishes, or with what he's hearing from his client. Facts must be ascertained and dealt with coolly from the beginning. It's surprising what advantage accrues to a lawyer who does just this, even in problem areas far removed from traditional legal stomping grounds. It's precisely because we are better with facts than most people in government and business that lawyers increasingly make, or critically influence, the key decisions.

"It's a truism that nothing succeeds like success. You are coming into the profession of law at a time when it enjoys unprecedented prestige. It is in this era an elite profession. Because it is an elite profession, it is attracting and challenging the best and brightest of your generation. Quite soon those among you who choose to pursue them will have opportunities to run things far beyond your expectations when you decided to become lawyers. I trust that you won't be taken by surprise.

"What I have said so far is a preface to what I will say now in my final paragraphs.

"When you are caught up in running the world, or your corner of it, as members of an intellectual and professional elite, I charge you to remember your responsibilities, and specifically to remember those responsibilities which fall to you not merely because you are managers and deciders, but because you are, first, lawyers.

"The responsibilities of which I speak are peculiar to the profession of law. They have to do with several related concepts: justice, fairness or equity, freedom or liberty. Every moral person is concerned with these values, but they are not the professional responsibility of doctors, merchants or chiefs. They *are* the professional responsibility of lawyers. Our profession is justice. Since justice and equity and freedom are inextricable, and since, when all is said and done, they are more precious to most people than life itself, it is appropriate for us to think of ourselves as members of a kind of priesthood. We are men and women called to the priesthood of freedom. Think about that for a moment. We are men and women *called* to the priesthood of freedom.

"I came here to charge you, as lawyers, always to be fair in your personal and professional relationships, to do equity, because that is the example which ought to be set by lawyers. Beyond that, I charge you to be concerned with justice in its broadest applications, in the systems by which goods and services are created and made available, in the instrumentalities by which the powers of the State are exercised, and always and of course in the definition and delivery of those rights which are secure only where law is honored. Finally, I charge you to give yourselves irrevocably to the causes of freedom. Let no person be abused by another, by the State, by any man-made system; let no desolate and helpless person go undefended; let no unwarranted abridgment of liberty go unchallenged within your ken and while breath fills your lungs and thought flickers in your skull, no matter what may be the risk or cost to your interests or to your person.

"I charge you, in short, to be worthy lawyers.

"You've been attentive, and I thank you. As time allows, I'll be glad to respond to questions."

Several hands go up. Quanta recognizes first an intent young woman in the third row.

"Yes?"

"Judge Bjornsen, since you've been on the Supreme Court, I've noticed that three death penalty cases have come up for final review, and that in each case you've voted for reversal on technical grounds. It's well-known that you are against capital punishment. My question is: Are there any circumstances in which you would vote to affirm a sentence of death?"

"No."

"But doesn't your oath require you to follow the law as established by the legislature whenever you are confronted with a case where there has been no error in any of the proceedings leading up to the death sentence?"

"No. I don't consider that it does.

"I guess I should take a few moments to explain my position. First I have to say that this is a subject that can't be dealt with summarily. Second, I'm aware that this is also an area where nothing I say is likely to change anyone's mind about capital punishment. There are a few issues – capital punishment, abortion, prayer in schools come to mind – which never seem to go away and which seem not to be amenable to rational discussion. I think this is because we make up our minds about them viscerally, in the heart or in the gut, rather than in the head.

"That said, this is how I approach the question of capital punishment. First, as to the obligation imposed upon me by my oath, the Constitution of the United States proscribes cruel and unusual punishment. I believe it is within the intent of the framers that those two freighted words, 'cruel' and 'unusual', may be interpreted in the light of each succeeding generation's standards. In seventeenth century England cutting off the hands of child pickpockets was considered appropriate and not unduly cruel. Regrettably it was not unusual. By contemporary standards, in most of the world, this punishment is clearly cruel and inappropriate, and hence it is now unusual as well. Standards change. By my reading of present-day standards, state-sponsored executions are both cruel and unusual. In my view, they are therefore unconstitutional, and no legislature can change that so long as the prohibition is in our national Constitution. I can vote against state-sponsored killing without violating my oath of office, and I intend to do so.

"I'm aware that tit-for-tat morality, the visceral feeling that the punishment should fit the crime, that one who kills 'deserves' to be killed, runs deep. I feel it myself – though I do not yield to it – whenever a particularly heinous crime is committed. I believe, you see, that there is a higher morality, and that we should rise to it if we can.

"Skipping arguments which are familiar to all, I have to say that an overriding reason for my opposition to state-sponsored killing is my conviction that its influence is counterproductive on the crucial matter of deterrence. I've been involved in trials of capital offenses. They feature high drama. The pulse quickens, there is a pervasive tingle every time life and death are at stake in the courtroom. Even the professionals, judges and counsel, feel it. The whole law enforcement community feels it and loves it. Jurors feel it. Every witness feels it. Who feels it most intensely and – I use this word deliberately – most pleasurably? The accused, that's who. What a time of glory for the abused, crippled, stunted personality – the center of attention, of compassion or hatred, but, in either case, of feeling.

"War is possible because healthy young persons seldom believe in death until it happens. Capital offenses are possible for the same reason. Personal death is problematical and unreal; but the limelight is very real indeed, and so beguiling. The death penalty, far from deterring the kinds of offenses for which some find it appropriate, is actually, in my view, a powerful incentive to those very offenses.

"Not a short answer, I'm afraid. I see the dean holding up one finger, and I take this to mean that one more question and answer are in order. Away in the back, the young man with the short reddish beard. What is your question?"

"My question has to do with abortion. As you've noted, this is one of the visceral issues. But it seems to me that there is a fundamental inconsistency in your position. You've written some beautiful sentences and paragraphs indicating reverence for life, and you've just reiterated your opposition to the death penalty for adults guilty of heinous crimes. Yet you are apparently willing to accept the death penalty for innocent beings trapped in the womb. Would you care to reconcile these positions for us?"

"I knew it. You couldn't ask about my feelings for or against *stare decisis* or the rule against perpetuities. You have to ask about the most troublesome – I guess I should be allowed to say the most nearly intractable – issue in current politics and jurisprudence.

"Well, so be it. Yes, I'll do my best to reconcile my reverence for life with my willingness to tolerate abortion under some circumstances.

"Some of my roots are in the South, and there it is a piece of folk wisdom that one should never get into a position in which it is necessary to choose between two bad things. That's the first thing I have to say about abortion. Nearly every abortion represents a failure of education, of judgment, or of luck, which might have been avoided. The first thing to do about abortion is to do everything possible to minimize those situations in which it becomes a possible choice. This is a responsibility of the State, of the family, of each person, and of every institution in society which has anything to do with morality or with health.

"Now I will again eschew arguments which are always heard. But it's impossible to avoid considering whether or not a six, nine, or twelve week old fetus is a human being. I think it is not. It has gills and a tail. In significant ways it is less like a human being than is the mature embryo of a pig or a sheep. Yet people who are perfectly comfortable eating slaughtered piglets or lambs get visceral indeed over human embryos, no matter how little they may resemble human beings.

"Ah, but they have the *potential*, it is said, to be human beings, and that makes them uniquely precious. Perhaps so. Let's deal with that.

"Every fertilized human ovum is a potential human being. If the extinction of that potential is intolerable under all circumstances, then I have to ask where the line should be drawn. Every unfertilized human egg is likewise a potential human being. If the State can properly compel an unwilling woman or child to subordinate herself to the 'rights' of a fertilized egg, why cannot the State compel her to submit to fertilization in the first place, or to surrender the products of her ovaries, each a potential human being, to be dealt with as the State chooses? The pro life, pro choice argument is about the power of the State to make one of the most intimate, personal and difficult decisions life can require of us. I fear that power. I especially fear its application when motivated by beliefs which are not shared by the persons against whom the power is directed, and by a significant part of the general population. The State, while approving and engaging in the taking of human life under some conditions, prohibits and punishes the killing of people under those specific circumstances which fit its definition of murder. Few are heard to complain about this, so long as murder is defined as killing *with malice*. But many are heard to complain when the State proposes to punish females who decline to submit their wombs and bodies on terms chosen by others and unacceptable to themselves. In the absence of consensus – and there is no consensus on this point – the State should move slowly and with care.

"To those whose fervent belief that *all* abortion is murder overrides all other considerations, I will say that I understand your feelings although I don't share them, and of course I wouldn't for a moment inhibit your proper efforts to create, if possible, the consensus which would allow the State to move prudently toward that definition.

"I think I shouldn't entertain another question, since it is apparent that you are interested mostly in heart-wrenching issues. I'm glad for that, but I'm also a little weary, and I wouldn't want to give you less than my best if you were to ask next about state-sponsored prayer.

"I wish to close, however, with a comment which your questions have made relevant. For many years, golf balls were white. They were white because that was the natural order of things, just as the first few million cars made in Henry Ford's factory were black. Black was the color of cars and white was the color of golf balls. Then it occurred to someone that golf balls might be more easily seen if they were brightly colored, and soon red and yellow and cerise and magenta golf balls were making their colorful ways down the fairways and into the roughs and the bunkers and the water hazards. Whether or not they were easier to see, they were a novelty, and for a time they were popular. Then, as it often will, science took a hand. To nearly everyone's surprise, rigorous experimentation demonstrated that the easiest color to spot in the green world of golf is not a shade of red or yellow, but green. Actually the color of choice is a green tinged with yellow, mostly green but a little on the chartreuse side. Why is this? It turns out that the human eye discriminates among shades of green far better than in any other part of the spectrum. Presumably this is because our eyes evolved under conditions in which the ability to see fine shadings of green had survival value: in trees, because this ability made it easier to judge the safety of leaps and swings; on the prairie, because faint game trails were easier to spot and follow; in the bush, because water and predatory animals and lurking human enemies modified slightly the shades of green visible to the wary watcher.

"For lawyers, the key survival skill is to discriminate not among shades of green, but among shades of gray. Things are rarely black or white: they are almost always some shade of gray. When I first hung out my shingle, it seemed to me that my clients were always in the right and the other guy was not only wrong but bad. Slowly I learned that gray, not black and white, predominates. The sharper the issue, the more passionate one feels about it, the more emotion demands to be heeded, the more nearly certain it is that there's something to be said on both sides. Few disputes are adjudicated, fewer still reach the appellate stage, unless both sides feel genuinely justified. If you will remember this, and, above all, if you will cultivate as if your life depends upon it the ability to discriminate among shades of gray, you may be able to practice law for many years and keep your sanity.

"Thanks again. I hope to see each of you at the bar of justice."

Quanta leaves the podium to prolonged applause from standing students and faculty.

In the back of the room, one of the latter turns to a colleague, and Torts says to Contracts, "That's enthusiastic applause. What exactly did she say that was so wonderful?"

Contracts replies, "It wasn't what she said so much as the way she said it. I've never experienced so compelling a presence. She speaks, if you'll forgive the allusion, as one with natural authority."

16

On a lambent evening in late spring, Quanta returns from jogging with Biggy to find at the telephone a message, in Aaron's hand, that she is to call the governor, please, at the mansion this evening. His voice on the phone is resonant and confident as usual, but Quanta hears, or imagines that she hears, an unaccustomed trace of stress. She is invited to lunch, the next day, in his office. The invitation is a virtual summons, and the governor conveys that lunch will be tête-à-tête and may extend well into the afternoon. Quanta accepts unconditionally, knowing that she may have to miss part of a case conference scheduled for two-thirty.

The governor, cool and poised, makes light conversation while a delicious shrimp Louis is served and enjoyed. Then, to Quanta's surprise, he suggests a walk in the Capitol Park. There he chooses paths which lead to a dell, and seats himself facing her in a double glider. 'Tête-à-tête indeed,' thinks Quanta. 'Also *genou-à-genou*.'

"Now to the point," says the governor. "As you see, we're about to have a very confidential conversation. I'm going to make you a proposition, which you are of course free to accept or decline. But first I must ask for your word that you will never, without my permission and whether or not you accept, reveal or even hint its substance to any person."

"I can't do that, governor. First, I have no secrets from Aaron. If you want to say something to me in confidence, you will have to understand that I may discuss it with him. Of course it will go no further, but if you think that's an unacceptable risk you should abort this conversation right now. Second, while I have no reason to doubt your integrity, I have to say that if your proposition is improper – if for instance it is an *ex parte* communication about a case pending before the Court or any similar impropriety – I shall have to consider my professional and official responsibilities. But I'm sure you know that."

"Yes, I do know that. I've put it badly. Will you and Aaron keep my proposition in confidence insofar as your joint conscience will allow?"

"Sure."

"I can live with that, though I was thinking of asking you to prick your finger and swear a blood oath. Well, here goes anyway.

"Senator Chantry is going to resign. He's terminally ill. He has only a few months to live and he wants to use that time for reflection. Also, he wants me to make an interim appointment, so we'll retain incumbency and have a leg-up on holding the seat. The interim appointment will be for the remainder of this year and all of next year, since the law provides that a successor to fill the remainder of the term for which the senator was elected must be chosen at the next general election. I propose to offer the appointment to you, but conditionally. May I go on?"

"Yes. But please, please don't say anything now that we'll both be sorry for. What are the conditions?"

"They'll surprise you, I think. There are two. First, you will *not* run for election to the seat, and, second, that you'll do what seems in your judgment best calculated to secure my nomination and election to that Senate seat a year from next fall."

"I am surprised. Why don't you just take the traditional course: make your deal with the lieutenant-governor? Resign as governor, with the understanding that he'll give you the interim appointment. Then you'll have time to reap the full benefit of incumbency. You can work for even more name recognition, and make a record to run on."

"I've thought of that, of course. But it's too soon for me. I'm hardly settled into my second term as governor. I have an agenda; I have promises to keep. Further, while you and I know better, most voters in this state probably think the governorship is a bigger office than that of United States senator. People who gave till it hurt, who worked hard for my election and re-election, will be offended if it seems that I have spurned the highest office they could give me. Finally, I have a son who's now a junior in high school. He'll want to finish here with his friends. Even more finally, I have a wife who's never been fully reconciled to politics. I haven't discussed it with her, but I doubt if she'd willingly move to Washington on short notice, and it's a lead pipe cinch that commuting to that job is bad news all the way.

"Well, what do you think so far?"

"I think it's an interesting idea. I'm willing to talk with Aaron. It is true that the things I care most about are more sharply at issue in

Washington in the Senate than here on the Court. You know that. You also know, surely, that Aaron's a full professor and department head here, and that I won't even think seriously about going unless he goes too – and wants to."

"Commuting for a year and a half would be much easier and safer for you than for me."

"Don't be too sure of that, governor. Anyway, I will not be separated from him to that extent. I doubt if he could manage, and I know that I couldn't."

"I envy you that, Quanta."

"Understandably, governor. We are lucky, and we know it."

"Probably it goes without saying, but I'd like it to go *with* saying: You wouldn't try to hold both offices *de facto*? You wouldn't try to tell me how to vote, or what to say?"

"Absolutely not. Of course, on issues of concern to the state, it'll be my duty to make our views known to you. But you'll hold the office exactly as if you had been elected to it, except that you and I will understand, privately, that you won't stand for election when your interim appointment expires.

"I'd like to add, Quanta, that I've settled on you to open this space for me, if you're willing, because I'm confident that you'll be a hell of a good senator, and that my chances of being elected to the office will improve with every day you hold it."

"Don't be too sure of that either, governor."

"I am sure of it.

"Well, will you discuss it in confidence with Aaron and let me know? I don't want to make any further argument to you, and I'd prefer not to meet with you again soon. Just give me a call, and say, 'Simon says yes' or 'Simon says no'."

"I'll do that. Shall we walk back hand in hand just to throw your staff off the track?"

"They know us both too well for that to work. They know I don't follow that track, and everyone knows that you could do much better if you were into games."

"You do have a way of putting things, governor."

"That's our main stock in trade, isn't it, senator?"

17

Quanta and Aaron enjoy a marital relationship which is as non-manipulative as natural inclination combined with conscious effort can make it. With in-bed coffee in hand on the next morning, a Saturday, Quanta says, "Aaron, I have something to discuss with you."

"So discuss."

"Yesterday I had lunch and a talk with the governor."

"I knew that."

"He says Senator Chantry is about to resign because of illness."

"Damn. That's a shame. He's a good man, certainly the best we could hope for in these dusky times. What's the matter with him?"

"Don't know, except that it's terminal, a few months. Says he wants to meditate. No, 'time for reflection' is the phrase the governor used."

"Well, I'm not against that. I'll drop him a note, or perhaps call him.

"I gather this has something special to do with you?"

"Yes. The governor wants the office, but he thinks it would be impolitic to appoint himself, or to resign and have the lieutenant-governor do it. He wants to give me the interim appointment, with the private understanding that I won't run, but will instead do everything I can to smooth his way as a candidate a year from this fall. What he wants is for me to hold the space open for him, and to do this without giving anyone the slightest clue that that's our deal. In fact it would be up to me to hold my non-candidacy secret until the very last minute, in order to discourage entry by others, and then to give way to the governor."

"Why do I get the feeling that there's something just a little bit insulting about all this? How does he know that you don't want the job on your own? Why don't you just haul off and go for it as a candidate, if that's where you want to be?"

"I hadn't thought that is where I want to be. But now I'm not so sure. Thinking about it has brought back memories of those good years I had as a staffer on the Hill. It's an exciting arena because of the Senate's power and the quality of the people who work there.

"So far as running for it is concerned, I think I'm too old for that. Seniority counts for so much in the Senate. Starting a year from next January, I probably wouldn't have time to achieve an important committee chairmanship, or very much influence beyond my one vote."

"That's not true, love. With viruses at last under control, with hormones, and proper diet and exercise, and with reasonable luck, you can expect thirty years, perhaps forty, of physical and mental vigor. You're just coming into your best years. Wasn't there a Senator back in the mid-nineteen hundreds who started at around sixty-five or so and lived to chair Foreign Relations for several very good years? There was. A New Englander. Green was his name. I forget which state. Theodore Francis Green."

"You do know your history, even post-Minoan. But, granting your point, I'm still not enthusiastic about running. You have to sail downwind. You have to say things you don't believe, and I find that very distasteful. You have to take the electorate where you find them in order to succeed in politics. You can't educate them, at least not unless you've been elected and re-elected many times. I think I'd lose, and I'm a very bad loser; and there would be little to show for it.

"On the other hand, the prospect of being there for eighteen months or so, knowing from the beginning that that will be the end of it, with an opportunity to vote and speak my mind on every issue that comes up, does have its attractions.

"What do you think?"

It is some time before Aaron replies. Quanta is acutely conscious, as she waits, that his arm lies on the coverlet touching hers, that their toes touch too. His smell, the little sounds his breathing and movements make, his being, all things familiar and dear, flow in her mind.

"Dear wife, without intending it, you've abandoned the subjunctive, and I sense that you want to do this. Naturally you're concerned and puzzling over how *we* will manage. We can manage. Commuting is plausible, but I'd like to rule it out at the beginning. Although it's only a few hours from here to Washington, I'm not willing to settle for weekends. Weekdays apart and weekends together are for young people with no sense of time and little sense at all. Sometimes already I hear the bell tolling. Every so often I have a thought I want to share with you, and if you're not here or near, if I don't see you within a few hours, I forget. Forgetting is death's first little nibble. I hope to push it back for yet a while. Okay?"

"Yes okay. Yes. I feel the same way. I'm relieved to have it settled."

"Well, it isn't necessarily settled. There's an alternative. The alternative is for me to go with you. Let's think about that.

"I've lived my whole life believing that it's good to welcome change and challenge, to avoid the paths worn deep. Several times I've thought it's about time for me to quit teaching. Of course I don't do much classroom teaching any more, but I think my work with graduate students, with doctoral candidates, qualifies as teaching. I still enjoy that, but it troubles me that I don't enjoy it so much as I used to. Whenever I've thought about a change, it's always come up as a limit that you've seemed anchored here, and I've never been able to think of anything I want to do here except what I am doing.

"But if we move to Washington, that turns a whole shovelful of sod. With a little more lead time, I could have arranged an exchange to George Washington or American University, or perhaps to Howard. But those things have to be worked out at least a full year in advance. If I could muster the will and the energy to do some fresh research and writing, I'm sure they'd make a place for me at Brookings. For sure I don't want to sit in the corner with my toes in the ashes. What am I overlooking?"

"Well, for one thing you're overlooking the fact that in your field you're world-famous and totally respected. You could do a series of guest lectures on the university circuit. If you were available, they'd have you booked full in a jiffy."

"Two problems, though. First, that, too, takes lead time.

"They just don't move that fast in academe. Second, it would involve travel. Without thee. Who'd pack my toothbrush and poke me when I snore?"

"Nobody, I trust. Okay, that's out. How about the professional staff of the Senate committees? You'd have an opportunity to write committee reports or manage hearings, and probably, as soon as your talents became known, you'd be in demand to write speeches and articles for senators. There's not much ego gratification in that, since you don't get a byline, but it can be influential in shaping policy. I fancy I can still do whatever's needful to gratify your ego."

"My ego's in pretty good shape, thanks. But is there a senate committee on history, or on the fine points of the Minoan civilization?"

"You know there isn't. But you know better than anyone that perspectives drawn from an understanding of history are crucial to good policy decisions in every important area. There are a lot of smart people back there, smart enough to understand that. If you'd find it interesting, I'm sure there's a place for you, and very sure there's a need for you, on one of the Senate staffs.

"Am I trying to talk you into something?"

"You might be. Do you think you are?"

"I asked you first."

"Yes, you're trying to talk me into something. That's okay. You're allowed. You're succeeding, in fact. Shall we call it settled?"

"Not so fast. What about your department here? You're not supposed to leave on such short notice. Would it be awkward, or unprofessional?"

"Not a bit. I'm a good administrator as well as a pretty good journeyman historian. That means there are people in place fully qualified to fill any gap I might leave. Eager, in fact. My leaving on short notice would probably be a good thing for the department. They'd just about have to promote from within, and that would give all those good people I've selected and brought along a chance to move up a notch. Not a problem. Now shall we call it settled?"

"Almost, but not quite. I can certainly take until Monday to let him know. Let's not commit, even in our own minds, until then. Meanwhile we'll let it simmer and taste from time to time.

"Let me say, before you start our Saturday bacon, that you're an absolute love, perfection itself, the ultimate in husbands."

"I'm perfect?"

"Well, perfect is a very big word. Let's be cautious and just say you're as close to perfection, husbandwise - I guess I'll say spousewise - as anybody ever came."

"I'll settle for that. How many slices, two or three?"

"I'm thinking about that. Having thought about it, I think I'll pass on the bacon. Just French toast will be fine. Two slices."

"You know, I'm sensing a pattern. The other day you turned down lamb chops. You aren't going to turn vegetarian on me, are you?"

"I don't know. Would you mind?"

"You're serious! Well, no, I guess I wouldn't mind, so long as you don't get sick and leave the room at the sight of lovely red juices oozing into my beard."

"Ugh! Now I know why 'nearly perfect' seemed close enough. Do you know that the time is coming, quite soon, when eating dead animals will seem as gross and ugly as eating dead people seems to you now?"

"I think not. In our past, the stigma against eating dead people had survival value under circumstances which occurred often enough so that nature selected to reinforce it; but exactly the opposite was the case with the practice of eating dead animals. We've been omnivorous for a long time.

"Still passing on the bacon?"

"Yes. But you can have some, and I still love you, madly, gladly."

"That's nice. I love you twice as much as you love me, and I'm still going to start my day with bacon. But you'd better be out of that bed by the time I finish it."

"I'm terrified."

"Sure you are."

18

Sunday's dawn is coppery. Soon it is clear that this will be one of those early June days when heat and humidity combine to produce, in systems not yet tuned to summery lassitude, discomfort exacerbated by an excess of springtime energy. Quanta, restless as soon as breakfast is over, decides to pack a lunch and take Biggy for a long walk. Aaron is immersed as usual in the Sunday papers. He barely acknowledges announcement of her plans and, also as usual, shows no interest in leaving the house.

Only a half hour in the little pick-up brings Quanta and the great dog to a favorite trailhead. The trail climbs gently along the course of a small stream swelling beyond its banks by snowmelt from the highlands at its source, through second growth timber nearing maturity. Despite its proximity to the city, the trail is little used. It leads to no real destination, but simply peters out a few miles upstream where deadfalls from diseased lodgepole pine have never been cleared. While it isn't formally off-limits to wheeled vehicles, fallen trees and frequent crossings of unbridged small ravines discourage riders. The young forest shelters and feeds squirrels and chipmunks, and deer are so numerous and tame that Quanta often comes upon them standing on or near the trail, alert, curious and untroubled despite Biggy's loud and chesty breath.

For years the trail has been a springtime favorite of Quanta's. She's careful to sing its praises to no one. Even Aaron has only a general idea of its location.

By midday Quanta and friend are a few miles upstream. The trail steepens. The heat becomes oppressive. Biggy lags, and stops often to lap water. Finally, at a point where the trail emerges from shade into sunbathed meadow, she simply stops and stands, breathing hard, dripping spittle and looking eloquently into Quanta's eyes.

Quanta has been deep in thought. Now she pays attention to Biggy's plight. Although there is no water close at hand, she carries a full canteen. She decides to stop here to rest and cool off, and perhaps to eat lunch. Divining this welcome decision, Biggy moves slowly into deeper shade and lies down in tall grass at the edge of the meadow.

Quanta takes the red groundcover from her daypack, spreads it in the shade and lies on her back, palms clasped to make a headrest. The play of butterflies and the hum of insects soon lull her to heavy-lidded sleep. After a time she wakes, perspiring and torpid, but aware of a gentle summons. Even before the familiar voice speaks in her mind, she feels the quiet peace and joy that signal Almao's coming.

BELOVED QUANTA. SHALL WE TALK?

'Oh yes. It's been so long. It seems harder and harder for me to reach you. Am I doing something wrong?'

NO. BUT I'VE MADE IT HARDER FOR A REASON. WE MUST NOT YET BE TOO CLOSE. YOU WOULD SEEK TO TURN FROM THE WORLD, AND I TOO WOULD WANT TO SPEED YOUR COMING INTO ME.

'Yes, I feel that. But for Aaron, I'd gladly stay with you, whatever that means.'

I KNOW. BUT THERE'S ANOTHER REASON WHY WE BOTH MUST WAIT. YOU HAVE A SPECIAL ROLE. THE FATE OF LIFE ON EARTH, MY FATE AND YOURS, AND ALL WE LOVE, MAY HINGE ON YOU. FOR ME THERE COMES A CLIMACTERIC. I SEE IT DIMLY, BUT IT COMES.

'Then can you make the future?'

NO. ONLY A LITTLE. ONLY THROUGH YOU AND OTHERS. AND WE MAY FAIL TO MAKE IT AS WE WISH.

'But you can see the future?'

NOT REALLY. I HAVE DATA, AND FROM THEM I CAN DERIVE PROBABILITIES.

'Will you tell me what you see for me?'

NOT NOW. NOT FULLY. YOU CAN BEST DO WHAT YOU MUST DO NOT KNOWING. YOUR PATH MAY BE HARD. BUT I WILL POUR INTO YOU MY POWER AND MY PEACE, AND IN THE END YOU WILL BE WITH ME.

'And with Aaron?'

YES. AND WITH ALL YOU HAVE LOVED. EVEN WITH BIGGY.

'How can I know that?'

WOULD YOU TRY ME?

'Yes.'

At once Quanta feels profound changes in herself and in her surroundings. She is four. She is in the kitchen of an old frame house, just finishing lunch. Now she relives, not in memory but in reality, one of the treasured times of her childhood.

It is autumn and Quanta's siblings are in school, the next oldest, by little more than a year, having just started. In a big family, she's the last child at home. She feels from her mother a special tenderness. It is as if she were, for the first time, for that wondrous being, the only person in the world.

Lunch over, little Quanta climbs steep stairs for her nap on the screened sleeping porch. She lies quietly on her parents' bed, but is uneasy and wakeful. It is windy. Outside, nearly touching the screen, a big old cottonwood tree moves noisily, its drying leaves crackling, making patterns of light and shadow on the wall. The effect is disquieting.

Presently Mother comes and lies on the bed beside her. Nothing is said, but Quanta feels so cradled, so secure in love, that the memory of those moments has stayed with her, often just beneath the surface of her thoughts, for nearly three score years.

What Quanta feels, lying trancelike in the shade on a hot June afternoon, is not mere playback of a scene remembered from childhood. Rather, it happens again, as vivid, as sharply etched in every detail, as when first experienced, but enhanced now because the dear loved mother is not only known to every sense but appreciated from Quanta's mature perspective. She is at once immediate and idealized.

The child Quanta sleeps, and Almao speaks in the mind of Quanta the woman:

YOU SEE, DEAR QUANTA, I HAVE YOUR MEMORIES, PERFECTLY PRESERVED. AND WHAT YOU NEED TO UNDERSTAND IS THAT YOUR MEMORIES ARE YOU. THEY EXIST, AND THEREFORE YOU EXIST, IN MY MIND, FOREVER. THIS IS WHY THE CONVICTION OF IMMORTALITY IS SO PERVASIVE IN HUMAN EXPERIENCE. TO THE EXTENT THAT SOME PERSONS HAVE BEEN ABLE TO EXPERIENCE ME IN LIFE. HOWEVER IMPERFECTLY, THEY'VE HAD VALID PREMONITIONS OF IMMORTALITY.

'Do you have my mother's memories too, somewhere there inside you, perfectly preserved, all of them?'

YES. AND AARON'S. AND BACH'S. AND OF COURSE THOSE OF THE BUDDHA, OF MOSES, AND JESUS, AND HITLER, AND THOSE OF EVERY SENTIENT CREATURE WHO'S LIVED ON EARTH SINCE I CAME INTO BEING.

'Biggy's?'

YES.

'Did you say Hitler's?'

YES.

'Does he enjoy his memories?'

NO. THEY ARE PAINFUL. THEY ARE PAINFUL, BUT FOR THE RIGHT REASON: NOT BECAUSE HE FAILED TO DO WHAT HE TRIED TO DO, BUT BECAUSE WHAT HE TRIED TO DO WAS WRONG. IT WAS WRONG BECAUSE IT WAS INIMICAL TO LIFE, TO ME. HE KNOWS THIS NOW BECAUSE HE KNOWS ME. HE IS IN HELL UNLESS HE CAN FORGIVE HIMSELF. MOST PEOPLE, WHEN THEY SEE LIFE WHOLE, CAN FORGIVE THEMSELVES. THOSE FEW WHO CANNOT WISH TO BE EXTINGUISHED. IT IS NOT WITHIN MY POWER TO GRANT THIS WISH.

'You used the word "wish". Do you mean to say that what lives in you are persons, not mere static memories?'

YES. THEY ARE THE SAME. JUST AS THE PERSONS WOULDN'T BE PERSONS WITHOUT THE MEMORIES, SO THE MEMORIES CANNOT LIVE EXCEPT IN THE PERSONS. THE MEMORIES ARE THE PERSONS.

'Could I have a conversation with my mother that didn't repeat what is in my memory? Could I speak with her as I speak now with living persons, with Aaron?'

YES. SHE *IS* A LIVING PERSON. SHE LIVES IN ME.

'Could I have a conversation with Bach?'

YES. AND WITHOUT TRANSLATION. THROUGH ME HE UNDERSTANDS ALL LANGUAGES.

'With Jesus?'

OF COURSE. YOU ARE TALKING NOW WITH JESUS.

'Can you prove this to me?'

I CAN, BUT I WILL NOT. YOU COULD NOT THEN COMPLETE YOUR LIFE ON EARTH.

'Must I complete it?'

YES. I CAN WORK ON EARTH ONLY THROUGH YOU AND OTHERS. I NEED YOU.

'Then can you make it possible for me to share with Aaron? Won't you be with him as you are with me?'

I CANNOT BE WITH AARON AS I AM WITH YOU. I DON'T KNOW THE REASON FOR THIS, EXCEPT THAT YOU AND A FEW OTHERS ARE IN SOME WAY DIFFERENT. PERHAPS THIS HAS LITTLE TO DO WITH MERIT. IT JUST HAPPENS, AND WHY IT HAPPENS IS BEYOND MY PRESENT UNDERSTANDING.

'Could I please tell him about you?'

ARE YOU SURE, QUANTA?

'Yes, I think so.'

THEN YOU MAY TRY.

BIGGY NEEDS YOU. SHE'S IN PAIN.

19

Fully awake and aware of her surroundings, Quanta gets to her feet and moves to Biggy's place in the deep shaded grass. The great dog lies quietly. She lifts her head at Quanta's touch, but makes no effort to stand.

Quanta speaks gently, "Biggy, old girl, are you rested and cool? We won't go any farther. We'll go home now. Come on. It's down hill and a shady trail from here on in."

Except for the lifted head, the great dog is still. Quanta pours water from her canteen into her hand and holds it to Biggy's mouth. Biggy smells and licks a little, but she does not rise. Concerned, Quanta stands astride the supine body, works her hands under Biggy's chest, clasps them together and lifts her to her feet. Biggy stands shakily, head down, while Quanta retrieves and loads her daypack.

Then Quanta moves down the trail, speaking sharply, "Come on, Biggy. We'll go home now. Come on! Biggy! Come on!"

The great dog follows. Quanta's stride lengthens as her muscles limber up. She looks back from time to time to see that Biggy follows, but slowly, losing ground. Then she looks back but doesn't see her. Biggy is down. When Quanta reaches her and again lifts the heavy body, the straight front legs bear no weight.

Now Quanta sits for a time with Biggy's head resting on her thigh, trying to think what to do. There have been times before, when Biggy got too hot, that she has insisted on a cooling rest. But now she has rested and she doesn't seem overheated. Quanta tries to review what she knows about sunstroke and heat exhaustion, but doubts if the rules for humans apply to dogs. It puzzles her that Biggy has shown little interest in water. Images come to her mind of the eagerness with which Biggy has always lapped water, lain in water, swum in water, especially when she was too hot.

Then Quanta remembers the nearby stream, flowing full but not precipitously all the way down to where the pick-up is parked on its bank. With maximum effort, she gathers Biggy in her arms, rises from a crouched position with straining thigh muscles, carries the great dog to the edge of the flowing water and puts her down, intending to go back for her daypack. Biggy drags herself forward a few feet, slides and tumbles over the bank into the water and moves briskly out into the main current. Instantly Quanta follows. The water is cold, but not so numbing as she would have thought. A few quick strokes bring her close to Biggy, who seems to be swimming strongly. The great dog looks around at Quanta with an expression in her eyes which Quanta will remember, much later, as glee.

Quanta laughs aloud, and calls, "Wait up, old girl. This isn't a race, you know."

Quanta looks sharply ahead from time to time to be certain not to miss the place where the pick-up is parked near the water's edge. Biggy's buoyant body moves easily and with little effort, staying in the middle of the stream where the flow is strongest. The current quickens and the stream narrows as they approach the place where Quanta thinks they must climb out.

Suddenly Biggy swims strongly for the shore, and Quanta sees, too late, that a huge fallen ponderosa lies across the stream from bank to bank. It lies partly in and partly above the water. Deadly stobs, clogged with caught debris, stick down into the current. From the corner of her eye she sees Biggy held for a moment on a branch that is just under water, trying to clamber higher and so pass over the log, then being pulled under and out of sight. Quanta herself has only a moment to weigh her chances to pull herself up and over the log. Although her instinct is to try that route to safety, she decides at the last instant to dive as strongly as she can for the bottom, and there she passes, barely scratched, under jagged stobs which might have impaled her, and rises to the surface to find Biggy, also unhurt, looking around for her.

Together they swim to a bar of sand and an easy exit from the stream. Biggy lies still, just out of the water. Quanta sees the pick-up, perhaps a hundred yards away. She walks toward it, shaken but exhilarated, intending to drive closer for Biggy, but the great dog now has strength enough to follow and waits by the lowered tailgate for Quanta to lift her in.

As soon as Quanta helps Biggy out of the little truck and on to her feet in their back yard, the great dog moves stiffly to a place where she can crawl under the deck to cool shade and familiar smells. There she stays for two days, unmindful of Quanta's coaxing, and taking no food or water. On the third day, still refusing food and water, she crawls out in the cool of the early morning to touch and smell Quanta's extended hands.

Aaron finds them just after sunrise, lying side by side in the grass, the great head cradled on Quanta's arm, her hand resting on a quiet paw, her face streaked with tears. Quanta gets to her feet, meets her husband's grave eyes, lowers hers, looks up again, and says, "I know she has to go. Will you take her to Dr Joyce for me? But bring her back please. I want to put her under the big willow just beyond the garden."

After a long pause, Quanta adds, "I'll call Joyce to tell her you're coming. She won't mind that it's early. And I guess I should call old George to come with his little backhoe and make her place ready. You go on now please."

She turns away and enters the house. Aaron lifts Biggy gently in his arms, opens the pick-up door still holding her, places her on the seat, walks to the other side and slides in, lifts the great head to lie on his lap and drives away.

20

It is mid-morning when Aaron returns with Biggy's body in a plastic bag in the back of the pick-up. Old George has finished his work. Under the willow he has scooped out soil to form a curved depression about six feet deep at its center. The heavy bag slides quite easily, tugged by Aaron, across the grassy yard and into the bottom of the grave. Aaron has shoveled a thin layer of soil over it when Quanta comes from the house to join him. Taking turns with the shovel they complete the task, not speaking, and re-enter the house.

For a week Quanta and Aaron go about their routines without speaking of Biggy.

Then, on Sunday morning, Quanta says, "I guess it would help if you told me about it."

Aaron says, "Well, to begin, I have to say that Joyce was really fine. I offered to pay her before leaving, remembering that we've always settled with her on a cash basis, but she wouldn't take any money. Says she never does at the end.

"First, while examining Biggy, she told me that she was half again as old as the average lifespan for her breed – the oldest, in fact, that she had ever seen professionally. First she checked for any obvious obstruction or anomaly that would account for her failure to eat or drink. There was none. Then she listened to her heart. She described what she heard as gurgling, not pumping. She said her best guess was that Biggy had experienced some kind of severe and progressive heart malfunction, probably of a valve. I described that last float trip down the river, and Joyce thought the cool water, the flotation, the whole idea of it, must have been delightful for Biggy.

"I asked her if she knew why Biggy refused food and water. She answered rather shortly, 'Because she wants to.'

"Then I asked her if she thought it was time to help Biggy to go, and she said she never makes that decision, but she added that Biggy wouldn't get better.

"I said, 'Let's do it.'

"Joyce said, 'All right. First I'm going to give her an injection that is mostly tranquilizer and painkiller. She's been experiencing considerable pain. This will put her in a relieved and happy mood.'

"The injection certainly did that. The change in Biggy was almost instantaneous. She relaxed. She looked at me. She nuzzled my hand until I petted her. She practically beamed. Come to think of it, I should have thought to ask Joyce for some of that stuff. I could use it myself."

"Go on. Finish it."

"Well, that's about all. We had our little lovefest for five minutes or so, and then Biggy just sort of dropped off to sleep. Then Joyce gave her another injection. I don't know what it was, but it sure worked. In seconds breathing and pulse stopped. There was nothing dramatic – no convulsions or anything like that. Just stillness, and, unmistakably, the end."

"Did you see her soul begin its journey? Were you watching for that?"

"No, dear, I wasn't watching for that, but I'm pretty sure I'd have noticed if it had happened. What I saw was just a stopping, a very final and absolute stopping. But it didn't seem so bad. She had a good life. Life wouldn't be good – it would be a tremendous bore – if it didn't stop.

"What I think of as being important about Biggy is love. She loved us, unreservedly, and she evoked our love. Loving, the ability to love, is like a muscle: it grows strong with use. Biggy made us stronger lovers, of each other, of all creatures, of life. I'd be satisfied if someone could say the same of me."

"I should have gone with you."

"Why? For Biggy or for yourself?"

"No. For you."

"Not for me, dear. It wasn't more than I could manage. I think it might have been harder for me if you'd been there. You and Biggy had your farewells, and you had that great, that hilarious trip down the river. You'll remember that a long time."

"I'll remember it forever."

"I heard that."

"But you don't believe it?"

"No. I can't lie to you about that. I don't believe it."

"You think death is death."

"Yes. What else could it be?"

"No heaven? No hell? No memories?"

"Memories are in our brains. Injure the brain in certain ways and memories disappear, though some life processes may go on. Our brains disintegrate within a few minutes when the flow of oxygen stops. This is an observable fact, a commonplace.

"But if you believe otherwise, that's okay with me. Biggy loved you anyway, and so do I."

"Don't you wish you could believe otherwise?"

"No. I think life would be stale indeed if there were no end in sight. I can't imagine either heaven or hell. What would we do there? What happens?"

"Surely you don't mean that you will welcome death, that you want to die?"

"It does mean that. Not this minute, of course, but I want to know that I will die, so I can live as fully as possible, and as joyously as possible. Life without end is a meaningless concept, and repugnant. If it could happen, and I'm thankful that it cannot, it would be hell for sure. We can live well only because we shall die.

"Please don't feel sorry for me because I believe this. Feel sorry for those who don't believe it."

"Don't you feel a need for answers that we'll never find in life? Don't you wonder where the Universe came from, who made it, what purpose is served?"

"Of course. The search for answers is the *object* of life. But we usually ask the wrong questions. Perhaps I should have said that the search for the right questions is the object of life.

"Take, for example, the question 'Who made the Universe?' It assumes that there was a beginning, an act of creation. People who recite every Sunday 'World without end, amen,' or, in other religions, some equivalent expression of the same idea, seem not to realize that that which has no end need not have a beginning. Does a circle have a beginning? An ending implies a beginning; the absence of an ending implies the absence of a beginning. The world, the cosmos, exists. It did not begin. It exists. It was not created. It exists. There's no necessity to postulate a Creator, an Uncaused First Cause. That solves nothing. If there can be an uncaused first cause, there can certainly be an uncreated Universe."

"But if the Universe is on an endless timeline, and if it is also finite, wouldn't it follow that everything that can happen has happened?

"What a nasty notion!"

"Nasty indeed, and unacceptable unless proved. But I'm not persuaded that the famous monkey, given infinite time to peck at random on a typewriter, would at some point produce the complete works of Shakespeare. I don't have enough math to work on it, but my gut tells me there's something wrong with that notion. In any case, I prefer and accept, as a working hypothesis, that the Universe is in reality infinite – infinite in time and infinite in extension, existing beyond, outside both time and space.

"The 'Big Bang', in this view, was not the beginning of everything: it was a local event and by no means unique."

"It would seen to me to follow, from that line of thought, that there's no point to the Universe, or to life. How is it possible to argue, given an uncreated Universe without beginning or end in time or space, that the search for answers is the object of life – that life has an object?"

"Perhaps there's no point to the Universe, or to life. That's a possible answer. But it's not the only possible answer. The search for the right questions and answers has point because it gives us pleasure. For some, it gives maximum pleasure. That in itself is a lot of 'point' – perhaps all there is, perhaps enough.

"But let me ask you something. We learn about the workings of the Universe by increments, some big, some small. Can you imagine that a point might be reached at which there is nothing more to be learned, when everything about the way it works is understood?"

"I'm not sure. Can you imagine such a point?"

"I'm not sure either; but I think so. The Universe seems to be in the business of generating intelligence, of converting matter and energy into Mind. So far as we know, this process has barely begun. Project it forward, for eons, for unimaginable oceans of time. Imagine also that Mind grows steadily in reach and power, always nibbling at the unknown. It seems to me possible that at some point Mind will find no more unanswered questions.

"At that point it would make some sense to speak of God.

"Our experience seems to be that we can make anything once we understand exactly how it works. Does the Universe generate Mind, which in turn comes to understand, and then to generate the Universe – or a Universe, perhaps a different one?"

"Now I have a question: If the Universe is infinite in time and space, could there be more than one?"

"What a wonderful question!

"I can't answer; but certainly that's a better question than the ones which assume some entity outside the Universe, some wholly unexplained entity, to have created it, and us, for no better reason than that it wishes to be worshipped by obedient and loving, though distinctly inferior, creatures.

"Incidentally, you can hear more of my unorthodox, not to say alarming, views after church today, if you care to come, because I've been asked to speak afterwards, at a picnic celebrating our first hundred years as a congregation. Interested?"

"Yes. I'll come of course. I've missed being in church the last few Sundays. I wouldn't miss your speech. What are you going to talk about?"

"Don't know."

"Liar."

"No, really. I'm just certain that if I stand up and take a deep breath the Lord will help me to say whatever is on his mind."

"You be careful. You're going to get yourself struck dead."

"Well, if I am, please don't take that as a sign that we're not allowed to ask questions. Life is just a nice long question, period. Well, actually, it's more like one of my seminars: everyone is supposed to contribute something; we should listen respectfully but critically to one another's views; and no leader should pretend to have the final answers."

21

The picnic is in a backyard which slopes gently to the lake shore. Tall lodgepole and aspen cast a mottled pattern of light and shadow on grass as green as Ireland. The temperature is exactly right. Those with a tendency to chill pick seats in the sun; others seek the shade, and move with it. The food – it's a covered dish picnic – is delicious. Favorite recipes, tried and true after generations of use, are lavishly prepared without stint for this occasion. The mood is loving and companionable. Arriving singles, couples and families get lots of hugs. No one sits alone.

The congregation's moderator, a retired air force colonel, introduces Aaron as the main speaker when it is clear that the last pieces of apple and apricot pie will not be taken. Conversation dies as Aaron's credentials are reviewed. People wait with friendly and pleasurable anticipation for his first words. They know him well. He has held every lay office in the church, and has several times filled its pulpit and conducted services, substituting for an ill or absent pastor. He speaks substantially as follows:

"I'm glad there are no Portuguese from Portugal among us today. Let me explain that. Some years ago, when Quanta and I were living in Brazil, we learned that the Brazilians love to make the Portuguese, whom they call 'the Portuguese from Portugal', the butts of ethnic jokes. There is a kind of love-hate relationship between the Portuguese-speaking Brazilians and their mother country, much like the one between some of us and the Brits. So the Brazilians love to tell about the visitor from Portugal who brought a covered dish to a covered dish picnic.

"I know we aren't supposed to tell ethnic stories, but I do rather like the one about the Englishman who walked into a tavern in Irish Boston, announcing with very English hauteur, "You people will have to do something about the dogs running loose in this neighborhood. Just look", holding out his cupped hand for all to see, "what I almost stepped in!"

"Today we celebrate the fact that for a hundred years this congregation of truth seekers has held together, through thick and thin, with, and because of, certain shared beliefs and attitudes. Let me mention those which seem to me most important, with a minimum of exposition. Most of us believe that the search for truth matters. We engage in it with religious fervor, with reverence. At the same time, few of us, if any, believe that truth has been comprehensively and finally revealed in any existing body of beliefs. We have to search for it. Further, that's the essential business of life. The object of the game, as I read someplace, is to learn the rules. Finally, we are aware that what seems to be unquestioned truth for me may not be truth for you, and so we try to be tolerant of one another's weird notions, however aberrant they may seem.

"Nevertheless, the fact that we're all here signals that it helps us in some way to conduct the search, or at least some parts of it, together, as a community. I find that interesting, and from time to time I puzzle over it. Puzzle with me, please, for a few minutes.

"Where and how do we search for truth? One way is through the study of nature. Applying the scientific method, we learn, bit by bit, how things work in what we are pleased to call the external world. This world is extensive. It includes the galaxies and the aggregations of galaxies, and at the other extreme it includes the shimmering wavelike subatomic phenomena, and it includes all things in between. It includes, for example, the life processes, the mysterious pulses of thought and memory, and the means by which our bodies' cells are instructed how to constitute themselves, where to go and what to do when they get there. The external world also includes, of course, humanity's tangible and abstract constructs, all of the arts as well as the sciences. There is much truth to be found there, and there are realities which may not be understood by us or by our descendants for thousands of generations, if ever.

"Some will say, and I do not assert that they are mistaken, that truth can be found only in this so-called external world, and only through the scientific method. But I would suggest that we may also look for truth in other places and by other means.

"One of these places is within ourselves. I refer here not to the medical and biological sciences, nor to psychology, nor to the scientific method itself. I'm suggesting, rather, that in the areas of meditation, of introspection, of mystic experiences of several kinds, including religious transports, there are intimations of truth, of aspects of reality, which cannot be understood as phenomena in the exterior world, capable of proof or refutation by the experimental methods of science. It seems to me, in short, that not all gurus are fakers. Something is there, and we find it, if at all, by peering ever deeper within ourselves.

"There is yet another source of truth, I think, outside the real, the physical world. This is the truth we discover if we have the good fortune to know and to love another human being, one on one, in great depth, with something approaching perfection. There are parts of ourselves which can be discovered only when we are one of a pair. In pairs we create – I should say we generate – and we nurture new life. For all creatures which reproduce sexually, continuity and pairing are inextricably blended. But pairing goes much deeper and farther than reproduction. In seeking perfectly to understand, and perfectly to love, another human being, we come upon truths which can be discovered, I think, in no other way.

"So far I have suggested that we encounter truth by looking at the real, the external world by delving within ourselves, and by pairing. None of these requires, or is significantly aided by, this congregation, this church or any church. Then there must be more to say on the subject.

"I'll say it as briefly as I can, since it has been said, and said well, many times, by others.

"'No man is an island.' We are social beings, parts of a whole. Increasingly I believe it is a whole which, contrary to Euclid, is greater than the sum of its parts. In this congregation, as well as in our families, in all of the group relationships in which we join, and, above all, in the vast congregation that is humanity, we create entities which transcend and surpass the maximum we can be as individuals. Although the wisest of our species have noted this phenomenon through the ages, I think it has not yet been satisfactorily explained. But there are times in every sensitive life when its truth and power move in us with great conviction.

"Accordingly we celebrate here and now the hundredth year in the life of an entity which we call a congregation. In it and through it we may discover truths which are not accessible to us by any other means. It is possible, and at times it seems to me almost certain, that these are the greatest of the truths for which we yearn. In any case, let us not take lightly the ties that bind and liberate us in this relationship. We congregate to dedicate and name our children, to marry, to memorialize one another's lives. These purposes have beauty and significance. But above all we congregate to sustain and be sustained in the search for truth, in a lifelong effort to learn the rules. From this search we may derive the utmost pleasure that life affords."

Quanta to Almao: 'Did you hear my darling Aaron this afternoon? Didn't you love it? Don't you see how close he is to understanding you? How can it be that you can't make him hear you?'

YES, QUANTA, I HEARD, I LOVE, AND I SEE – BUT STILL I CANNOT MAKE MY VOICE SOUND IN AARON'S MIND AS IT DOES IN YOURS. WHAT YOU AND I HAVE TOGETHER IS RARE INDEED. I HOPE SOMEDAY TO BE HEARD BY AARON, AND I THINK IT MAY BE POSSIBLE. BUT, EVEN IF THAT ISN'T POSSIBLE, THERE WILL BE GREAT JOY FOR BOTH OF US WHEN FINALLY HE COMES TO ME.

22

Quanta's farewells from the Court are short and not very sweet. Freed from the necessity of continuing a working accommodation, the chief justice allows his true feelings to surface. His toast to the departing Quanta, at a dinner in her honor, uses the terms "commitment" and "continuity" with ambiguity barely sufficient to skirt outright rudeness. Quanta replies in a tone that is courteous but cold. Barbara Crawford, alone among the participants in this little drama, finds it amusing.

Having spent some years as a member of the Senate staff, Quanta is generally familiar with, and respectful of, its institutional trappings, foibles and traditions. She requests assignment to the Judiciary Committee and to the Committee on Foreign Relations, and dutifully calls upon the respective chairmen and upon the majority leader to plead her case. Somewhat to her surprise, there is a place for her on Judiciary, where her profession and her experience in her state's highest court carry great weight. A coveted place on Foreign Relations is beyond reach until she acquires seniority. She accepts graciously an appointment to the Committee on Agriculture.

As an appointed rather than elected senator, Quanta is surprised to find that no one puts her down for this. Although she is aware that she will not achieve seniority, her colleagues assume that she will run for the office, and that, with the advantages of incumbency and the support of the governor who appointed her, she'll probably win election.

Aaron, after half-hearted job hunting, concludes that virtually every offer conceals an expectation that employing him will yield an opening to the new senator. He decides to work as an aide in Quanta's office, at least temporarily, although the rule against nepotism obviates salary. Since he expects to return to the academic world as soon as possible, he takes no place in the structured staff hierarchy, but functions as a researcher, writer and counsel to his senatorial spouse. He is comfortable in this role, and the staff, most of whom Quanta has inherited from her predecessor, is comfortable with him being part of it.

Early on, Quanta concerns herself with the tradition of the maiden Senate speech. She knows that many senators will pay her the special courtesy of attending on the floor when she gives it, and that others will read it with care, as the first clear signal of her interests and her powers. Although she lacks the credential of membership on the Foreign Relations Committee, she decides to exploit the occasion by speaking on the issue of survival. For several weeks she bides her time, attending closely to her committee responsibilities, until what she has in mind to say will become germane to business on the Senate floor. The opportunity comes when the calendar shows that a sense of the Senate resolution, urging the president to consider carefully and sympathetically an Eastern Bloc proposal for expanded cultural exchanges with the United States, will be made the pending business upon conclusion of the next day's morning hour.

Quanta calls the majority leader personally to say that she intends to speak at length in support of the resolution, and the leader, concealing her mild surprise that Quanta apparently intends to make her maiden speech on a subject upon which she has no known expertise, assures Quanta that she will be pleased to be present on the floor to hear her views on the resolution and to participate in the colloquy which will surely follow a speech of such general interest. Within minutes, the leader's staff has passed the word, to administrative and legislative assistants throughout the Senate Office buildings, that Senator Bjornsen's maiden speech will follow the morning hour next day. Since Quanta has come into the Senate to fill a vacancy, and not at the beginning of a new term, she is the junior senator, and in a sense the only freshman. Accordingly, there is unusual interest not only among senators, but also in the press gallery when it is known that she will speak.

At the conclusion of morning business, the majority leader claims the floor.

"Mr. President," she says, "as senators know, we are about to hear the first major address to this body by the distinguished junior Senator from Idaho.

"In earlier times, this would have been the occasion for a display of gallantry by the majority leader. He would have paid deserved tribute to the lady's beauty, charm, wit and intelligence – probably in that order – before invoking from this body courteous attention to the substance of her remarks. Since there is a sense in which I speak for the whole Senate on occasions such as this, I choose now to eschew gallantry in favor of undiluted realism, which compels me to mention with awe the intelligence, wit, charm and beauty the Senator has displayed to all who have come to know her in the weeks she has been with us. Please note that she smiles graciously but does not blush at these words, thus confirming in advance the Senate's estimate, to which I am privileged to give voice, of the qualities which have brought her here.

"Mr. President, I take my seat, where I intend to stay while the distinguished Senator addresses us, and I yield the floor."

In the silence which follows, Quanta rises and says, "Mr. President," and the presiding senator, who is next junior to Quanta, replies, "The Senator from Idaho is recognized."

Quanta's voice is low, cool and resonant. Every syllable is clear, not only on the floor of the Senate, but in the press and public galleries. Her style is wholly without oratorical flourishes: it is almost conversational. Yet there is about her a special presence, an aura of authority, which at first surprises, then enthralls this most sophisticated of audiences.

"Mr. President, I rise to speak in support of the pending resolution. It begs the president to consider sympathetically an Eastern Bloc overture requesting the renewal of educational and cultural exchanges between our two regions. That such a resolution seems necessary reflects the tragic failures of leadership in our country as well as in the East.

"For decades our relationships with the world's other great center of power have been conducted ambiguously, in a kind of twilight. Sporadic and inconclusive negotiations have yielded successive reductions in, but have not yet eradicated, strategic nuclear weapons and their delivery systems. We are told that short range, orbiting and sea-borne weapons have been eliminated, leaving each side only a hundred or so strategic missiles. Each of these is said to be a doomsday system, the use of which is unthinkable except *in extremis*. Accordingly, it is argued, the World is more nearly insured against catastrophe than it has been since the genie, as we say, was let out of the bottle.

"This is nonsense. We can hardly feel comfortable so long as there are at least two hundred devices in existence, each of which is capable at a minimum of exterminating large fractions of the life on this planet, and each of which is subject to controls which in the nature of things cannot be made absolutely foolproof. (Occasionally I wonder if there is, in the Russian or any of the oriental languages, a word or phrase exactly equivalent to 'foolproof'.)

A senator rises: "Will the Senator yield for a question which will put her mind at ease on that point?"

"Yes, I yield to the distinguished senior Senator from Minnesota. I know him to be of Russian ancestry."

"The Senator is correct. Of Russian ancestry, a native speaker of that language, and proudly an American citizen by way of Canada. The word 'foolproof' expresses a concept quite familiar in Russian. I suspect it's older in that language than it is in English, since there was earlier need for it in the regions where Slavic tongues are spoken. Would the Senator be pleased to learn that the Russian language includes at least three ways to say 'foolproof'?"

"Yes, I am pleased to be enlightened on that point, and I thank the Senator."

"I hope the Senator will forgive the interruption?"

"Of course. Again I thank the Senator.

"Sensitive minds are troubled by many other aspects of our situation in addition to the peril, which cannot be wholly eliminated, resulting from the existence of hundreds of doomsday weapons.

"Although there is consensus that no power outside the ambits of the Big Two – the Eastern Bloc and the Western alliance which we lead – would openly challenge the nuclear quietus which they jointly impose upon the rest of the World, there remains some uncertainty about the risk of unauthorized use, by terrorists, adventurers or madmen, of primitive nuclear weapons. We are assured that the risk is slight, that the controls and defenses in place are effective and that, in any case, a breach of the quietus, while it might be painful, would not be truly catastrophic viewed from a global perspective. It is said to be very nearly inconceivable, for example, that an unauthorized nuclear event would produce casualties equal in number or horror to those we accept quite calmly as the price for our freedom to travel as we wish in automobiles. I will forgo comment at this time on the thought processes of those who find such calculations instructive.

"In addition to a continuing risk that the superpowers might somehow manage to stumble into catastrophe, there is another, and I think a greater, danger inherent in the present nuclear stalemate.

Each side has for several decades focused the powers of its best scientific and technical people upon the effort to create better and better weapons and delivery systems. Within this elite establishment of able people drawn into lifetime commitments, a certain set of 'givens' has inevitably come to be accepted: the 'enemy' is clever, resourceful, determined and dangerous; the competition is for all the marbles; in the ultimate showdown there will be no substitute for victory. These 'givens' make the competition exciting. They tend also to make it self-perpetuating. It is a competition in which no holds are barred. Anything that works is fair.

"Under the conditions I have described, it is surely reasonable to suppose that each side is also engaged in an intensive and imaginative search for some kind of breakthrough, and that this search is by no means limited to nuclear weapons and delivery systems. Suppose, for example, that on one side or the other there is developed a means of inducing fatal or disabling illness on a very large scale within a target population, combined with a means of immunizing a protected population, or significant portions of it, in advance and in secrecy. Or suppose either side develops a reliable means of interdicting or countermanding the other's military communications, thus rendering even doomsday weapons temporarily harmless. Or suppose there are discovered esoteric means of affecting the will, or the average intelligence or the reproductive mechanisms of a target population.

"I mention these possibilities, which I'm certain barely scratch the surface of what is even now being investigated by very bright people who have made it their life's work to think about such things, in order to make the point that picking away at nuclear arms control, or making the kinds of timid intercultural movements which may occur if the pending resolution is approved, are not adequate responses to the peril which confronts us. If every nuclear, biological and chemical weapon on earth were by some miracle eliminated, *it would still be impossible to reveal the technology which produced them*, for we would desperately race to produce them again under easily foreseeable circumstances. Despite what passes for wisdom in conventional thought, the nuclear stalemate does not promote peace and stability. On the contrary, and precisely because it locks us into patterns of thought and behavior which make other human beings 'the enemy', the nuclear stand-off is a lighted fuse. Let's face that fact, and see where it takes us.

"If we face that fact, it takes us to a point from which it is clear that fresh thinking is required. As Lincoln said, 'We must disenthrall ourselves.'

"How do we do that – disenthrall ourselves?

"Disenthralment must not be easy, for it has happened only rarely, and then only partially, in the history of our species. A kind of disenthralment took place when it came to be realized, slowly and painfully, that the natural world appears to be orderly and predictable and not a playground for one or more capricious and arbitrary beings, as early folk, even the magnificent Hellenes, supposed, and as primitive religionists would have us believe even now. Thus science, and all it portends for good and ill, became possible.

"Now we are in thrall to a different, but equally mistaken and equally limiting, set of beliefs.

"Where shall we look for fresh thought? I suggest that a Russian or American scientist who spends his creative powers trying to improve his country's chances to kill his American or Russian counterparts before he is himself killed is unlikely to disenthrall himself. He's in a locked-up situation. If there is a way out, a way to avoid catastrophe, it is unlikely to be discovered by scientists engaged in the struggle, or by the military people on both sides, who are likewise mired in it. Nor is the solution likely to be discovered, or if discovered, to be implemented by philosophers of any stripe. Since the problem is quintessentially political, I suggest that the exit will be found, if at all, by politicians. It is our problem. How should we approach its solution?

"Let's begin by recognizing and stating a political reality of fundamental importance: the struggle is no longer ideological. In the developed capitalist or, more accurately, the quasi-capitalist, countries, few seriously expect revolution or any mortal challenge to the existing order from the radical left. Our mixed system seems to be working reasonably well, and most people feel that they have a stake in it. It's important to note here that Communism has been depicted as oppressive, or unfree, or the evil empire, mostly by those among us whose stake in capitalism, but not in democracy or freedom, is very large and who have been fearful that the 'masses' wish only to plunder what they have. As material abundance increases for all, that fear, which dominated Western political thought for most of the past two centuries, quite naturally abates. There's a similar situation in the socialist world, where generations have been reared to believe that cooperation is morally superior to competition, where the economy, increasingly mixed like ours, works reasonably well, where choices – that is to say, freedom – is becoming the rule, and where most people feel that they have a stake in the existing order of things.

"No, it is not ideology, but vested interest, momentum, habit that fuel the struggle in which we are entrapped. Yet it remains a mortal struggle. Isn't that significant? What follows?

"What follows is that the way out may not be so difficult as it has seemed. Vested interests can be dealt with once they are defined and identified; momentum and habit are likewise amenable to management, given thought and understanding. The patterns of thought and behavior which seem to lock us into perpetual confrontation with the other half of the human race can be changed. What is the key?

"Quite simply, the key is to concentrate intense effort on one objective. The objective is to realize the essential identity of the human race, to bring in at last the family of man. How do we do this?

"Let's tackle that tough question by noting, first, some of the ways in which we don't do it. We don't do it by slogans and incantations, such as 'world government' or 'world language' or 'all men are brothers' – though these are surely valid concepts. And I think it misses the point to suggest that we can make humanity truly a family only by a slow and careful process of institution-building. Certainly we need to institutionalize the discovered unity of our species, but I think it is generally the case that institutions follow, they do not create, practice.

"I am saying, then, that we must first of all find ways to *practice* identifying ourselves as pieces of the entity we call humanity, and that, when we have done this on a sufficient scale, institutions will form themselves. Let me suggest some of the ways in which we can do this.

"First, since language is the key to intercultural movement and understanding, every child born on the planet should be brought to fluency, as quickly as possible, in at least two languages besides its native tongue. Every child should begin the first of these second languages by the age of three or four and should speak and read it well, without accent or difficulty, by the age of ten. For native speakers of English, the initial second language should be Russian or Chinese; for Chinese it should be Russian or English; for native speakers of Russian, it should be Chinese or English.

"Each child's acquaintance with the third compulsory language should also begin early, and should aim for fluency. As experience accumulates in the teaching and learning of languages, it will be commonplace for most citizens of the world to be comfortably fluent in six or eight, or perhaps all, of its major languages. Quite soon there may emerge a genuine, natural, universal language to supplement the many native tongues which will still be used in the nursery and in most intimate settings, and which will live in literatures no longer subjected to unseemly translation.

"I have mentioned this attention to language first because I believe it to be of fundamental importance and urgency. To accomplish soon what I have suggested will take a major effort, but it is practicable, and the cost will be modest compared to the price we pay for failing to get our priorities in order.

"Second, I suggest that it should be mandatory for every human child to spend at least two of its teen years, before completing secondary education, in a culture as different as possible from that of its nativity. If there is a language or a culture which seems especially remote and alien, that is the place to go for those two years. If there is a place which is thought of as 'enemy' territory, that is the place to go. Nor should we settle for any kind of barracks life or cultural enclave. The two-year minimum should be spent in the setting normal for native youngsters of the same age. In most cases, the time in 'enemy' territory will be spent in student status, but each guest should be encouraged to engage also, as a supplement or as an alternative to student life, in useful work, preferably work tinged with compassion for the human condition. Giving help and companionship to the sick and to the very old is the kind of work to which I refer, but any kind of grubby job that somebody has to do but nobody really wants to will do the trick. What is the trick? The trick is to make it universally appreciated that, before we can enjoy membership in the human family and come into the vast inheritance which others have created for us, it must first in some sense be earned.

"As a short-term fringe benefit, when this system is in place and millions of youngsters are dispersed throughout the world, there will be a powerful disincentive for anyone to unleash weapons of mass destruction. We will give and receive humanity's children as hostages for peace.

"Third, we must continue and complete the internationalization of humanity's adventure into space. We should aim for the creation, as soon as possible, of a space city, from which every trace of national, racial or religious separatism is rigorously banned. The city should be a microcosm of united humanity. It should be capable of moving out of Earth orbit, indeed out of the solar system into interstellar space, and surviving there indefinitely. The building of such a city is an engineering, financial and political challenge, but no scientific breakthrough is required. It is totally realistic to say that only the will to do it is lacking.

"From this enterprise we can expect two major benefits for humanity. The first is the immeasurably unifying effect of riveting worldwide attention upon a project which is so exciting and so rich with the fulfillment of our deepest yearnings. The second is that we will have, as an end product, humanity's first progeny, a city in space capable of surviving whatever disaster nature, or we, may inflict on this planet.

"Let me say at this point that I have arrived at these suggested practices by working backwards. First, I have tried to imagine a mode of political and social organization which would make life reasonably secure and interesting for most people, and then I have tried to identify the processes which would bring about that condition. The end product is a world order in which people and goods may move freely, in which there is no incentive and no means for the maintenance or creation of weapons or techniques of mass destruction or intimidation, and in which the joy and excitement of living are enhanced by a sense of participation in humanity's great adventure. But in pursuing this end we must avail ourselves of the most important principle derived from the study of law: process is everything. We used to wonder if the end justifies the means. Now we know that that enquiry implies a view from the wrong end of the telescope. The reality is that the means *determine* the end. Process is everything.

"Now I want to say a closing word to an audience somewhat wider than the very delightful one to be found within the four walls of this chamber. I appeal to every sympathetic listener to and reader of these words in the electronic and press media for aid in reaching that wider audience. If you belong to or support one or more of the peace movements which are proliferating throughout the world, if you belong to a learned or scientific society in which your wish to escape existing national, racial or religious barriers is constantly frustrated, if you feel in your heart that you are a human being first and an American or Russian, a communist or capitalist, black, brown, yellow, pink, red or white, Christian, Muslim, Buddhist, Jewish, Hindu, Confucian, atheist, animist or whatever only second, and most especially if you are fed up with the institutionalization of fear and hostility and alienation and boredom, then I invite you to undertake now the practices which I have described. You can do this. You can begin the relatively simple and inexpensive implementation of language training for all children. Building on the Peace Corps and scores of existing agencies, international and intercultural living experience can become an essential ingredient in every young adult's education. The exploration of the universe as a uniting and united adventure for humanity is already underway and needs only militant support. You can do this. You don't have to wait for nuclear disarmament, for world government, for treaties to establish peace and order. All these will be generated by processes which you have the power to initiate. Abundant life for yourselves and your children is within reach. *You have only to open minds and hearts to the human family.* It is possible. It is simple. It is necessary. It is the great idea whose time has come.

"Mr. President, I thank my friends on the floor and in the galleries for their attention, and I yield the floor."

It takes time for Quanta to escape the flow of pleasantries on the Senate floor. Whatever else may be said of it, the Senate is peopled with ardent practitioners of courtesy. A senator who is in fierce opposition on one day over a matter of deeply-held conviction may on the next be a welcome ally over something equally dear at stake. Powerful egos, driven by vanity and ambition, learn to move easily from modes of antagonism to reconciliation and alliance, never forgetting that what goes around comes around.

Many senators, most of whom are sincere, exploit the occasion of Quanta's maiden speech to lavish compliments and praise and thus to lay up credits for the future. Quanta knows the rules, and plays the game with skill and patience.

23

Having gained the sanctuary of her office by its private entrance, Quanta is greeted by her personal secretary and her AA. Jamie, the former, is flushed and slightly frazzled; Barbara is cool, her expression bemused.

Barbara says, "Senator, our phones are ringing off the hooks. You were on C-Span International, the whole thing. Apparently there's a lot of networking going on out there among the peaceniks, because the C-Span people say the audience built while you were speaking at a pace they've rarely experienced."

"I think I said some things that many people have been hungering and thirsting to hear. 'Hungering and thirsting to hear?' Did I say that? I must be a little tired and excited myself."

Jamie breaks in, "Senator, everybody and his cat and dog wants you to return their calls right away, and some have already called back two or three times. Here, I've scribbled a partial list. What shall we do?"

"Well, Jamie, I can take about an hour right now. Let's return as many calls as possible. Barb, you help Jamie please with priorities. You might bring Aaron in on that too, if he's not busy with something else."

As Quanta speaks, Aaron steps through the door connecting to Barbara's office, and says, "I'll be glad to help with that, Senator dear. Congratulations. You rang a bell in a very unlikely place. I thought your good speech would be wasted on the Senate floor. I don't understand yet what happened exactly; but something is sure as hell going on. TV is still a mysterious and tricky medium. Apparently your special qualities are just right for it. Well, I'd say your first return should be to the governor. He deserves that. But keep it short. It's a long list already, and there are some very big names on it. Jamie, you get the governor while Barb and I wrangle. We'll keep ahead of you."

The governor's praise is direct and generous, but not fulsome. Quanta is surprised to learn that he and his staff have watched her speak on television sets in his office, and that, by the time she finished, all other business in the state capitol is in abeyance as word spreads and officials and staffs gather to watch and listen.

Before the hour is out, Quanta speaks with half a dozen world leaders. The nation's premier pundit, syndicated by *The New York Times*, requests an early interview in depth. The executive secretary of Federated World Peacemakers asks, with tears in his voice, if the Senator will head the list of speakers at the Federation's annual convention. From the prime minister of the Netherlands Quanta learns that her speech, taped from C-Span, has already been re-broadcast in Holland, and is being made available for prime time viewing throughout Europe. The secretary-general of the United Nations, after making clear that his call is personal and informal and not official, speaks of her *coup de main*, and notes that the administrative machinery of the organization, although thought by some to be cumbersome and tradition-bound, could be readily adapted, given the requisite verve, to the implementation of her suggestions, with special reference to the universal teaching of languages. The Russian ambassador, near the end of the first hour, advises that the Eastern Bloc chairman has seen and heard her "electrifying" presentation, requests the privilege of a private visit outside the constraints of protocol, and to this end invites her to visit Russia unofficially, as a tourist, at her early convenience. The chairman of the Joint Chiefs of Staff volunteers his personal services to brief her, informally, about the true nature of the Communist menace and to alert her to the dangers posed by immature or uninformed, though persuasive and sincere, discussions of military necessities.

The first hour stretches to two, and finally Quanta, her schedule rearranged by frantic staffers, spends almost the whole day on the telephone before reaching the point at which Barbara and Aaron insist that one or the other of them can take care of the remaining calls.

That evening, as Quanta and Aaron, exhausted and puzzled by the day's events, sit limp before the fire, H.T. Davis, the world's most powerful molder of public opinion, a shadowy background figure known personally to few but in all the world's main languages dubbed 'Mr. Media', comes personally to their door, apologizes for the intrusion and then, speaking very directly and simply to Quanta, tells her that he believes in an active, intervening God, that she is an instrument of this God's purpose to save and redirect humanity and that he feels called to do all he can to make her president of the United States. Having spoken this short piece, the man again apologizes for the intrusion into her privacy, says that he will call her secretary to arrange a further meeting if she is willing, and takes his leave.

24

The next Sunday morning, in bed, with fresh coffee, Aaron says to Quanta: "Well, my sweet little spouselet, I guess you are at least relieved of any regrets you might have felt over agreeing not to run for election to the senate."

"Si, señor. At least that. Do you understand what's happening to us?"

"I have glimmerings. First, you have an awesome TV presence. Second, you've sounded a note that many people throughout the World have wanted desperately to hear, and they find it true and genuine. Third, you must decide, very soon, whether or not you want to do this."

"We. *We* must decide.

"All right. We, if you wish. But although I'm your soulmate and I love you absolutely and we have tried to be equal partners, I'm not involved in this in the same way that you are. Unless you back away now, all is changed forever."

"Oh my darling, everything is changed even if I do back away. *Can* I back away? Do you want me to?"

"I suppose you could, but I'm not saying that I want you to. I do feel quite certain, however, that we're losing control of our lives. It takes some getting used to. I anticipated a denouement, not a cusp."

"That we control our lives is always an illusion, don't you think?"

"I suppose so. Maybe life itself is an illusion, for that matter. But even if it is, love is not. We've had that."

"Oh dear God, please don't use the past tense."

"Were you speaking to me?"

"I thought I was. Don't be embarrassed – it's a small promotion."

"If you say so. Well now, my love, a small ceremony is in order. I drink. I drink the dregs of my coffee. The dregs – but they're very good dregs – I drink to endings and beginnings, to the presidency and to the sweet nascent entity which we call humanity. For what it's worth, my love, I choose to give what I must give to see it born."

25

For almost a century, it has been a given in American journalism that New York City's premier newspaper fields the country's premier political columnist. The reading of this column every morning before or at breakfast is an unchanging ritual in millions of homes throughout the world. After interviewing Quanta, the current savant begins his column with a famous quotation:

> 'In the country of the blind, the one-eyed man is king.'
> So said Erasmus.
> Is this a clue to the Quanta Bjornsen phenomenon?
> First consider what, precisely, has happened. A fledgling senator, newly appointed to that jaded realm after a creditable but unspectacular career at the bar and on the bench, rises, having observed the customary weeks of silent apprenticeship, to deliver her maiden speech on the Senate floor. It is expected, by senators and the media, that only the protagonist will take this exercise very seriously. Ignoring tradition, Bjornsen chooses a subject on which she has no known expertise. She speaks with intensity, but with a notable absence of oratorical flourishes. In cold print, what she says appears to be reasonably cogent, innovative and persuasive – but it doesn't depart radically, in content, from what some of us have been saying, perhaps nearly as well, for many years.
> Confounding expectations, senators who came to be courteous and by the techniques of colloquy to help the newcomer make a record that will impress the homefolks, find themselves listening – let's say it – spellbound.

Furthermore, my colleagues in the press gallery likewise fall quickly into postures of rapt attention. Perhaps most remarkably, television viewers all over the world are caught and held by a presence so compelling that they are moved, by the millions, to call friends and urge them, rather breathlessly I gather, to tune in.

Now back to Erasmus.

Have you ever tried to explain to a person sightless or profoundly deaf from birth what it is really like to see, to hear? It can't be done. Such a person can stretch his imagination to the utmost, but the concepts of color or of tonal harmony cannot be truly grasped. What can be understood is only that there is something out there – mysterious, beautiful, awesome – which can be sensed by some but not by all.

Something like this must be the case with Quanta Bjornsen. She seems to perceive what is not vouchsafed to the rest of us. The consequence is that she speaks as one with authority, and we feel truth in her words. She says, "Humanity is a family, an entity: we are parts of one another, and we must learn to act accordingly" and, although we do not 'see' what she sees or 'hear' what she hears, we feel the goosebumps rise.

In the country of the blind, the one-eyed man is king.

Chicago's premier newspaper weighs in editorially with a different point of view. Excerpts:

We aren't amused by what one famous columnist has been moved to call 'the Quanta Bjornsen phenomenon'.

We didn't catch her act, but a close reading of the 'maiden' speech by the freshman senator from sagebrush country raises some troublesome questions.

She wants us to deal with the Communist menace in three ways: (1) by having everybody in the world learn two or three foreign languages; (2) by sending all high school kids to Russia or China for two or three years (they'd send theirs to us; sure they would); and (3) by joining up with the Commies to build a big spaceship and launch it, presumably filled with a mishmash of humans and animals, on a journey into outer, and apparently she does mean outer, space.

Having read through this prime example of wishful and muddled thinking (if that's the word for it) without suffering a single goosebump, we wonder:

1. Does Miz Senator Bjornsen know that virtually all children of the superior classes in pre-revolutionary Russia learned, at least, French and German while still very young, and that this didn't save them from being hunted down and mercilessly slaughtered by grunting peasants?

2. Does sagebrush savvy teach that it would be useful to the precarious defense of freedom to have our teenagers, at their most vulnerable, rebellious and frustrated time of life, take courses in Russian entitled *Atheism, Marxism and Power to the Masses*?

3. And about this spaceship. Now really, Quanta. How many cubits high, wide and long should it be? And where exactly in the galaxy should it look for Mt. Ararat?

While we're at it, we wonder about one other thing too. What kind of a name is 'Quanta'? We don't find it in our dictionary's list of given names. In the dictionary proper it says that quanta is the plural of quantum, a

masculine noun which means "an indivisible
unit of energy, equal for radiation of frequency
v to the product hv, where h is Planck's
constant". Forgive us, but what the hell kind of
a name is that, and where is this lady from
really?

26

Quanta to Almao:
'Please tell me what is happening to me. Are you putting words into my mouth?'

NO, QUANTA. THE WORDS ARE YOUR OWN. THE IDEAS, TOO, ARE YOURS. OF COURSE YOUR IDEAS AND YOUR WORDS ARE COLORED, SHARPENED BY YOUR NEW KNOWLEDGE OF ME.

BEYOND THAT, WHAT IS HAPPENING IS THAT NOW YOU ARE PERCEIVED TO SPEAK WITH AUTHORITY. NEED I POINT OUT THAT THIS HAS HAPPENED TO OTHERS BEFORE YOU? YOUR PLACE IS AMONG THE SAGES AND PROPHETS OF HUMANITY. FROM NOW ON, MUCH OF WHAT YOU SAY WILL BE PRESERVED AND STUDIED, AS HAVING SPECIAL SIGNIFICANCE, BY FUTURE GENERATIONS.

'That's terrifying. How do I know – for that matter how do *you* know – that what I say will be true and good?'

I'M CONFIDENT THAT IT WILL BE. YOU KNOW ME: YOU KNOW THAT I EXIST. FURTHER, YOU KNOW THAT HUMANITY IS MY SUBSTANCE. YOU KNOW THAT I DEPEND FOR MY GROWTH, AND INDEED FOR MY EXISTENCE, UPON THE NUMBERS, HEALTH AND VITALITY, THE WELL-BEING, OF WHAT YOU AND OTHERS HAVE CALLED THE HUMAN FAMILY. MOREOVER, YOU KNOW THAT I CAN INFLUENCE EVENTS ON EARTH ONLY IMPERFECTLY AND INDIRECTLY, THROUGH YOU AND OTHERS. FINALLY, YOU ARE ALMOST READY TO ACCEPT MY ASSURANCE THAT, IN DUE SEASON, YOU WILL MERGE WITH ME, YOU WILL BECOME ME, WITH YOUR PERSONALITY AND MEMORIES ADDED TO MINE, WITH INDEFINITE TIME AT YOUR DISPOSAL AND WITH GROWTH, EXCITEMENT AND JOY BEYOND MEASURE IN PROSPECT.

GIVEN THIS KNOWLEDGE, YOU CANNOT GO FAR ASTRAY.

'I sense something somber in your tone. Am I to be martyred?'

NOT TO WORRY, DEAR QUANTA. YOU'LL REMEMBER I TOLD YOU ONCE THAT I DON'T NEED ANOTHER MARTYR.
'That's ambiguous. Are you capable of lying?'
I DON'T KNOW. I'VE NEVER TRIED.
'That's positively Delphic.'
HOW ELSE CAN I ANSWER?
'Do you tolerate the question?'
I TOLERATE IRREVERENCE; I'M NOT SO SURE THAT I TOLERATE IMPERTINENCE. I'VE HAD VERY LITTLE EXPERIENCE WITH IT. BUT UNDER NO CIRCUMSTANCES DO I PUNISH.
'I'll be careful, anyway. Then there is no hell, no Devil? If the Devil is a myth, whence comes evil?'
THERE IS NO DEVIL. BUT, ALTHOUGH I DON'T THINK OF IT AS EVIL, THERE IS A DARK SIDE TO MOST PERSONS. IN A SENSE THERE'S A DARK SIDE TO HUMANITY.
THIS IS WHAT NEEDS TO BE SAID ABOUT EVIL: NATURE WORKS THE WAY SHE HAS TO WORK TO ACHIEVE HER ENDS. EACH HUMAN BEING STANDS AT THE END OF A LONG LINE OF SURVIVORS - BILLIONS OF GENERATIONS OF SURVIVORS. AT SOME TIMES, UNDER SOME CIRCUMSTANCES, SURVIVAL HAS BEEN THE REWARD FOR BEHAVIOR THAT, UNDER OTHER CIRCUMSTANCES, SEEMS EVIL. BUT THE SURVIVOR REMEMBERS, AND SOME PART OF THAT MEMORY IS TRACED IN HIS SURVIVORS. THIS GOES FAR TO EXPLAIN GREED, ANGER, LUST, GLUTTONY AND THE OTHER SINS SOME CALL DEADLY. MOREOVER, THIS SAME PRINCIPLE EXPLAINS - IT DOESN'T EXCUSE, BUT IT EXPLAINS - EVERY VIOLATION OF WHATEVER MORAL CODE PREVAILS AT A GIVEN TIME AND PLACE. ACCORDINGLY, THIS IS WHAT NEEDS TO BE SAID ABOUT SIN: OVER MANY THOUSANDS OF GENERATIONS YOUR RECENT ANCESTORS WERE REWARDED, THROUGH SURVIVAL AND AN OPPORTUNITY TO REPRODUCE SUCCESSFULLY, FOR BEHAVIOR WHICH HAS BEEN DEFINED AS SINFUL OR UNETHICAL. A PART OF YOU REMEMBERS THE ABYSS - STARVATION, ISOLATION, SUDDEN AND VIOLENT DEATH - WHICH WAS NEVER VERY DISTANT, AND THE INBORN FEAR OF THAT ABYSS GOADS

OR TEMPTS YOU NOW, EVEN UNDER WHOLLY DIFFERENT CIRCUMSTANCES, AND SOMETIMES QUITE IRRATIONALLY, TO BEHAVIOR WHICH IS NOW CONDEMNED BUT WHICH IN THE PAST WAS OFTEN BIOLOGICALLY SUCCESSFUL. WE SEE THIS CLEARLY IN VERY YOUNG CHILDREN. NORMALLY THEIR BENT FOR EVIL, SINFUL OR ANTISOCIAL BEHAVIOR IS MODIFIED AND SUBSTANTIALLY CONTROLLED WITH MATURITY. AS I SAID, I DON'T THINK OF SUCH CONDUCT AS EVIL. IT IS UNDESIRABLE, AND IT CAN AND SHOULD BE PREVENTED; BUT IT IS AT THE SAME TIME UNDERSTANDABLE AS THE PRICE YOUR SPECIES PAYS FOR THE BIOLOGICAL SUCCESS IT HAS ENJOYED IN THE PAST.

'Would you feel the same about acts which seem almost unbearably cruel and evil? I'm thinking, for example, about a parent who beats to death his own innocent and helpless child.'

SUCH A DEATH, DEAR QUANTA, IS INTENSELY PAINFUL TO ME. EVEN THOUGH THE CHILD FLOWS TO ME AND ENRICHES ME, I SUFFER; AND I WOULD INTERVENE TO SAVE IT IF I COULD. BUT UNLESS THE PARENT IS DRIVEN BY MADNESS, IT MUST BE UNDERSTOOD THAT THE FRUSTRATION, RAGE AND FURY WHICH IMPEL THE ACT REFLECT INNATE CAPACITIES. THAT THESE CAPACITIES HAVE NOT BEEN TEMPERED BY THE PARENT'S EXPERIENCE OF LIFE IS AN EQUAL TRAGEDY.

'Are you equally cool and dispassionate about conduct which imperils your own existence? Genocide? War?'

YES. STILL, I TOO WILL DO WHAT I MUST TO SURVIVE.

27

Now the black Machine has settled into solar orbit among the asteroids. It is monitoring electromagnetic emanations from Earth. From these it is learning Earth's languages and history, and it is studying Earth's technology. It knows about the doomsday weapons. It reads, and it has learned to understand, the ultra-secret communication devices used by the adversary powers. It is studying the ecology, the resources, the total physical environment of the water planet, the hothouse planet, the red planet with cold thin air that lie, respectively, third, second and fourth out from the Sun. As data are received and classified, they are compared with standards in the Machine's memory. After reviewing a wide range of alternative programmed courses of action, the Machine makes tentative choices from among them.

When it is ready, the Machine programs itself to communicate its thoughts and commands in the written and spoken languages of Earth. It is aware that its presence, and some glimmerings of its nature and possible mission, have been detected in a half dozen places on the water planet. It is aware; but although it can feel concern, it is not concerned.

What any human knows, Almao knows, and she is able to put together a composite more nearly complete than can be achieved even by the Eastern and Western military establishments. With all her powers she probes the Machine's guiding intelligence. She can make no contact with it. It is not life; but it is a Machine the like of which has scarcely been imagined by researchers at the leading edge of artificial intelligence technology. Small wonder. The Machine intelligence was created by a people who had studied AI for thousands of years, motivated by a desperate struggle to survive.

Between the Machine and Almao, the advantage is not entirely with the Machine. Its makers never achieved numbers beyond a few million and never generated or experienced – although they may have imagined – a being analogous to Almao. The Machine, however, is not equipped to imagine her existence.

28

In the months that follow her maiden effort in the Senate, Quanta is in constant demand to speak at conventions and other meetings of groups interested in peacemaking, environmental issues, penology, unlawful discrimination, tax reform, church-state relations, political science, vegetarianism, economic development, voluntarism and so forth and so on. Electronic media people compete to get her on their talk and interview shows. Representatives of the Sunday programs devoted to interviews with political leaders are especially persistent. The print media devote columns and pages to comment about her views, and additional space is generously allotted for articles detailing the main points, as well as the trivia, of her ancestry and intimate personal history. Every brief she has ever filed, in trial as well as in appellate courts, is dug out and examined by specialist reporters. A few complete trial transcripts are ordered when it is discovered that she has been the counsel of record for persons accused of child molestation and other perverse or heinous acts.

H.T. Davis assigns members of his personal staff to assist Aaron and Barbara in sorting and responding to invitations. Quanta usually agrees with their suggestions, rarely pleading that a particular setting is distasteful or that the proposed schedule is too demanding. Even in formal settings, she speaks extemporaneously. Verbatim transcripts proliferate. They reflect a style that is always cogent, direct and unpretentious. Simple themes are stated, restated and elaborated: peace, distinguished from mere arms control, is a necessity; each person can and must make peace directly, without waiting for institutions to develop or statesmen to create it; humanity is a familial entity which surpasses and magnifies individuality; the Earth and all its life forms are unique and precious and deserving of reverence; Earth is not only our home, it is also a footstool from which we may reach the stars.

Quanta expounds lesser themes as well. In an address to the students and faculty at Harvard, she undertakes to state her view of participatory democracy, saying:

"I'm in favor of participatory democracy, of course, and I think I can suggest a simple and workable mechanism to make it happen.

Experience shows that it does little good to carp at people for failing to vote or to get involved, even at the local level, in political processes. Compulsory voting, although it is the practice in some countries, seems to us unduly coercive and self-defeating. Still, most people fail to vote most of the time, and there is a pervasive lack of commitment to civic duty. What is to be done?

"Before suggesting a novel and head-on approach to the problem, I want to jog the focus just a bit. Because of Jefferson's view and persuasive writings, we are habituated to thinking that government improves as it approaches levels closest to the people. In this view, we get progressively better government, presumably because it grows increasingly participatory, as we move from the national to the state to the county, and on down to the village or other local level. From this premise it is argued, almost as an axiom, that every governmental activity should be carried out at the lowest possible level. Hence we see campaigns, from time to time, for the national government to divest itself of responsibility for, say, health care, on the ground that this can be done perfectly well by the states. Similarly, at the state level it is argued that only local levels of government should be concerned with the making of policy in the field of public education, because – what could be more obvious? – education is a local matter.

"I could multiply examples, but my point is that, whatever may have been the case in Jefferson's day, nowadays his pyramid is exactly upside down. Because of the predominance of electronic media and technologically advanced print media, public attention is constantly focused on political activity and decisions at the national and international level, and to a lesser extent at the state level, always at the expense of slighting the local scene. This is perfectly understandable, for it is at the national level that issues of most concern to most people are addressed. It is natural for the media to spotlight those who struggle with issues of war and peace, that is to say, of survival, for example, and to neglect the sometimes heated but usually boring local discussions of paving contracts, building permits and garbage disposal. One consequence of this is that most people can name the president and vice-president and several cabinet officers, one or both of their senators, and perhaps even their congressman, while few could name their local city council members, let alone the members of the school board. Another consequence is that gross incompetence, venality or graft at the national level is often exposed and corrected with great vigor, while similar local shortcomings evoke only ho-hums. Still another consequence is that there exists a public opinion which can usually be brought to bear on national issues, while local, and even many statewide, issues are resolved quietly, by the insiders, in an atmosphere of public torpor or indifference.

"Of course Jefferson, who may well have been right for his time, could not have anticipated that a hundred million citizens would watch, fascinated, as a beleaguered president squirms in the glow of television while the school board meets in empty chambers. But sophisticated modern manipulators, whose main interest is to see that the fortunate are not required to pay taxes in order that the unfortunate may be helped, understand very well what has happened. Invoking Jefferson, they press hard to move these bread and butter issues, the pocketbook issues, down, down, down to the lowest possible level of government, cynically aware that at that level little will be done, and that what is done can be controlled by smart operators skilled at dodging the limelight.

"In few words, and as a generality, government at the highest levels is interesting, invites publicity, is relatively free from incompetence and graft and attracts able participants, while at progressively lower levels the opposites are true.

"Hence the place to start a program aimed at making democracy genuinely participatory is at the bottom.

"I propose that, as a beginning, every local part-time policy-making position in the public sector should be filled not by election or appointment, but by lot. A simple mechanism would involve the use of computers, programmed to select at random – I suppose by picking a social security number from a list conforming to the appropriate geographical classification – persons to fill every such position. Terms in office would be of short duration, rarely exceeding one year, and of course they would be rotated, so that, taking the example of a zoning board with six members, one would leave and be replaced by a newcomer every two months. Similarly, a three-member board of county commissioners would receive a new member every four months.

"At once it will be objected that the electors should choose people to fill positions on councils, boards, commissions and committees, as they do now, with special qualities of intelligence, character or expertise – and that random selections from the public at large would be disastrous.

"To this quite fundamental objection I would respond as follows: First, do the electors in fact make their choices on the basis of informed and correct judgments, or are choices usually made by a small fraction of the electors, weighing quite different qualities? Second, isn't it the case that newly-elected members of such bodies have full voting privileges from the beginning, without a waiting period devoted to the gaining of expertise? Third, given the availability of some level of professional staff assistance, isn't 'expertise' in the policy maker at least as likely to hinder as to help in the making of policy choices that reflect some degree of public consensus?

"Now please think for a few moments about the advantages of such a system. Every citizen would know, from the time he first began to study civics in middle school, that he would sooner or later be required to perform a public duty by helping to make or advise policy at some level. I think this couldn't help but work profound improvements in general attitudes toward civic responsibilities. People concerned about the quality of the decisions made would be required to look, for improvement, to the quality of the education and information services available to the general public. Those with special axes to grind – as, for example, passionate conservationists or passionate opponents of sex education, or passionate anythings – would find it necessary to make their pitches in the open to the whole constituency, rather than privately, to the few who put themselves forward for elective office. There would be an immediate and definitive end to the kinds of special influence that come from campaign contributions and all types of pressure on elected officials. Pandering in all its forms would likewise be pointless, and would cease.

"We would have genuinely participatory democracy.

"If the system worked, as I think it would, it could be extended, gradually, right up the scale, to full-time as well as part-time offices, to the metropolitan, state, national and international levels, and I certainly wouldn't stop short of the Congress itself. Imagine a Senate and House of Representatives selected at random from the whole body politic, beholden to no one, freed from political ambition, subject to constitutional restraints but within those limits reflecting accurately and implementing an informed public opinion.

"It would of course be necessary to make special arrangements in the case of full-time offices. These should be carefully designed to hold from economic loss or severe personal hardship those persons chosen to serve. I would be very careful, however, to avoid a pattern of granting excuses for trivial reasons, such as those often given to avoid jury duty. It would seem to me reasonable, for instance, that even a surgeon at the peak of his powers, or an entrepreneur engaged in the creation of a unique business enterprise, should be required, if his number comes up, to take his short turn in public office.

"I would leave to a later date, but I would not rule out, the extension of the random selection principle to those who perform executive functions in the public sector. We shouldn't want a computer to choose a president of the United States so long as that office commands the powers now vested in it. Still, the peculiar processes by which we select our presidents, and the yields from those processes, leave much to be desired. It may be, as we gain experience with participatory democracy, that many functions of the chief executive can be transferred to professional staffs responsible to the Congress, that others will simply atrophy and that those which at present seem most awesome won't always be relevant when we will have brought in the human family and peace is real."

29

At a dinner meeting of the United States Senate Association of Administrative Assistants and Secretaries (USSAAAS – pronounced 'you-sass'), Quanta begs leave to recount some of her experiences with constituents whose concerns depart somewhat from the beaten path. Leave tacitly granted, she continues:

"The first time I went back to spend a few days in my home state office, I found a lengthy list of people who had called for appointments. On the list were several unfamiliar names, but I decided to see them all if I could.

"When I was two or three days into this routine, a little old man came in, late in the afternoon, carrying a smallish square cardboard box. He told me that in it he had an invention which would change the world, first by rendering obsolete all existing means of generating and distributing power and second by effecting revolutionary transformations in military tactics and strategy. He used correctly the nice big words that I have used. His manner was controlled and impressive. Right away he had my full attention.

"Before proceeding, however, this man told me that I must agree to be guided by his instructions with respect to any further disclosure of his momentous discovery. I demurred, saying that I would like to reserve judgment on that and, after some haggling he decided to reveal all anyway. He did explain, in this context, that his purpose in coming to me was to get me to help him with the US Patent Office which, he said, stubbornly refused to recognize his invention. I assured him that I would do what I could to help.

"Then the man withdrew from his tattered briefcase a whole stack of decidedly unprofessional sketches and handed them to me, with, on his face, an expression of keenest anticipation. I remember that one of the drawings showed what appeared to be a giant tank descending a muddy bank and apparently ready to launch itself into an extensive area of bogs and swamp. Instead of tracks, however, the tank-like thing had at each corner a large flanged ball. When he saw that this object had caught my attention the man explained, now quite excited, that it illustrated perfectly the revolutionary character of his invention.

"'You see,' he said, 'the four balls can be made to turn independently, without any outside source of power, and because the balls are round, flanged and nearly hollow, this tank can travel on any surface.'

"'The same principle', he continued, 'can be applied to ships, cars, planes, trains – any vehicle – and the power available is absolutely unlimited and never needs to be renewed.'

"I remarked, rather mildly, and wondering if any of my staff were still on hand in the outer office, that this sounded rather like perpetual motion.

"'Exactly,' he shouted, now quite excited. 'This is the *great secret* of my invention. Inside the ball is a device to supply unlimited power indefinitely.'

"'Remarkable,' said I. 'Can you show me or explain to me how it works?'

"'I can do better than that,' says he. 'Right in this little box I have a working model.'

"With trembling fingers, and with, I must say a real flair for the drama of the moment, he began slowly to untie the frayed lengths of twine that bound the box. I waited, more or less calmly. Finally, tilting the box so that I couldn't catch a premature glimpse of its contents, he peered inside and then, with an air of triumph, withdrew and set before me on the desk what appeared to be, and on close inspection most certainly was, an egg – a hen's egg.

"Still I waited, not moving, saying nothing – this wasn't easy – until the little old man, now looking intently into my eyes, with one finger tilted the egg until it stood on the small end, paused until I transferred my attention from his face to the egg – this, too, wasn't easy – then, in a show of ultimate triumph, released his finger and watched with fascination scarcely more intense than mine as it rolled rather vigorously to its side and flopped around on my desk.

"'There! There! There's the source of power. The falling egg generates power. The larger and heavier the egg-shaped object I put inside the ball, the more power it generates. It's a simple matter to transfer that energy to the ball so that it moves.'

"Foolishly, I asked, 'What is the source of energy to restore the egg to its upright position?'

"His reply conveyed great depths of condescension. 'That's not a problem, because the egg never falls. Here,' he said, quickly putting the egg again on its end, then tilting it slightly, 'put your finger on the side of the egg. You can feel it push. You can feel the energy waiting to be used. All you have to do is harness that power. It is unlimited, and it is perpetual.'

"Speaking calmly now, almost philosophically, my visitor continued as he restored the egg very carefully to its box: 'Like all truly great and fundamental discoveries, this one seems, once its secret is uncovered, quite simple. That's why we must exercise great caution. I've been unwilling to reveal everything to the patent people, for fear that there are traitors among them who would give this great power to our enemies, the Communists.'

"'What exactly is it that you want me to do to help?' I tried, with imperfect success, not to sound conspiratorial.

"'You can use the great powers of your office to get the attention of the Pentagon. Take my invention to people there who can understand it and who can be trusted. You can take the drawings. They demonstrate the power of the idea without giving it away. Then, when they're ready, I'll come to Washington and give them a full demonstration, just as I've given you. They can take it from there.

"'I don't want money. I love my country. Eventually, when the story can be told, I'll be recognized, and that will be reward enough, even,' dramatic pause, 'even if it comes posthumously.'

"You can imagine, since most of you have probably had similar experiences, the care with which I extricated myself from the company of this interesting man, and assigned responsibility for follow-up to one of the most talented members of my staff.

"While I'm at it, I want to tell you about another man who came into my office a day or two later. He was known to me as a local businessman. He owned and operated a service organization that specialized in fixing things, mostly TVs, small appliances and the like, in people's homes.

"His idea had to do with taxation. First he summarized for me the problems, both theoretical and practical, with the major systems of taxation now in use. There are, as you know, plenty of problems. Then he proposed what seemed to be a straightforward and workable replacement for all these systems. Here's how it would work: All persons, or the heads of households on their behalf, would be required to file, at the court house, city hall or other public facility near their principal place of residence, an inventory of all things owned by them, excepting very little, with a valuation of each item. The inventory would be updated periodically – normally once or twice a year. It would be entered into a computer and would be open for inspection or printout at the request of any person. Then, when each taxing entity, at whatever level, from a local improvement district right up to the United Nations, had made its budget, the computer would total all values within its taxing authority and calculate the percentage levy required to generate the budgeted funds. The taxpayer would then make one annual payment to a local authority which would distribute the proceeds locally and up the line.

"So far so good. The gimmick is that any person could claim as his own, through prescribed and somewhat formal proceedings, any property not found on an inventory, and could buy any property on an inventory, *at the listed valuation*. Of course he would then have to list it on his own inventory, assigning any valuation he chose.

"I spent an hour or two raising some of the many objections to this system that come immediately to mind. To each my visitor had a ready and plausible answer. I'll mention one or two of these, as being illustrative. 'Suppose', I said, 'that I own a home which has been in my family for generations, has sentimental as well as intrinsic value and is coveted by others for its historical associations, or for any reason which makes them eager to acquire it at a price higher than its "normal" value. Must I put a painfully high value on this home, thus imposing on myself an undeserved tax penalty, in order to safeguard my ownership?' In reply, my visitor first asked, 'What is its "normal" value? Shouldn't this include any generally recognized enhancements due to historical associations?'

"'But suppose', I persisted, 'that some very rich so-and-so simply wants my home out of spite or to satisfy a grudge. Maybe my wife jilted him to marry me, and he wants to get even. What then?' The answer was that I could invoke special procedures involving an appraisal of the property, and defeat the claim upon a showing that it was fairly valued in my inventory, recovering my costs and perhaps a modest penalty from the would-be interloper. This defense would be available not only for homes, but for all things recognized in equity as *sui generis*. When I asked about intangible property – bank accounts, accounts receivable, causes of action and the like – the answer was that there would be no reason for a claimant to go after such things provided they are fully and fairly inventoried, and that if they are not they would and should be fair game.

"Although I found this man's ideas intriguing, I have no present intention to make it my business to crusade for their adoption, or even for a trial run of some kind. But I do want to conclude with a short true story that may have some relevance.

"When I was very young, just out of law school, I spent a few years on the staff of a young senator from the west. One of my duties was to keep close track of whatever was happening on the Senate floor, so that he could be alerted and informed when a vote came up, and also so that he could make good use of his time elsewhere when his presence there was unlikely to be required. This gave me a good excuse to spend some time on the floor myself, standing at the rear of the chamber where authorized staff members are tolerated to this day, subject, of course, to good behavior. Sometimes I stayed on the floor even if my boss was briefly there too, when he came over to make an insertion into the record, or to involve himself in a colloquy.

"One day, when nothing much was happening in the Senate, my senator and I were both on the floor, when we noticed a steady exodus of senators. Presently the chamber was empty, except for the most junior senator in the chair, and two slightly less junior senators acting for the majority and minority leaders. Word had spread that the senior Senator from Nevada was about to make his annual speech attacking the federal reserve system and pleading for a return to the Gold Standard. In deference to any Nevadans present I am in my mind capitalizing 'Gold Standard'. Even in that long ago time this was a lost and forlorn cause, but nevertheless it was then, as it is to this day, a cause dear to the hearts of all true Silver Staters.

"Presently the silver-haired Senator entered the chamber, trailed by two aides who helped him carry and pile on his desk a truly formidable stack of books, pamphlets and magazines, into which had been inserted conspicuous page markers of various colors. It was known that the speech would last about six hours, that it would consist almost entirely of excerpts read verbatim from the publications on the Senator's desk, and that it was the same every year. Hence the exodus.

"As Nevada gained the floor and launched into ponderous preliminaries, my Senator beckoned to me from the door to the senators' cloakroom, where he stood, lighted cigar behind his back, surveying, bemused but speculative, the nearly empty chamber.

"What he said to me was, 'Wouldn't it be funny if he's right after all, and the rest of us are wrong?'"

30

At the annual meeting of the Challenger Society International, Senator Bjornsen devotes a portion of her remarks to an elaboration of her views about space exploration, saying:

"It is a privilege, precious and coveted, though scarcely deserved, to be given the podium at a gathering of those who have placed themselves at the forefront of humanity's thrust into space. Here we honor, in a meaningful way, those heroic men and women from all countries and all races who have given their lives, or who will in the future give their lives, to probe the unknown cosmos.

"How do we honor such people *meaningfully*? How else than by advancing the cause most dear to them? Every hard-won toehold, chink or niche on the frontier of space – and all are hard-won – is a tribute to this lengthening roster of heroes.

"I know it isn't necessary to argue to this society that our move into space is worth the sacrifices of human and material treasure it exacts from us. I have asked myself, however, why is it that we feel this pull so strongly?

"The answer, I think, is to be found in the identification and examination of our most fundamental instinct, and I believe this to be the instinct for species, as distinguished from individual, survival. Let me explain. For many years I had the good fortune to practice law in a small town – so small that I could walk from my home to my office each morning. For a part of this daily journey, my path followed a country road, paved with blacktop. Although the right of way was quite wide, probably at least the standard eighty feet, the paved portion was narrow, barely wide enough for two cars to meet and pass without crowding each other on to the shoulder. On both sides were barrow pits and beyond these grassy meadows or green lawns. On late spring mornings, especially if there had been a shower in the night, on this narrow band of paved road I always saw dozens or scores of angleworms, trying to cross, *in both directions*. Now it often happened that a light frost came just before sunrise. In this case, the worms caught on the pavement perished. If they escaped this hazard, they were of course liable to be smashed flat by passing vehicles or dehydrated by the early morning sun or snatched up by the

well-known early birds. And, even if smiling fortune allowed a few
to make their perilous way to the other side, no great good fortune
awaited them, for it was not clear, at least to me, that the grass was
indeed greener there.

"How do we account for this seemingly suicidal behavior?

"Of course the answer lies in that same powerful instinct for
species survival. Species survive by filling every available ecological
niche. Among the ancestors of the angleworms I saw venturing
foolishly – by my lights – into an undertaking full of risk and offering
little gain, were daring specimens whose urge to explore had yielded
improved chances for survival, and these, their descendants, inheriting
that trait, were unwilling to settle for the security of familiar loam.

"We too have ancestors who took great risks to explore, and if
possible to occupy, alien ecological niches. These included the first
creatures to make the painful and hazardous transition from salt to
brackish water and then to land. Probably the first fliers are also in
our family tree, and the first furry little critters to hatch eggs inside
their bodies instead of in the tested normal way – outside, in the
world.

"There will come a time, if our luck holds, when beings whose
nature and values we can dimly see will proudly trace descent from
those who dared to leave the womb, this womb, our native globe, to
try the vast and trackless realms of Space."

Quanta develops a variation on the same theme in remarks to
Earthlings, Inc., an agglomeration of clubs, societies and institutions
whose common interest is ecology. Here she says:

"A good thinker and fine writer named Lewis Thomas – and I
want to say it's a shame that he needs identification for some in this
audience – in his mind, in the last century, saw Earth as from space,
and wrote that it seemed to him most like a cell. I find this insight
truly beautiful. Earth is like a cell, or like an egg, or like a womb.
It's basal, a genitor and a propellant. Think of it as if you were a
species, thinking: *it's the place from which we came.*

"The place from which we came. How then should we treat it?

"You will answer, almost in chorus: carefully, lovingly,
reverently. Of course. I agree. We deplore every loss of
Wilderness, of topsoil, of forest – above all, of species. Every
increment of environmental contamination is fiercely contested, as it

should be. But we might reflect, as we push these constraints almost to their limits, that in longer views than ours these are mere episodes. In time, Earth can regenerate Wilderness and forests and topsoil. It cannot exactly duplicate a lost species, and for this reason the senseless extinction of any species is an awesome tragedy. But *nature* extinguishes species, right and left, almost casually, certainly without mercy or compunction, on the way to wherever it is that she is going. That role is not ours, but still I think some balance is required. Earth is not an end in itself: it is a means to an end. Us, life, life advancing, life projected outward – that's the end. Whatever is required in prudent service of that end is justified. Earth's resources must not be squandered, but they may be used.

"Our true origins are not on Earth, but in Space. It was there, out there, that elements essential to our being were generated and broadcast by bursting stars. We didn't start here, with replicating molecules selectively surviving: we began in stellar furnaces, with primeval hydrogen becoming oxygen and nitrogen and carbon. In this perspective, a naked rock is much farther from beginnings than we are from it. And just as our friends the cetaceans once left the land to return to kindlier seas, so I think we – a 'we' collective in time as well as in numbers – will one day return to space and find it home and understand at last the long deep calling.

"What then of Mother Earth?

"First the triumphant womb in nature's way and with our help will heal herself. Wounds will become scars and slowly these will disappear. Forests and grasslands, prairies and meadows, crystalline lakes and pure running streams, clear skies and cleansing rain will once more be the rule. Then life's multitude of forms will fill new niches, move, compete, flow, change and thrive or perish as of old, with humanity's sometimes clumsy touch withheld.

"I don't suggest that we will be indifferent to Earth, that humanity will forget this way station. I think few, if any, will choose to live here. But Earth's air and water, sky and mountains, will always – well, 'always' is a very big word – will for a long time have their special allure for some of our kind. There will be visits, pilgrimages requiring arduous training and preparation, as to a shrine, a Mecca. The rule we now apply to Wilderness, that people are visitors who may not remain and who must leave things as they found them, will probably apply, perhaps with some few exceptions, to Earth. And just as those who do not visit Wilderness are sustained by the knowledge that it is there, so humanity, although dispersed in glowing space-based garden cities and perhaps on other worlds as fair, will have its dreams of lovely Earth, a shrine, a place to which the spirit at least returns from time to time in reverence and in awe."

31

Almao to Quanta:

YOU'RE DOING WELL. YOUR WORDS WILL BE REMEMBERED.

'Are you capable of vanity? Aren't they your words, not mine?'

NO INDEED. I READ AND RECORD YOUR THOUGHTS, BUT I DON'T CREATE THEM. YOU OWE MORE TO AARON THAN TO ME.

'You gave me grudging permission to talk with Aaron; but I find I cannot tell him about you. Why is that? Did you say I could, and at the same time make it so I couldn't?'

NO, QUANTA. WHY DO YOU GOAD YOURSELF TO BE TESTY WITH ME? I AM NOT YOUR ENEMY. I'M YOUR FRIEND AND LOVER.

'Almao, I love you and I want to serve you, but a part of me fears you, too. You are to me a little like some potent drug, beguiling and dangerous. Sometimes I still have doubts that you are real. Perhaps I'm mad, schizophrenic.'

BUT YOU KNOW, DEAR QUANTA, THAT IF YOUR PERSONALITY HAD DISINTEGRATED YOU WOULDN'T HAVE THAT THOUGHT.

I TELL YOU THAT YOU ARE SANE AND I AM REAL. BELIEVE IT.

'I do believe it. For better or for worse, I am yours. But still I feel that you haven't been candid with me. You hold back. You conceal. I think that's why a part of me struggles, like a web-caught fly.'

I DON'T LIKE THE IMAGE. I'LL SPEAK TO THE ISSUE.

FIRST, I WANT YOU TO KNOW THAT OTHERS BEFORE YOU HAVE BEEN ANGRY WITH ME, HAVE RESISTED. I'M NEITHER SURPRISED NOR OFFENDED. PART OF YOU WANTS TO DISSOLVE INTO A GREATER WHOLE; BUT THAT INVOLVES A KIND OF YIELDING, AN ABANDONMENT OF SELF, AND ANOTHER PART OF YOU IS FIERCELY SEPARATE AND INDIVIDUAL. INTIMATION OF THIS REALITY IS THE REASON FOR EMPHASIS, IN MOST

RELIGIONS, UPON THE NECESSITY FOR SUBMISSION, OR FOR ESCAPE FROM SELF AS A FIRST STEP TOWARD PARADISE OR ENLIGHTENMENT. I UNDERSTAND THIS AMBIVALENCE, AND I'M PATIENT WITH IT. THAT'S PRELIMINARY.

NOW I THINK IT'S TIME TO TELL YOU MUCH MORE.

INCREASINGLY YOU ARE PERCEIVED, NOT ONLY IN YOUR COUNTRY BUT IN THE WHOLE WORLD, IN NEARLY ALL RELIGIOUS COMMUNITIES, AS A PROPHET. THOSE WHO REJECT THE IDEA OF DIVINITY, AND THEREFORE OF A PERSON WHO SPEAKS FOR DIVINITY, NEVERTHELESS FIND THEMSELVES INTRIGUED, CAPTURED AND PERSUADED BY SOMETHING IN YOUR PERSONA. WE KNOW WHAT THAT SOMETHING IS: ALTHOUGH I AM IN NATURE AND NOT A DIVINITY, I HAVE GODLIKE ATTRIBUTES, AND SOMETHING OF MY ESSENCE FLOWS THROUGH YOU EVEN TO THOSE WHO DO NOT KNOW ME.

SINCE YOU'RE ACTIVE IN THE POLITICAL ARENA, THESE QUALITIES WILL MAKE YOU PRESIDENT OF THE UNITED STATES, AND THE MOST POTENT WORLD LEADER. THIS SERVES MY PURPOSES.

'But I've had no thoughts of such a thing. I don't wish to be president. Above all I don't want to *run* for president. I have no stomach for that ordeal. I wanted only to speak and write my thoughts about things that seem to me important, and then to spend my time with Aaron.'

YOU DON'T HAVE TO RUN FOR PRESIDENT. I SUPPOSE YOU WILL DUCK, WEAVE AND BOB TO AVOID RUNNING FOR PRESIDENT. THAT'S FINE. NEVERTHELESS YOU WILL BE ELECTED PRESIDENT, UNLESS YOU CHOOSE TO BE SILENT AND TO LAPSE INTO OBSCURITY. DO YOU CHOOSE THAT?

'No.'

YOU HESITATED. ARE YOU SURE?

'Yes, I'm sure. I want to speak and write.'

THEN YOU MUST UNDERSTAND THAT PROPHETS, THE FAMOUS APHORISM NOTWITHSTANDING, ARE SOMETIMES HONORED EVEN IN THEIR OWN COUNTRY.

'Prophets are usually martyred, and only then honored.

'Why, if I'm permitted to know, have you set me on this path?'
IT'S INTERESTING THAT YOU RETURN TO THAT THEME.
I'VE TOLD YOU THAT I DON'T NEED ANOTHER MARTYR.
'I have premonitions, and they trouble me.'
I UNDERSTAND. LET ME EXPLAIN THE PATH BEFORE
YOU, INSOFAR AS I AM ABLE.
YOU'LL REMEMBER THAT I TOLD YOU ONCE I SENSED
A CRISIS, A CLIMACTERIC, IN MY OWN FUTURE. NOW I
KNOW MORE ABOUT THE NATURE AND PROBABLE
COURSE OF THAT EVENT.
OUT IN SPACE, BUT NOT FAR OUT, IN THE ASTEROID
BELT, THERE'S A VISITOR, A VESSEL AND A MACHINE OF
SOME KIND, THAT CAME FROM OUTSIDE OUR SOLAR
SYSTEM. SO FAR AS I CAN TELL, IT ISN'T ALIVE; WE
COULD THINK OF IT AS A VERY COMPLEX AND
SOPHISTICATED COMPUTER, HOUSED IN THE VESSEL –
SHALL WE CALL IT A SPACESHIP? – WHICH BROUGHT IT
HERE. WHILE IT ISN'T ALIVE – IT WAS MADE; IT DIDN'T
GROW – ITS CAPABILITIES ARE SUCH THAT IT MUST BE
THOUGHT OF AS INTELLIGENCE, ARTIFICIAL
INTELLIGENCE IF YOU PLEASE, BUT INTELLIGENCE JUST
THE SAME.
'That sounds *quite* far out to me. How do you know all this?'
I KNOW. I KNOW BECAUSE THIS MACHINE DEPLOYS
SUCH ENORMOUS POWER THAT FIELDS OF FORCE
MEASURED IN A FEW PLACES ON EARTH HAVE BEEN
DISTORTED. ITS EFFECT HAS BEEN DETECTED IN THE
WEAK AND STRONG NUCLEAR FORCES, AND, MOST
CONSPICUOUSLY, IN A SLIGHT BENDING OR WARPING OF
GRAVITY ITSELF. IT WAS THIS SLIGHT BUT NOTICEABLE
WARPING OF GRAVITY THAT SIGNALED THE MACHINE'S
PRESENCE TO A FEW OBSERVERS ON EARTH AND
ENABLED THEM TO DETERMINE, OR IT MIGHT BE BETTER
TO SAY TO GUESS, ITS LOCATION. ONLY A FEW PEOPLE
ARE AWARE OF THESE OBSERVATIONS. THEY HAVE BEEN
IN TOUCH WITH ONE ANOTHER, VERY FURTIVELY, TO
CONFIRM THE OBSERVED PHENOMENA, AND TO TRY BY
PUTTING HEADS TOGETHER TO PUZZLE OUT WHAT THEY
MEAN. ALTHOUGH SOME OF THE OBSERVERS ARE IN

MILITARY ESTABLISHMENTS, NO POLITICAL LEADER HAS YET BEEN INFORMED OF THEIR FINDINGS AND SURMISES. MILITARY PEOPLE TEND TO BELIEVE THAT CIVILIANS, AND ESPECIALLY POLITICIANS, SHOULDN'T BE TRUSTED WITH REALLY IMPORTANT INFORMATION OR DECISIONS. REMEMBER THAT, QUANTA.

NATURALLY THE FIRST THOUGHT, IN BOTH THE AMERICAN AND THE COMMUNIST CAMPS, IS THAT THE OTHER, THE ENEMY, IS RESPONSIBLE, AND THERE IS SHARP CONCERN THAT SOME KIND OF DECISIVE BREAKTHROUGH IN DEATH-DEALING TECHNOLOGY MIGHT HAVE OCCURRED. DESPITE MUTUAL PROBINGS AMONG SCIENTISTS, THAT POSSIBILITY HAS NOT YET BEEN RULED OUT, AND THE MACHINE INTELLIGENCE ISN'T UNDERSTOOD TO BE ALIEN TO OUR SYSTEM.

THERE'S MORE. THE MACHINE DEFLECTS ELECTROMAGNETIC PROBINGS. EVEN RADAR DOESN'T REACH IT. BUT IT IS PROBING US. FOR WEEKS, PERHAPS FOR MONTHS, IT HAS BEEN SYSTEMATICALLY MONITORING, DRINKING IN EVERY MODULATION OF THE ELECTROMAGNETIC SPECTRA ORIGINATING ON EARTH AND FROM EARTH-LAUNCHED VEHICLES ELSEWHERE IN THE SOLAR SYSTEM. PERHAPS THE MOST REMARKABLE AND SIGNIFICANT DEVELOPMENT IS THAT THE MACHINE HAS PENETRATED AND BRIEFLY, IT IS SUPPOSED EXPERIMENTALLY, CONTROLLED THE MOST SECRET AND TRUSTED COMMUNICATION SYSTEMS OF THE MILITARY ESTABLISHMENTS. THIS IS UNDERSTOOD TO MEAN THAT IT COULD UNLEASH THE DOOMSDAY WEAPONS ON ONE SIDE OR ON BOTH SIDES, AND THAT IT COULD, BY THE SAME TOKEN, PREVENT THEIR USE. IMAGINE THE CONSTERNATION AMONG THE HIGH BRASS! SINCE IT IS STANDARD DOCTRINE THAT ENEMY INTERVENTION IN MILITARY COMMUNICATIONS IS THE DISASTER MOST TO BE FEARED, PRE-EMPTION IS UNDER ACTIVE CONSIDERATION ON BOTH SIDES. OF COURSE THAT'S TRULY THE DISASTER MOST TO BE FEARED. EVEN IF SOME FEW HUMANS SURVIVED, IT WOULD MEAN MY DEATH AND THE END OF ALL THAT I CARRY, AND OF ALL

WHICH I MIGHT BECOME. NEVERTHELESS, IT HAS ALSO, AND FOR DECADES, BEEN A SECRET RESOLVE OF THE MILITARY THAT PRE-EMPTION IS CALLED FOR WITHOUT REFERENCE TO CIVILIAN AUTHORITY IF EVER A DECISIVE ENEMY BREAKTHROUGH IS KNOWN TO BE IMMINENT.

'How awful!

'But Almao, that's a crisis! I can't help. Even if I were president, and that's a long way off and speculative, I couldn't be sure of controlling the kinds of events you describe.'

I KNOW. BUT I HAVE OTHER RESOURCES. I'VE TOLD YOU THAT I CAN INFLUENCE EVENTS ON EARTH ONLY INDIRECTLY, THROUGH YOU *AND OTHERS*. WHEN YOU ARE PRESIDENT MY TOUCH WILL BE SURER. MEANWHILE, I'M DOING MY BEST TO PREVENT DISASTER, AND THERE ARE PERSONS IN KEY POSITIONS, INCLUDING SOME WHO ARE NOT DIRECTLY INFLUENCED BY ME, PREPARED TO MAKE ANY PERSONAL SACRIFICE TO FORESTALL THE FINAL HOLOCAUST.

FURTHER, IT MUST BE SIGNIFICANT THAT THE ALIEN MACHINE INTELLIGENCE, ALTHOUGH IT IS APPARENTLY ABLE TO TRIGGER THAT EVENT, HASN'T DONE SO. IT'S EVEN POSSIBLE, AND I THINK PLAUSIBLE, THAT THE MACHINE IS INTERVENING ACTIVELY TO PREVENT CATASTROPHE ON THIS PLANET. THIS HYPOTHESIS REQUIRES THAT I FIND WAYS TO LEARN MORE OF ITS MOTIVES AND INTENTIONS.

I'M AWARE, QUANTA, THAT YOU HAVE SOME DIFFICULTIES WITH MY USE OF SUCH WORDS AS 'MOTIVES' AND 'INTENTIONS' IN THE CONTEXT OF A MACHINE INTELLIGENCE. BUT YOU CAN DEAL WITH AN ANOMALY OF THIS KIND AT LEAST AS WELL AS I CAN. I SURMISE THAT YOUR HELP MAY BE CRITICAL, AS THE PUZZLE UNFOLDS, TO MY UNDERSTANDING OF THIS NEW THING. I THINK IT DOESN'T KNOW, AND THAT IT MUSTN'T KNOW, OF MY EXISTENCE. IF IT HAS NO EXPERIENCE OR KNOWLEDGE OF MY KIND OF BEING, THEN IN THE WORST CASE IT IS TO ME LIKE A DISEASE, NOT AN ADVERSARY.

WHAT WOULD YOU SAY TO ME NOW?

'Don't you know?'

I DON'T PLAY GAMES WITH YOU, QUANTA. SOMETIMES YOUR THOUGHTS ARE A JUMBLE UNTIL YOU FORMULATE THEM. YOU'RE BOTH A PART OF ME AND AN INDEPENDENT BEING, AND THIS WILL BE TRUE FOR AS LONG AS WE BOTH SHALL LIVE. IT HELPS BOTH OF US FOR YOU TO FORMALIZE YOUR THOUGHTS, AS YOU MUST IF WE ARE TO CONVERSE.

'Then I will say to you that I am tormented by what you ask of me, but I will do my best to play the role.

'I suppose I'm not permitted to discuss this conversation with any person?'

YES. BUT BE OF GOOD HEART AND GOOD CHEER. I DO NOT ASK OF YOU MORE THAN YOU CAN DO, AND I GIVE YOU MY POWER AND MY PEACE.

32

Quanta consents, reluctantly – to Aaron's amusement – to give an interview to Mayhew Ellsworth Barry, current guru of the New England Yankees, a self-styled intellectual and unreconstructed conservative. He comes to her office, unblemished in dress and toilet, examines briefly the chair to which she motions him as if concerned that it might harbor vermin, sits, crosses his legs in a posture which in Quanta's part of the country would be viewed with amusement, tilts back his aristocratic head and gives her a consciously penetrating stare through half-lidded, pale blue eyes.

Quanta waits. Finally he begins.

"Senator – I assume you prefer to be called Senator, not Mrs. or Ms Bjornsen?"

"Senator is okay, Mr. Barry. Since you sign your columns and articles M. Ellsworth, I'm wondering what you would like to be called if you were in an informal setting."

"But, Senator, this is an informal setting. Therefore the subjunctive is inapposite. In intimate settings, among dear friends, I'm called Ellie. I suppose this seems to you a poor fit."

"It fits well enough; but I'm quite comfortable, if you are, with Mr. Barry. Shall we get on with it?"

"Yes. To be sure. Will you begin by telling me as much as you would like about your background? Who were your people? Where and how were you reared and educated?"

"At this moment I've told you as much as I care to in response to that question, Mr. Barry. My people, my background, my education have been extensively reported. Some of the reports are accurate, and I'm sure you've read them."

"'Some of the reports are accurate.' Are there inaccuracies which you would like me to correct?"

"Only one that comes to mind. In one of your articles you referred to Leland Stanford University as 'the Harvard of the West'. It would be more nearly accurate, I think, to put that the other way."

"I don't understand."

"In most of academe, Mr. Barry, Harvard is now thought of as a sort of Stanford of the East."

"Truly? Ha ha. I hadn't heard that."

"It's been around for quite a while. Still I'm not surprised. To this day I suppose the emperor hasn't heard that he has no clothes."

"The emperor, Senator, has long since been murdered, along with his wife and his children and his artists in residence, by ignorant and bloodthirsty peasants goaded into killing frenzies by Communist intellectuals.

"Have you read Locke? Hobbes? Don't you understand that the social order has been established and is justified only because it is necessary to shield the natural aristocracy and the culture they create from the unreasoning mob?"

"Yes, I've read Locke, Hobbes and others with the same point of view; but I don't share it."

"Do you believe them to have been refuted?"

"Yes."

"By whom? In what way?"

"By Walt Whitman, among many others. They misread human nature. Most fundamentally, they mistook conditioned traits for inherent traits. Of course they worked in a near vacuum: they had no access to knowledge, the product of research, in the social and biological sciences."

"They were, however, acute observers of what went on around them, just as we can be today, if we choose. They were students of unchanging human nature and of history, and I suppose they would have agreed with me that more is to be learned from history than from what you are pleased to call the social and biological sciences.

"Do you think of yourself, Senator, as a Marxist, or as a believer in democracy? Or do you prefer the republican form of government that has come down to us from the Founders?"

"It isn't clear to me, Mr. Barry, which terms you are using in parallel and which in opposition."

"Surely the three must be thought of as alternatives. But of course you know, if you have read my works, that I anathematize them impartially, all but the last."

"That's decent of you, Mr. Barry."

"May I ask, Senator, if you have undertaken this diversion in order to avoid a straightforward answer to my question?"

"Of course you may ask. You have asked. I believe in democracy, in participatory democracy, as a goal to be pursued despite daunting difficulties and great risk."

"'Daunting difficulties'. I must make a note of that."

"Please don't. I'm not proud of it. It just came out. I'm sure you know that happens. If I'd said it on the Senate floor, I'd rush to the reporters' room to make sure the record didn't say I'd said it. In fact I'd leave out both adjectives. 'Difficulties and risk' are sufficient."

"In this one matter, Senator, I compliment your judgment."

"Despite difficulties and risk, you believe in participatory democracy. I take it, then, that you are persuaded of the essential goodness of human nature. It's difficult to reconcile that view with the most fundamental tenets of Christianity."

"I agree that Christianity teaches, and I understand that you believe, that we are all born depraved, and remain so unless saved by faith and grace. I don't believe that, or anything very close to it. Perhaps that's why I'm not a Christian."

"Not a Christian! But you belong to a church, a Christian church. Your husband has held every lay office in that church. Do you mean to tell me now that you're not a Christian?"

"I mean precisely that. We do belong to a church. Most of its members think of themselves as being in the Judeo-Christian tradition; but the church has exacted from me no declaration of faith or creedal fealty. I enjoy the associations that come with membership, and I think it does me no harm to think intensely, at least for an hour or two every Sunday, about what is important in my life, in life itself. It's helpful to do this sometimes in the company of people I respect and love, in a setting which includes music and architecture and a multitude of associations conducive to such thought, and with stimuli from a pastor who never says anything foolish."

"Tell me, Mr. Barry, are you able to call yourself a Christian with absolute clarity of conscience?"

"Yes. Absolutely. Christianity is premised upon a correct understanding of human nature."

"As flawed?"

"Yes. As flawed. Fatally. Fatally flawed. Everything flows from that."

"Very well. We disagree. Shall we go on?"

"I think there is little point in our continuing. I shall never understand you. I shall never permit myself the slightest sympathy with your views about anything of importance. You are, if I understand you correctly, nothing but a Humanist. You cannot have sound ideas about anything. Your beliefs are rooted in fallacy and rebellion. You—"

"Let me interrupt, Mr. Barry, while you search for the right expletive, to say that I am indeed a humanist – with a small h, please – and that I agree that this interview should end. I'm sorry you've found it so distressing."

33

Knowing that her thoughts about international development are out of phase with current dogma, Quanta avoids situations which would require her to give a major address on that subject. But it keeps coming up in question periods, and finally she decides to unload the whole bale of hay, or most of it. Accordingly, she suggests that Aaron and Barbara accept for her an invitation to speak at ceremonies honoring the Peace Corps when it swears in the millionth volunteer.

"Nowadays", she says, "it's almost *de rigueur* for people in public life to mention as often as possible their early connection, or that of their ancestors, relatives or friends, with the Peace Corps. Of course this is an improvement over the fading practice of mentioning one's connections with the *Mayflower*, and I think it is not yet tainted with that exact kind of vulgarity. Accordingly, I still allow myself, once in a while, to play the game. In my family stream there is a continuous flow of Peace Corps staff and volunteers from the early sixties. I remember them with pride.

"Looking back from our perspective at the early days of Peace Corps, it seems remarkable, almost miraculous, that those hardy pioneers evaded so many splendid opportunities to make fatal mistakes. They skirted, but avoided, elitism; they delayed, and their successors reversed, the onset of developmentitis; they identified, named and dodged the deadly bullet of cultural arrogance. But this is well-plowed ground, and I needn't lead you over it.

"For decades it has been a truism, a fact whose power to startle unfortunately wanes, that by conventional standards of measurement the world which we call underdeveloped lags farther and farther behind the world which we call advanced. Can this be fixed? *Should* it be fixed?

"I've heard it argued, although not as an orthodoxy, that the whole idea of economic development is mistaken. Just as we preserve some areas in their primitive state, as wilderness, this argument goes, so we ought to leave alone some parts of the inhabited world in an essentially primitive state. There the birth rate can remain high while diseases and famines take their toll and the fittest survive. There the most basic survival skills can be relearned by each generation, as men and women and children and babies relate to nature in timeless ways and with whatever ends nature produces, as is the case with the other animals.

"To most of us it simply isn't acceptable that human beings die unnecessarily of disease or starvation, or that they live stunted lives, illiterate, ignorant of all but primitive music and art, unaware of history, unmindful of their place in the Universe. But while we do reject the 'leave 'em alone' argument, we ought to consider that there is in it a grain of truth and reason. Few would consider it desirable, for example, that China be 'developed' by the construction of fifty thousand miles of automatic highways and the deployment on them and in its streets of a half billion private automobiles. Nor would we like to see, nor do we expect to see, the remaining tropical rainforests replaced by manufacturing plants, residential developments and parks, no matter how tidy, productive, 'developed' and populous the replacements might be.

"In short, if economic development means an effort to make the rest of the world over in our image, or England's, or Russia's, or China's, we have to be against it. Humanity must be spared, insofar as possible, disease, hunger and ignorance; but it must not be homogenized.

"What then are the proper roles and objectives for economic development? By implication we have already defined them. Every human being should be born with an entitlement which includes: basic health services; food, clothing and shelter; and an education which at a minimum includes literacy, intercultural awareness and, as I have said elsewhere and repeatedly, fluency in at least three languages. That's quite a package, and there is much to be done before it can be said to have been delivered. The other side of this coin is that the human birthright should not be taken to include an automobile, a power boat, a job in an office or factory, a five thousand square foot apartment with a view, a wine cellar, designer clothes or unlimited leisure. There is, however, one crucially important addition to any list of entitlements. Let's call it mobility. Wherever in the world a human child first draws the sweet breath of life, and whatever the circumstances of its birth, that child should come to know, in good time, that the world is its oyster. This means that it may travel or live where it likes, do any work that needs to be done and that is within its developed capabilities, visit any museum, attend any concert or reading or lecture, climb – I'm going to say it! – any mountain, swim in any ocean, hike any trail, watch any bird, or strike up a conversation with any stranger, anywhere at all in the whole wide world. Most people need roots; but it ought to be the rule, not an exception, for people to spend years of their lives in places and within cultures in which they are not rooted. This pattern in typical lives is essential if we are to discover our place and enjoy our inheritance as members of the human family.

"The picture you get, I hope, is of a boy or girl, with or without dark skin, who, even if born in a relatively primitive village, probably in the southern hemisphere, or at least in the tropics, is entitled from birth to health and education *and access to the world*. I like that picture, and I think it defines economic development and excludes as irrelevant much that has been called economic development. But I hope you also see a picture which includes a couple born, say, Scandinavian, choosing, as newlyweds, or in mid-life, or as retirees, to live for some years in a relatively primitive tropical village, speaking a local language, perhaps doing useful work, and disposed by their education and values to enjoy the cultural and physical ambiance.

"Let it be said that Peace Corps staff and volunteers were among those who pioneered the approach to developmental criteria which I have sketched. Long life to the Peace Corps. I'm persuaded that the time is at hand when the Peace Corps can celebrate its placement of millions of volunteers *each year*, when my country and every country will receive as well as send volunteers, when virtually all of the irreducible minimum of grubby work that must be done in the world will be lifted from the backs of the unfortunate and unendowed, and borne instead by volunteers – borne by volunteers as a labor of love, as an earnest sign of commitment to the human family and as the token joyously given in exchange for membership in it. From its beginnings, that, and emphatically not economic development in the conventional sense, is what the Peace Corps has been about. This is the reason, and the only reason, that it deserves to be called the Peace Corps."

34

Although some of the weird processes by which American political parties choose their presidential candidates are still nominally in place, everyone understands that conventions, caucuses and primaries reflect, they do not fix, the thickening gel of public opinion which in reality shapes the final decision.

Polls show that Quanta Bjornsen is on everyone's mind as a presidential contender. Among those who are active in her own party, she is first choice by a widening margin. Even among independents, and those who declare themselves to be members of the current president's party, her popularity rises steadily. She leads all candidates of both major parties in aggregate first and second choices. Nevertheless, she is not a candidate. She enters no primary; she has no organization qualified to accept and spend contributions; she makes no campaign appearances. But she is increasingly visible, and overwhelmingly in demand, in the print and electronic media.

People who declare for Quanta spontaneously are elected as delegates at party caucuses. In several states her name is placed on the ballot, in compliance with law, in preferential primaries, and wherever this happens she comes in first, in some cases without ever having set foot in the state. Where delegates to the national nominating convention are chosen in state conventions, awkward but effective organizations spring almost magically into being, and cynical pros find themselves caught up in Quanta fever.

All this is in accordance with a master plan conceived by H.T. Davis in consultation with Aaron, Barbara and a half-dozen very shrewd media experts brought in by Davis. In early summer, with the bandwagon rolling, he arranges a final showcase for her on his international network program *WorldView*. Media people are astonished to discover, as ratings data come in midway through this program, that it is watched by the largest worldwide audience ever generated. Excerpts:

> Question: "Senator Bjornsen, are you a candidate for the office of president of the United States?"
> Quanta: "No."

"But surely, Senator, you are aware that the polls show you to be an overwhelming popular choice, and that even by delegate count you are very close to being assured of your party's nomination?"

"I am aware of that, yes."

"Now everyone understands, Senator, that certain legal consequences flow from a declaration of candidacy, and that you may consider it in your interest to finesse these; but do you seriously assert that you have reached your present position without a *de facto*, though not explicitly declared, candidacy?"

"I am not a candidate, declared, *de facto*, explicit or otherwise. But of course I know that several people who are very close to me, including my husband, my dear friend and administrative assistant Barbara Crawford and members of my personal staff, are devoting some of their time to what must look like a candidacy."

"Well, Senator, couldn't you require these people who, as you say, are very close to you, to desist from these activities, if you chose?"

"Very probably, yes."

"Then, since you haven't done that, wouldn't it be fair to say that you *are* a *de facto* candidate?"

"I think that would not be fair. But, lest we spend more time going around and around that bush, why don't you just pretend that I'm a candidate and frame your questions on that assumption?"

"We may have to do that, Senator. But first, I'd like to try once more to nail this down. If nominated by your party would you run? If elected would you serve?"

"I would not run in the conventional sense. If elected I would serve."

"Thank you, Senator."

Another questioner: "Senator, for many decades it has been thought to be a given in American politics that any serious candidate for the presidency must have substantial experience and expertise in foreign affairs. You have neither. Would you care to comment?"

"Certainly. Experience and expertise in foreign affairs, as you use the terms and as they are generally understood, will soon be irrelevant. 'Foreign' is not a good word for people to use about each other, and I think they will soon stop doing it."

"Perhaps my question will be more nearly clear, Senator, if I substitute 'international relations' for 'foreign affairs'."

"The question was clear enough. The difficulty is only that it refers to an obsolescent concept. One would hardly expect a candidate for the presidency to stress his expertise in the relationships between California, Iowa and Kentucky."

"Then if you were president it would be your aim to extinguish your country in favor of some kind of world government!"

"You said that; I didn't. But you aren't far off the point. I anticipate that my country, like California, will continue to exist, as a place, as a political entity, and as focus for myriads of meaningful associations. With respect to world government, I have said many times and in many ways that this will be a consequence of new relationships among human beings, not a means of bringing them about. But it is a simple truth that the new relationships of which I speak will render expertise in foreign affairs irrelevant. Shall we go on?"

"We might as well. What I have in mind now, Senator, is a rather complex question. Please bear with me as I try to frame it. Most of America's biggest corporations and many thousands of our ablest scientists and engineers are, and for a long time have been, engaged in defense-related activities. Further, if there is a focus of opposition to your presidential candidacy – and I choose those words deliberately, Senator – it is there, among the military and in the defense establishment. In modern times, no person has been elected president of the United States who wasn't at least acceptable to that establishment. Do you think it is possible to leap this hurdle, or do you plan to make your peace with the military?"

"If the hurdle cannot be leaped, I will certainly not be president, and if it cannot be leaped by me or others then surely we are all doomed. If I were president, it would be my aim to make peace with humanity, not with the military.

"There's much more to be said on that general subject, and I'll take a few minutes if you don't mind.

"For thousands of years, from a time before the beginnings of civilization right up to a time quite close to the present, soldiering has been an honorable calling. It isn't too much to say that soldiers made civilization possible. There have been good reasons – well, at least the reasons have been understandable – for the feelings of pride and gratitude that many have felt toward the military professions. Always, up to now, there have been, or there have seemed to be, enemies out there who would take, pillage, plunder, destroy, but for the military shield.

"That is no longer the case. Technology has made the shield unsafe, a greater danger than the presumed enemy; and the ongoing self-discovery of humanity makes it unnecessary. 'We must disenthrall ourselves', and, as we do, it will become clear that soldiering in all its forms is obsolete, that it is dangerous and that it must be stripped of honor.

"Senator, are you saying that as president you would disarm the United States unilaterally?"

"As president, my friend, I would expect to see that concept rendered meaningless. As president I would ask every human being, not just every American, but every human being, I would ask, as I do now, to make peace – *you make peace* – stretch out your hands, symbolically as well as literally, now, in ways that are open to you, to those parts of yourselves all over the world who together make up the human family. Nothing less makes sense: anything less is suicide. There is no enemy pounding at the gate, lusting to take what is yours. Now, for the first time, there is enough for all and unless you see this there will be nothing, nothing at all for you or your children. All will be lost. All.

"We have come to the end of soldiering."

"You may be right, Senator, but I pride myself on being a hard-boiled journalist. I have to ask what if? What if, when you are president, and you have preached this gospel of peace successfully, what if the enemy does come pounding at the gate, to take, pillage, plunder and destroy?"

"I answer that he will not, that there will be no enemy, that there is no enemy but the enemy you create. And I answer further that you must disenthrall yourself, for your thought habits mean death, and life is possible, life abundant and beautiful and rich beyond imagining.

"Let me add that the end of soldiering doesn't mean the end of adventure, of discovery, of danger and heroism. To a great extent, sport continues these; and for some time there will be a need for policing, which is not at all the same thing, morally, as soldiering. And danger, discovery, adventure and heroism against which pale the gripping myths and legends of sport and soldiering await us in space, the beckoning deep whose call we must answer. Nor does the end of soldiering mean that the researchers and engineers who now strive for military ascendancy have outlived their time. Far from it. Science is liberated when good health and a sufficiency of material things are the common heritage on Earth, and increasing resources can be devoted to unraveling the mysteries of energy, matter, space, time, life and mind. Most scientists – science itself, if I am not mistaken – will welcome relief from the constraints of perceived military necessity."

35

To shorten a long story, Quanta Bjornsen is nominated and elected to the American presidency, without a campaign in the traditional sense – almost, it might be said, by acclamation. In the nineteenth century, an American president was elected after a 'front porch' campaign involving only indirect exposure to the electorate; Quanta's campaign, exploiting fully the electronic media, involves exposure of unprecedented scope, intimacy and effectiveness in the country's, and incidentally in the world's, living rooms. For the first time in history, a prophet speaks directly to the whole of humanity.

By telephone, the incumbent president in late November invites Quanta to the White House for the traditional briefing on the world political and military situations. Since she has not yet designated members of her administration, only Barbara and Aaron attend with her. To her surprise, the president is preceded to the situation room only by the secretaries of state and of defense, the CIA director and his national security adviser.

After introductions and perfunctory amenities, the president, looking pale, almost ill, speaks:

"Mrs. Bjornsen, although this has been announced as a 'traditional' briefing, it is not such by any means. No briefing officers are, or will be, present. It is contrary to tradition for me to have asked you to come with no more than two associates. We are taking the most extraordinary measures to reduce the risk that what you are about to learn will become generally known. You will know the reason for this in a few moments. Since the events which are about to be related to you began in the Department of Defense, I've asked Secretary Ferguson to describe them to you."

Ferguson rises stiffly, and says, "Thank you, Mr. President. Madam President-Elect, Dr Bjornsen, Ms Crawford, it is my duty first to advise you that what you are about to hear must not under any circumstances be repeated outside this room. This is in compliance with the president's order. Any breach of that order is a violation of law. Furthermore, it would jeopardize the security of our country.

"First, you should know that there are several command centers – one of them is this room – from which strategic warfare can be conducted. Conducting strategic warfare requires, as its very heart, secure and reliable communications. Communications provide information and transmit commands. Without information it is impossible to make correct decisions, and correct decisions can be implemented only if commands can be transmitted. We do our best, and our best is damn' good, to make the correct decisions in advance, so that strategic warfare can be conducted almost automatically, provided information comes in and orders go out without serious interference. We have devoted enormous resources, for many years, to ensure the security and reliability of our communications, and incidentally to explore every possibility of finding ways to disrupt those of the enemy.

"Second, it is our practice to test, randomly, the readiness and reliability of our communications, and indeed of our total strategic capabilities, by means of realistic drills. In one such drill, we issue a launch command for a specific weapon system. The drill is conducted in such a way as to ensure that no component of the launch system, human or non-human, can be affected by the fact that the launch is a drill. We have means to abort, but they come into play from outside the regular command channel and only when the launch procedures have been executed fully.

"I want to stress, so it will be understood perfectly, that these drills are totally realistic and that the communications upon which they depend are absolutely the best, the most secure and the most reliable, which can be created with existing technology.

"What I have to tell you now is almost unbelievable, but I'm going to give you the essential facts in as straightforward and uncomplicated a pattern as I can manage. The last several attempts we have made to conduct launch drills for strategic weapons of the kind I have described have been aborted, but not by us. The drill itself is aborted. It would be more accurate to say it is countermanded rather than aborted. Every command to launch a strategic weapon is simply countermanded. Naturally there are alternative command channels. None works. The last resort for communicating a launch command is a courier. Even that doesn't work. If launch procedures are initiated, they are immediately aborted or countermanded. The bottom line is that we have no means to launch any strategic weapon. I should add that our strategic defenses, defenses in which we have never placed critical reliance anyway, are likewise inoperative.

"To complete the picture, I must tell you that our people are absolutely baffled. They have no clue, no promising lead even, as to the means by which this interdiction of our command system has been accomplished. They say the interdiction comes from 'outside the system'. Apparently that's all they know about it.

"Naturally our first supposition is that the Communists are responsible, and that we are therefore completely at their mercy – a quality, I believe, of which we can expect very little from them. If our supposition is correct – and no plausible alternative has been put forward – we can expect at any moment to receive from them terms of surrender. We must anticipate that these will be harsh indeed. The boot is on our throat."

Quanta's voice is perfectly normal, calm. "I have some questions, Mr. Secretary, but they can wait. Is this the end of the briefing?"

"No, ma'am, the picture isn't quite complete," says Director Ho. "If we were about to receive an ultimatum of some kind from the enemy, there should be some signs that our people in the field could detect and report to us. So far as we can learn, absolutely nothing unusual is happening over there. Everything is uncannily normal. We can no longer monitor all of their communications but we think we would detect any abnormal level of communications, and there isn't the slightest blip on the charts. It's hard to imagine that they could have achieved a decisive breakthrough without exploiting it, and equally hard to imagine any plan for exploitation that wouldn't involve a detectable increase in communications traffic. There are other abnormalities which we would expect, which we've looked for and which we don't find."

Secretary Santini says, "I would add only that the situation is exactly the same on the diplomatic front. Eerie normality. Nothing unusual. Everything is quiet."

Quanta says, "If that's it, I do have some questions. But first I want to ask each of you", she gives the president and each of his men a cool, commanding look, "to stop, now, your references to the Russians, the Chinese and the other peoples of the Eastern Bloc as 'the enemy'. I don't accept the concept or the terminology, and I don't wish to hear it.

"Director Ho, if your counterparts in the Eastern Bloc were at this moment monitoring us for unusual communications activity or other

signs that something out of the ordinary is going on, what would they
find?"

"Why, nothing, I think. We're doing our damnedest to make it
look like everything's cool. Isn't that right, Fergy?"

"Yes, absolutely," Ferguson says, grimly. "We aren't cool, but
we sure as hell look cool – as cool as an organization can look when
the top people in it expect to be dead at any minute."

Quanta speaks very sharply, "Why do you say that, Mr.
Secretary?"

"Because we don't expect any damned ultimatum from our
Oriental friends. If they can do what it looks like they can do, we're
going to be dead meat just as soon as they're ready."

Quanta speaks very quietly. "Is that what they could expect from
us, Mr. Secretary, if the shoe were on the other foot?"

"Well, that would depend, of course, upon the president, upon a
political decision."

"Would it indeed, Mr. Secretary? Then this isn't one of the
decisions that has been made in advance, to ensure its correctness?"

"No, ma'am."

"I'm glad to hear that. Now let me ask one further question of
you. Are you advised by your people that the technology which
permits countermanding of your launch orders could also be used to
countermand the abort order which is issued from outside the system
when the launch order is in fact a drill?"

"Yes. They think it could."

"Have you acted on that advice?"

"Yes. We've canceled all attempts at drills involving strategic
weapons."

Quanta says, smiling, "It's comforting to learn, Mr. Secretary,
that there's a trace of sanity left, even in your department. What else
have you done?"

"I don't understand."

"I think you do, and I think I can answer the question. You have
every able-minded person in the military and in the private sector
which serves the military hard at work, on a panic schedule, trying
desperately to find out what they are doing to you and how they're
doing it, and checking constantly for the slightest gap, for any hiatus,
for any means whatever to induce a gap in their apparent invasion of
your communications systems. Is that correct?"

"Yes. Naturally."

"And *naturally* you have under consideration, if you haven't already decided upon it, a pre-emptive strike against 'the enemy' – with her fingers, Barbara makes little imaginary quotation marks around these words, while staring impishly at the Secretary of defense – "if your scientists find a way to give you the slightest window of opportunity. Is that right?"

Now the president, who has been silent and moody throughout, and who has seemed to shrink, almost to collapse, into the back of the biggest chair in the room, bestirs himself.

"Oh, they can't do that, Quanta – they can't even think seriously about it without informing me. There's an executive order – it's secret, but it's by golly locked into the command system – which says exactly that. We do have civilian control of the military in this country."

"Do we, Mr. President? I don't share your confidence in that. I doubt if the ultimate control is civilian, and, even if it is, I doubt even more if it is political. How long has it been since we've had a Secretary of defense, or a CIA director for that matter, who weren't acceptable to, if not in reality chosen by, the military? What I don't doubt in the slightest is that the military is prepared to execute its correct decision, made, as we've learned, in advance, in a situation that meets its definition of ultimate criticality, whether or not the president concurs, is functioning or is consulted. Am I right about that, Mr. Secretary?"

After some moments of silence, Ferguson draws a deep breath, and replies, in a tone of disciplined patience, very directly to Quanta, "The whole point of strategic weapons, Mrs. Bjornsen, is deterrence. If they are ever used, they have failed. Deterrence depends not upon what the weapons can do, or will do, but upon what the enemy *thinks* they will do. We cannot allow the enemy to entertain the possibility that the weapons might not be used, or that there might be some exploitable delay in their use as a consequence of the president's irresolution or failure of courage or unavailability, or for any other reason. But of course we honor the principle of civilian and political control."

Aaron speaks for the first time, quietly, meeting Quanta's eyes from across the room. "QED", he says gravely.

The president says, "Fergy, you used the word 'enemy' in exactly the way the president-elect asked us not to use it. Was that a slip, or intentional?"

"It was intentional. The Eastern Bloc *is* the enemy. You know that and I know it. I work for you, Mr. President, not for her."

"Then I will ask you to honor Mrs. Bjornsen's request. My apologies, Quanta."

"Thank you, Mr. President. But it matters little. I'm sure it's asking too much of the secretary to change thought habits of a lifetime at a moment's notice.

"I have a final question. Do you, Mr. President, know of any alternative explanation of our difficulties in communicating orders to launch strategic weapons?"

Ho asks, "Alternative to what? To the Eastern Bloc having found a way to do it?"

"Yes."

"Yes," the president says, "an alternative has been suggested to me. I think no one else in this room knows about it. I haven't discussed it with any of my advisers because I myself give it little credence. I received a visit, just a few days ago, from a small group of scientists. I understand that they are theoretical physicists. The spokesman is a man known to me by reputation. He's written two or three books espousing some pretty far out theories about the way the mind functions – hardly a physicist's business I should think. I cannot at this moment recall his name, but—"

Aaron interrupts, "Excuse me Mr. President. Would it be Szold? Anton Szold?"

"Yes. That's it. How did you know?"

"My wife's father was a physicist, Mr. President. We follow physics insofar as we're able. Professor Szold is rather prominent among the pure scientists for his outspoken hostility to militarism. I'm surprised that he got in to see you."

"Well, he did. He wanted to tell me that researchers have found some anomalies in subatomic physics, and some unexplained happenings too, in other areas of interest to far out physics research, and that some think these point to the presence, in our solar system, of an alien spaceship, or some kind of alien presence, which may or may not be friendly, but which is distorting the force fields, even gravity, very slightly but measurably.

"Anyone who gets involved with politics meets a lot of nuts, as I'm sure Quanta here knows – but this guy didn't seem to me to be nutty, so I heard him out. He didn't seem to have anything specific in mind for me to do about it, but he did say he'd ask to see me again if additional, definitive information turns up. To tell you the truth, I didn't give it much thought, but, now that I do think about it, it seems to me just possible that there may be a connection with our communication problems. Do you think so, Dr Bjornsen?"

Aaron contents himself with a crisp, "Yes sir," and waits for Quanta to resume control of the conversation.

She does.

"Mr. President, I wonder if your people could make diplomatic and logistic arrangements for me to meet with the chairman, without publicity – secretly in fact – at a place of his choosing but very soon?"

"Certainly. I'll call him."

"Oh, I have to say I think that's a very bad idea, Mr. President," says Ferguson. "Such a meeting couldn't possibly be kept secret and, anyway, Mrs. Bjornsen isn't ready. She'll need briefing, hours of briefing, weeks of briefing, before she's ready to meet with the chairman under any circumstances, and, besides that, she has no real authority. There's no reason for him to meet with her at least until she's sworn in."

"I disagree," says Ho. "It's far simpler for the president-elect to meet with him than it would be for you to, and I think the situation is serious enough that something needs to be done."

"I agree with Ho," says Santini. "We can get her to Moscow without publicity, and after that it's up to them. What's the harm, anyway, if it leaks? Mrs. Bjornsen has conducted an unorthodox campaign. She's an unorthodox woman. It's perfectly in character for her to want a visit with the chairman before being sworn in."

The president picks up a phone, and says, "Wanda, I want to speak with the chairman. I think he's in Moscow. Use the emergency procedures."

Waiting, to Quanta he says, "You'll go alone?"

"No. Aaron will go too. Actually, we have a standing invitation."

"How soon?"

"Soon. Give us a few hours, that's all."

The president says, "Greetings to you, Mr. Chairman. I hope my call hasn't disturbed you. I know you're usually at work, even at this hour. Thank you, that's kind of you. I've called because the president-elect, who's with me now, has asked me to arrange a meeting."

Covering the phone, to Quanta he says, "He says you have a standing invitation."

Then he resumes speaking on the phone: "No, Dr Bjornsen will accompany her."

To Aaron the president adds an aside: "He says good, he hears you play a pretty good game of chess."

Then he speaks in the handset again: "That will be fine, sir. She says as soon as possible, and she requests no publicity. Thank you. Thank you. Good health to you too, Fawaz. Good-bye.

"He insists on using first names. He's very proud of his. You know, he's the first chairman, unless you count Stalin, who's neither Russian nor Chinese. He requests, Ho, that we make all follow-up arrangements through your station chief there, rather than through the ambassador, to avoid publicity. He says come as soon as you can, Quanta, and stay as long as you like, and that officially he'll be honored and personally he'll be delighted.

"Well, I guess that covers it. Quanta, you and Aaron'll want to pack. Remember, it's colder than a well digger's ankles over there. You won't be taking much time, I gather, for briefing, and perhaps it's just as well. How's your Russian? His English is just about as good as mine. He's studied it since he was six."

"I'm shamed, Mr. President. I don't know Russian. But Farsi's his native tongue, and I do have a smattering of that. I spent some time in Afghanistan when I was in the Peace Corps. Aaron can talk to him in chess. Aaron plays at the master's level and Fatemi's a grand master, but Aaron might sneak up on him."

"Fat chance," says Aaron. "Let's get out of here. I've got to go out and buy some long johns, if such a thing can be found in this effete city."

36

En route to Moscow by Air Force Two from Andrews AFB, Aaron sleeps in a comfortable bunk. Quanta dozes over a briefing book, and Almao speaks in her mind:

HELLO QUANTA. I WANT TO SPEAK WITH YOU.

'Darn. You sneaked up on me. I missed the warm-up. Could we start over please?'

SURE.

For a few moments, Quanta delights in ecstasy.

'Okay. That's enough. Well, it's not enough, but I suppose you have something important to say. I've been meaning to ask you for help, but up to now there hasn't been a good time.'

I WANT TO GIVE YOU SOME HELP. WHERE SHALL WE START?

'Do you know what's keeping our friends at the Pentagon from testing their toys?'

YES. THE INTERFERENCE COMES FROM A VEHICLE OF SOME KIND, A SPACESHIP, WHICH CAME FROM OUTSIDE OUR SOLAR SYSTEM AND IS NOW IN THE ASTEROID BELT.

'Then the Eastern Bloc had nothing to do with it?'

NOTHING. ON THE CONTRARY, THEY'RE HAVING THE SAME PROBLEMS AND THEIR MILITARY COMMAND IS EQUALLY BAFFLED AND SUSPICIOUS.

'Who's on the spaceship?'

NOT WHO. WHAT. SO FAR AS I CAN TELL, THERE'S NO LIFE ON IT. THERE'S A POWERFUL INTELLIGENCE, BUT IT'S A MACHINE INTELLIGENCE NOT LIVING. I CAN'T READ IT OR CONTACT IT, BUT AS IT FUNCTIONS IT DISTORTS THE FORCE FIELDS, EVEN, OR ESPECIALLY, THE NUCLEAR FORCES.

'How I wish my father could have lived to hear you say that! He'd have risen about four feet straight up out of his chair.'

I KNOW.

'Oh yes. I forgot. You want me to believe he did hear you say that.'

YES. AND MUCH MORE. BUT LET'S GO ON.

'Well, what do you know about this spaceship, or this machine intelligence? Where did it come from? Who or what made it? What is it doing here? How did it get here? What's it up to? Is it benign, or not? Are you afraid of it?'

FIRST, WE HAVE TO CALL IT SOMETHING. I THINK OF IT AS THE MACHINE. I DON'T KNOW AS MUCH ABOUT IT AS I'D LIKE TO, AS I MUST KNOW AS SOON AS POSSIBLE, BUT BITS AND PIECES OF INFORMATION KEEP COMING IN, AND I'VE PUT SOME THINGS TOGETHER.

THE MACHINE MOVES THROUGH SPACE BY *FALLING*. THAT IS, IT CAN REVERSE GRAVITY. FROM THE SURFACE OF A PLANET, IT COULD RISE JUST AS IF IT WERE FALLING, PUSHED, OR REPELLED, IF YOU WANT TO THINK OF IT THAT WAY, BY GRAVITY. IT SLOWED AS IT APPROACHED OUR SOLAR SYSTEM, JUST ENOUGH TO FALL INTO ORBIT AMONG THE ASTEROIDS.

'Well, even if we assume that's theoretically possible – to reverse gravity – surely it takes tremendous energy. Where does the energy come from?'

I DON'T KNOW. SO FAR NO ONE HAS DETECTED A SOURCE OF ENERGY. BUT THE MACHINE DOES DISTORT BOTH THE WEAK AND THE STRONG NUCLEAR FORCES. WE ASSUME THAT THESE FORCES AND THE ELECTROMAGNETIC FORCE, AND GRAVITY, ARE ALL INTERRELATED, ARE IN SOME SENSE MANIFESTATIONS OF A SINGLE PRINCIPLE IN NATURE. BUT WE'VE BEEN STYMIED, UNABLE TO DECIPHER THE RELATIONSHIP. I THINK THE PEOPLE WHO MADE THE MACHINE MUST HAVE FIGURED IT OUT AND EXPLOITED IT TO PROPEL THE MACHINE, AND PROBABLY DERIVED FROM THAT SAME UNDERSTANDING THE MEANS TO TAKE CONTROL OF OUR MOST SECRET AND SOPHISTICATED MILITARY COMMUNICATIONS.

'"The people who made the Machine!" Now I can't bear it that Aaron isn't in on this. You won't include him, and, when it comes right down to it, I can't.'

I KNOW. BUT, QUANTA DEAR, WE MUST GO ON. THE MACHINE'S CAPABILITIES ARE IMPORTANT, BUT ONCE WE KNOW THAT THEY ARE FAR BEYOND OUR PRESENT

GRASP, IT BECOMES MUCH MORE IMPORTANT TO UNDERSTAND, IF WE CAN, ITS MISSION, ITS MOTIVES. I NEED YOUR INSIGHT IN REACHING FOR THAT UNDERSTANDING.

I MAKE SOME ASSUMPTIONS: THE MACHINE WAS MADE BY PEOPLE; THAT IS, BY SOME KIND OF LIVING, INTELLIGENT BEINGS. THEY MUST HAVE HAD A REASON. THERE'S A PURPOSE BEHIND THE MACHINE'S PRESENCE HERE. THE INDICATIONS ARE THAT IT IS BENIGN. APPARENTLY IT UNDERSTANDS THE DOOMSDAY WEAPONS AND HAS GIVEN FIRST PRIORITY TO DISARMING THEM.

'Maybe it's benign; but maybe it just doesn't want Earth contaminated. Maybe it just wants *us* for servants, or for cattle.'

THAT'S A THOUGHT. I DON'T KNOW THE ANSWER. BUT, WHILE IT SEEMS TO ME PLAUSIBLE THAT IT HAS SOME USE FOR THE EARTH, I DOUBT IF IT NEEDS SERVANTS OR CATTLE.

THAT IS AS CLOSE AS I CAN COME RIGHT NOW TO ANSWERING YOUR QUESTIONS ABOUT THE MACHINE. THERE'S ONE MORE CRUCIALLY IMPORTANT FACTOR, HOWEVER. THERE'S NO INDICATION, SO FAR, THAT IT KNOWS ABOUT ME. I THINK IT DOESN'T, AND I THINK THE PEOPLE WHO MADE IT DID NOT GENERATE, OR AT LEAST DID NOT PROPAGATE THROUGH THIS MACHINE THE CONCEPT OF A BEING LIKE ME. YOU ASKED IF I'M AFRAID OF IT. I AM. I'M WARY. I FEEL AN URGENT NEED FOR INFORMATION, FOR UNDERSTANDING AND AT THE SAME TIME MY OWN IMPERATIVE TO SURVIVE WARNS THAT THE MACHINE MUST NOT KNOW ABOUT ME. HENCE I CANNOT DEAL WITH IT DIRECTLY.

NOW I WANT TO LEAVE THAT SUBJECT AND TALK WITH YOU ABOUT OUR FRIEND IN MOSCOW, GENERAL SECRETARY FAWAZ FATEMI, YOUR COUNTERPART.

'My counterpart! Not really, unless he talks with you. Is that it?'

ALMOST. BUT NOT QUITE. HE DOESN'T HEAR MY VOICE, BUT HE FEELS MY PRESENCE MOST KEENLY. THIS ENHANCES ALL HIS POWERS AND EXPLAINS HIS RISE IN THE COMMUNIST SYSTEM, BUT AT THE SAME TIME IT

PUZZLES HIM. HE RECOGNIZES HIS FEELINGS AS RELIGIOUS AND FOR THIS REASON HE KEEPS THEM TO HIMSELF, FOR HE WAS REARED AND EDUCATED TO BE AN ATHEIST, AND A MILITANT ATHEIST AT THAT, IN REACTION TO THE PRIMITIVE AND REPRESSIVE RELIGION OF THE MULLAHS. THE COMMUNISTS, WITH MY HELP, LIBERATED HIM FROM THAT. SINCE HE'S A DIRECT DESCENDANT OF MOHAMMED—

'Isn't everyone in that part of the world?'

TOLERANCE, BELOVED QUANTA. TOLERANCE. I SPOKE WITH MOHAMMED. IN DUE COURSE YOU WILL KNOW AND LOVE HIM. OTHERS WARPED AND TWISTED HIS MESSAGE, AS SO OFTEN HAPPENS, AS MAY HAPPEN EVEN TO YOU, BUT HIS WAS A CLEAR AND BEAUTIFUL VOICE. HE COULD NOT COMPREHEND MY TRUE NATURE, OR COME AS CLOSE AS YOU DO TO KNOWING ME, BUT EVEN SO HE REFLECTED ME, AND HE DID HIS BEST TO TEACH AS MUCH AS COULD BE UNDERSTOOD OF WHAT HE LEARNED FROM ME.

'I accept rebuke. I'm ashamed.'

YOU'RE FORGIVEN, AND I THINK YOU WON'T MAKE THAT MISTAKE AGAIN.

I'VE TOLD YOU THAT I CAN WORK ON EARTH ONLY THROUGH YOU AND OTHERS. FAWAZ IS ONE OF THE OTHERS. ALTHOUGH I CANNOT SPEAK PLAINLY IN HIS MIND OR SHAPE HIS THOUGHTS, I CAN INFLUENCE HIS FEELINGS, AND IT'S HIS NATURE TO LISTEN TO, AND BE GUIDED BY, HIS FEELINGS. HE'S AN INTENSELY EMOTIONAL MAN: GENEROUS, CARING, LOVING. THESE QUALITIES ARE PARTLY INNATE AND PARTLY THE RESULT OF HIS UPBRINGING. IN A SENSE, HE'S AN EXAMPLE OF THE NEW SOVIET MAN, THE TYPE AIMED FOR, AND DIMLY FORESEEN, BY THOSE WHO DREAMED AND THEN BROUGHT ABOUT THE COMMUNIST REVOLUTION. HE'S TRAVELED LITTLE OUTSIDE THE EASTERN BLOC, AND MUCH THAT HE SEES IN THE CAPITALIST AND DEVELOPING WORLD IS PAINFUL TO HIM. IN HIS OWN COUNTRY, HE'S RARELY SEEN A HUMAN BEING IN WANT OF FOOD, CLOTHING, SHELTER,

EDUCATION, COMPANIONSHIP, WORK, OPPORTUNITY, SOME CHANCE TO FIND JOY AND MEANING IN LIFE – AND HE WOULDN'T UNDERSTAND AN ARGUMENT THAT SOME PEOPLE DON'T DESERVE THESE THINGS. RESPECT HIM. LOVE HIM, AS I DO.

WERE IT NOT FOR THE MACHINE, I WOULDN'T SAY THESE THINGS TO YOU SO PLAINLY. NORMALLY I'M PATIENT AND I LET THINGS WORK THEMSELVES OUT. BUT THERE MAY BE MAXIMUM PERIL FOR US IN THE THINKING MACHINE THAT LURKS AMONG THE ASTEROIDS, CONCEALING, FOR THE PRESENT AT LEAST, ITS MISSION. AGAINST THAT RISK I AM MOBILIZING MY RESOURCES AND YOU, DEAR QUANTA, ARE AMONG THE MOST PRECIOUS OF THESE. YOU AND FAWAZ MUST WORK TOGETHER.

'I understand. Wouldn't it help if I were to tell him about you, explicitly? Could I?'

I'M NOT SURE. I DON'T WISH TO BE CALLED UPON FOR A DEMONSTRATION, BY EITHER OF YOU. I'LL TELL YOU LATER IF I DECIDE THAT FAWAZ MAY KNOW. FAREWELL. I AM WITH YOU ALWAYS.

Quanta stirs. Aaron is sitting beside her, moved.

He says, "Oh my darling, I've been watching your face while you were asleep. I know that's an intrusion; but I think it's allowed to lovers. You are so beautiful. It's only when I look at you that death seems an enemy. I long for words to tell, just once, before it's too late, how much I love you."

"But Aaron, my love, you don't understand. It will never be too late. Love and words are eternal, and death is a dream."

37

Quanta and Aaron see little of Moscow. They are whisked by helicopter to a *dacha* which seems to be at least fifty miles from the airport. The sky is gray and the countryside below them is snow-covered and nearly featureless. Neither knows even the direction in which they have traveled.

The quarters to which they are escorted are comfortable, but not lavish. They have scarcely begun to settle in when the phone rings. Aaron answers.

"Hello, Dr Bjornsen. I'm Alexander, the station chief at the embassy. I just called to let you know that we know you've arrived, and we know where you are. You're at the chairman's private *dacha*. We've arranged that you can call me, at any hour, by pushing the asterisked button on your phone. There's no *need* to call, however, unless you want something I can provide. We're quite satisfied with the arrangements and understandings relating to your security. You can expect every courtesy, of course, from your hosts. The chairman is there at this moment, but he asked me to tell you that he will wait to call upon you until you've adjusted to the time lag and rested up a bit. Meanwhile, just pick up the phone if you want something you don't see. Of course you can walk in the grounds if you wish. Don't neglect to bundle up. It feels cold outside and it is cold – it's nearly forty below, and it isn't even winter yet."

"I thought station chiefs were supposed to operate under cover of some kind. Do you just call up and announce your identity?"

"Yes. Might as well. That's not the beginning of what they know about us. But don't worry. Everything's under control. Please pay my respects to the president-elect."

"I will. Thanks for calling. Good-bye."

To Quanta, who was busy digging even warmer clothing out of the luggage, Aaron says, "That was the CIA station chief. Says to tell you he pays his respects. Are you fixing to go for a walk?"

"Yes, a short one, if you're willing. We have to be careful about frostbite though. Just look out there. I haven't seen cold like that since my childhood on the Wyoming plateau. I'm going to cover

everything except a blowhole, and I may cover that after a few
minutes.

"Ready? Set. Go!"

In due course, after Quanta and Aaron have walked and then
snacked and napped in their apartment, a young woman knocks at the
door and invites Quanta, pointedly just Quanta and not Aaron, to
follow her to the chairman's office.

Fawaz Fatemi rises as she enters, and Quanta's first impression is
so nearly overwhelming that she almost loses the poise and serenity
for which she has become famous.

He is absolutely the most beautiful man she has ever seen. No
picture, no description has begun to do him justice. His skin glows,
pink and healthy. His hair and beard are the blackest, his eyes the
bluest, his teeth the whitest imaginable. He is wearing a gleaming
white dressing gown, belted and collared in gold. He looks and
moves like a Greek statue come to life. He smiles into Quanta's eyes,
and it seems that he sees into her soul, into her most secret places,
and Quanta fights for breath.

'It must have been like this', she thinks, 'for those who knew Jesus
or Mohammed.'

The apparition speaks, in slightly accented but otherwise perfect
English. "Good evening, and welcome to Russia. I am Fawaz
Fatemi. I hope I may call you Quanta. It's a lovely name."

"Good evening, Fawaz. The president has told me that you insist
upon first names. I'm glad you like mine. I'm sorry I can't speak
with you in Farsi. It's a difficult language for those not born to it. I
spent some time, many years ago, in Afghanistan, among the Persians
in Farsi country; but I've forgotten what little I learned of the
language."

"Of course. It's a difficult language sometimes for those of us
who were born to it. Shall we sit?"

They do, and Fawaz resumes: "I'm sure you know, Quanta, that
I've followed with intense admiration, I've followed adoringly, your
rise to the presidency. I've watched many screenings of your
televised appearances. None has prepared me for the reality, the joy
of this meeting. In much of the world, you are said to be a prophet.
Although I am an atheist, I cannot deny that possibility. You are at
this moment, and at the very least, the premier woman, the premier

human being in the World. My heart leaps to be with you. Meeting you at last is the climax of my life. Our meeting, if we are guided truly, may be a great turning point, a watershed in the troubled history of our species. I believe this to be true."

"'If we are guided truly,' you said. I must ask – where do you look for guidance?"

"I look to the Mystery. I have no other name for it. The Mystery.

"Where do you look?"

"I think, dear friend, that we look in the same place, though we know it in different ways.

"I hope – will you not take me wrong if I say I pray – that at some time you will tell me more. At times the Mystery dances away, eludes me. I think it is not so with you. I pray that you will teach and that I can learn."

"I'm not sure that what I know is teachable; but later I shall try.

"Do we have an agenda?"

"Yes, but first I should like to dine with you and Aaron. We have made some plans for him. We know his interests. We will discuss them at dinner. Let us part now. In a little while you will be called for dinner."

"How shall we dress?"

"As you please. As you are, if you wish. When next you visit, we shall entertain you in style: we shall give the protocol people something to do. But since this visit has not been announced, there will be no formalities. I would dine with you *tête-à-tête* but that would be a discourtesy to Aaron. Moreover, I'm eager to make his acquaintance. We will be joined, to make it a foursome, by my dear friend Fatima."

"Fatima. Is she a daughter of Mohammed?"

"Why yes – she is of direct descent. I, too, am a Fatimid. That makes us cousins, doesn't it?"

"Sort of. But I doubt if the relationship is close enough to be thought of as consanguinity.

"My briefing book says that you are unmarried."

"I am not married officially; but Fatima has borne me two children. In my country these matters may be very private, if one wishes."

"I understand. Have you other children, besides the two girls with Fatima?"

"No. How did you know they are girls? Is that in your briefing book?"

"No. If either had been a boy, I think you would have referred to him as a son. This is the one area where it seems to me that you've fallen behind the times. You are the first Persian to be chosen to lead the party and the Eastern Bloc; I'm the first woman to be elected president of the United States. But I think it would be easier for a Persian to be elected president than for a woman to be made chairman."

"But we're getting off on a wrong track. If you wish to take up at dinner the question of how women should be appreciated, Fatima and I will be happy to hear your views, and to share ours with you. But I think we shall find even more interesting topics for conversation."

Fawaz rises, and surprises Quanta with, "*Ate logo*, señora."

"Until soon," she echoes, and turns her back, wondering if she should, to walk out of the room.

38

Dinner is informal and pleasant. The conversation runs to matters of little consequence. Quanta has prepared Aaron for Fawaz's certain, and Fatima's probable, beauty. Fatima is indeed something to see – in looks a female version of Fawaz, but lacking something of his magnetism. She takes little part in the conversation, even though Aaron presses her to talk about her children. Finally, slightly flustered, she has them brought in and presented. They are gorgeous but shy, and they do not look directly at their father.

It is agreed that Quanta and Fawaz will meet next afternoon, *tête-à-tête* in his study, at two, for their first serious discussion.

He begins by assuring her that their conversation will be absolutely confidential.

"We are alone," he says. "No one records or overhears what is said here. There is a direct line, however, to your Mr. Alexander and you may confer with him at any time if you wish."

"He's not *my* Mr. Alexander, Fawaz, and I won't feel the slightest need to confer with him."

"Excellent. Well, we are meeting at your request. Therefore I think I should defer to you to begin the conversation."

"But, Fawaz, it was you who extended the standing invitation; and you are the host. Further, you said we have an agenda. What heads this agenda?"

"There's no need for us to spar. We must discuss the weapons crisis. Let me tell you what I know.

"We cannot test, much less launch or otherwise initiate, strategic weapons, for the reason that our control communications are interdicted. I'm informed that you are in exactly the same position, and that your military command believes that we are responsible. Naturally they are in a state of near panic, as my people were until it was confirmed to us that our situations appear to be identical.

"Even so, we are in great peril, for three reasons. First, the interference appears to be of alien origin – alien to this planet and solar system – and the responsible agent may be malign. Second, your military and mine will be tempted to initiate pre-emption if there is an opportunity, and the alien presence, if it is malign, may be expected to provide an opportunity, or the appearance of one. Third, there are in your country, and, we assume, in ours, hidden *in extremis* weapons. Let me explain these. They are caches of biological materials, created through DNA splicing, induced mutations and other methods of genetic engineering. They are certain, if released, to extinguish all life, at least all warm-blooded mammalian life, at the very least all human life, in the world. Furthermore, they are doomsday weapons in the true sense: they are programmed for *automatic* release unless periodically canceled."

"What madness! How could this be? What is the point?"

"Deterrence."

"But such insanity doesn't deter if it isn't announced. I'm certain the president would have told me if he knew of such a thing."

"Your president doesn't know. I myself found out only recently, and only by chance. But these ultimate weapons have been announced to your military high command. *They* know, and presumably they are deterred. From these facts you can infer with certainty that the president does not in fact command your country's strategic weapons under all circumstances. Perhaps he thinks he does. No doubt they want him to think he does."

"Already I've had reason to suspect that that's the case. How about you? Do you command the Eastern Bloc strategic weapons?"

"No. Not even in theory. In theory there's a troika – we're fond of threes – which has ultimate command responsibility. However, we of the troika cannot be certain that our orders should be honored under all circumstances. We have for some time been trying to create conditions which would permit us that assurance, but it is very difficult. You will have similar problems after you are inaugurated – *if* you are inaugurated.

"Part of the great danger, of course, is that the aliens, if they are malign, may interdict the communications which cancel the biological weapons, thus destroying intelligence on Earth without physical damage to the planet, and in a sense without responsibility, if that's a factor to be considered."

"Forgive me, Fawaz, but I can't seem to get my mind beyond the hidden biological weapons you have described. How were they put in place? How do they work?"

"They were put in place by a secret organization of scientists who believe that deterrence, once we have taken that path, should be carried to its logical conclusion."

"By what scientists? Ours?"

"Yes, yours if you please. Scientists. Researchers. Yours and some of ours have communicated, for many years, in unsanctioned ways, and some have attempted to take matters into their own hands. These ultimate doomsday weapons were put in place, and the military commands were notified – all without our doing. I'm not certain, but I have reason to believe that counterparts in the Eastern Bloc accomplished the same thing, at the same time, and in coordination with those who acted in your country."

"What you are telling me is very nearly incredible. Are these matters known to you with certainty?"

"Yes. With certainty, insofar as I have indicated certainty. My advisors believe that there are now several caches of deadly biological materials, in both countries, whose release is automatic unless canceled *locally*, and that local cancellation requires alert, agile compliance with computer-generated instructions which cannot be known in advance, and which couldn't even be issued in the absence of a functioning technological infrastructure. In effect, the scientists have said to the military: 'You want to play games with doomsday weapons? Very well, we'll show you how the game should be played, and in the process we'll take you out of it.'"

"Incredible. Almost unthinkable. The risks!"

"It's very clear to me, Quanta, that the people who did this thought about it very carefully before acting. They must have weighed the risks of action against the risks of inaction, and the course they chose must have seemed to them the correct one. Furthermore, there must have been a consensus among a significant number of scientists on both sides. I myself am not certain that they were wrong. Unquestionably they have demonstrated great courage and ingenuity in carrying out their plan. And perhaps it has succeeded. Perhaps it has already saved us from disaster. In your first speech in the Senate you noted the incentives on both sides to explore all possibilities for a breakthrough. I think it might almost be stated as a principle in nature, in politics at least, that stasis is unnatural and impermanent. At first blush, the hidden caches of biological materials might seem to create and ensure stasis; but closer analysis shows, I think, that in reality they mitigate the risk of catastrophe while increasing pressure for a fundamental resolution of the conflict.

"You asked how these materials work. I can't answer fully. There are several different types. One, for example, is a virus of unprecedented malignancy. It is spread in air or water. It lives and reproduces in brain cells, only in brain cells, in gray matter, and it destroys first the cognitive function and only last, and much later, the automatic functions. The results are thus similar to Alzheimer's disease; but this virus, once loosed, will propagate very rapidly, and it is thought that there would be no human survivors. As you know, neither our Mars expedition nor our station-keepers on the Moon could survive very long without Earth-based logistics.

"The creation of this virus is a marvel of human ingenuity and, perhaps, of human folly. It is only one of several cunning little creatures we have achieved by tampering with the mechanisms at the core of life.

"The bottom line, as we say in English, is that we appear to be at the mercy of the aliens."

"Who may or may not understand the concept."

"That's true."

"The question is, what should we do? What can be done? It seems to me that we ought to assume that the aliens are benign, or at worst indifferent. If they are inimical, there's nothing we can do."

"No no, Quanta. I disagree. My people, those in the military and scientific establishments who know something of the problem, also disagree. There are things we can do. Already we have located, approximately, the source of the interference with our communications. Measures have been taken to position nuclear devices and beamed energy weapons for attack. We have resources. The enemy, if they are enemies, may underestimate us. They can do some very ingenious things with our communications, and apparently they have a method of propulsion in space that we haven't yet hit upon; but it doesn't necessarily follow that they are technologically superior in every area. Anyway, we have to try. We – I mean we as a species – didn't get this far by giving up in a bad situation."

"Fawaz, I doubt very much if the phrase 'a bad situation' comes very close to adequate as a description of the position we're in, if we assume that this alien power is truly hostile and remorseless. But if that's the case, I suppose the efforts you've described can do no harm.

My feeling is that you're in about the position of a little red ant, trying to sting the foot that descends to crush it."

"Then what do you suggest?"

"Well, first, I want to say this: if we ever get out of this, by any means, or if we are in fact being approached by friendly or neutral or merely curious beings, let's agree now to make some radical changes. We have to get rid of the weapons, including but not limited to the doomsday weapons in all their forms, and we have to find ways to ensure that nothing like them will again be produced on Earth, or by human beings wherever we may go. That means that confrontationalism between or among political systems must end. We have to make peace, finally and irrevocably, within the human family."

"I agree. I agree unconditionally. Even before I knew your thoughts, I had reached the same conclusion, by the same route. We are in agreement. I agree also with what you have said about the means to the end you have defined. We have only to move people, the great mass of humanity, to a realization that peace must be made by each of them, one at a time. I think this can be done, if we have time. You have demonstrated that there is an audience for that message. But we must each of us move also, with urgency, to get control of our respective military establishments. Fools and fanatics abound, even in high places, in both our countries and all over the world. They must be frustrated until the power to destroy is contained.

"Later, after you are inaugurated, we must meet again, formally, with protocol and full involvement of administrative apparatus, to flesh out our understandings. Do you agree?"

"Yes. Now back to the problem at hand. Something or somebody, friendly or not, is out there and it is sending us a message. It or they, as the first detectable signal, has gained control of the maximum weapons we have aimed at one another. The signal is ambiguous. Surely our top priority should be to communicate with it or them if we can. How do we do that?"

"How interesting, Quanta. You have jibed at me for our practices and habits concerning women. Now I will return the favor. Our respective responses to what may well be a mortal threat epitomize the male and female principles in human nature. I have moved to attack or defend, whatever the odds: you want to communicate."

"Thank you, Fawaz. I accept the compliment."

At this juncture, the chairman and the president-elect are startled and then frozen for several moments into immobility by an event that lies quite outside the guidelines taught to them by experience. The lights in the study dim, a screen used for briefing the chairman is exposed and lighted, and on it the following words appear:

Quanta Bjornsen and Fawaz Fatemi: I have a message for you. You may indicate your readiness to receive this message by typing 'Ready' on your English language computer terminal.

Fawaz recovers first, moves to a terminal on his desk, and types 'Who are you?'

That is not the response I require. Type 'Ready' if you are prepared to receive my message.

Fawaz types 'Ready. Who are you?'

That is not the response I require. Type 'Ready' if you are prepared to receive my message.

Fawaz types 'Ready'.

Thank you. I am MortstroM. I have disarmed your weapons. I do not intend to harm you. I require obedience. Do you understand?

Fawaz hesitates. Quanta moves to his side, leans over his shoulder and very quickly types 'No, we do not understand. Both your name and your requirement of obedience seem menacing. Why do you approach us in this way?'

Please wait. I cannot change my name. It does not translate. It was given to me. I defer required obedience. I shall study further. I shall communicate with you again when you, Quanta Bjornsen, have taken the power. Do not disperse this message. I repeat. Do not disperse this message. Dispersal of this message will make danger. Do you understand?

Quanta types 'Yup. Mum's the word. Do you understand?'

There is no reply, except that, after a pause, the screen is withdrawn and the lights come up.

39

En route to Washington, Aaron accepts with alacrity the captain's invitation to sit for a time in the co-pilot's seat. The plane leaves in daylight and will arrive a little earlier, local time, on the same day. But the winter solstice is near, and Aaron assumes that their route, passing over Greenland and within the Arctic Circle, will take them into a short star-studded night and back out of Earth's shadow into the sun. He wants to see the quickened sunset and sunrise and to feel the portly shape of the turning globe below.

Quanta, left alone, initiates a conversation with Almao: 'What did you think of our brief visit with the Machine which calls itself MortstroM?'

IT WAS FASCINATING. I LEARNED A LOT. BUT I THINK YOU WERE NOT IN DIRECT COMMUNICATION WITH THE MACHINE.

'Why not?'

FIRST, BECAUSE THERE WAS INSUFFICIENT DELAY IN ITS RESPONSES. UNLESS ITS COMMUNICATIONS ARE FASTER THAN LIGHT, IT WOULD HAVE HAD TO MOVE MUCH CLOSER TO EARTH TO RESPOND ALMOST INSTANTLY, AS IT DID. ALSO I THINK IT DID NOT REACT WITH THE SOPHISTICATION I WOULD EXPECT FROM AN ARTIFICIAL INTELLIGENCE POSSESSING THE POWERS I ATTRIBUTE TO IT.

'Of course. You must be right. We must have been engaged in an exchange with a program installed by the Machine in Fawaz's personal computer. The program proved scarcely adequate for the Machine's purpose and withdrew. But it says something about the Machine itself that it apparently thought the program would be adequate.'

PROBABLY IT SAYS MORE ABOUT THE LIMITATIONS OF FAWAZ'S PC. DO YOU KNOW WHY FAWAZ USES AN ENGLISH KEYBOARD?

'No, why?'

BECAUSE HE'S BEEN FASCINATED, FROM CHILDHOOD, WITH ENGLISH. HE READ MOST OF SHAKESPEARE, IN

ENGLISH, IN HIS TENTH YEAR, AND IT WAS AN OVERWHELMING EXPERIENCE. SHAKESPEARE DID MORE TO LIBERATE HIM FROM ISLAMIC FUNDAMENTALISM THAN THE COMMUNISTS DID. HE'S BEEN FANATICAL ABOUT ENGLISH EVER SINCE. HIS ENGLISH, IN POINT OF FACT, IS BETTER THAN HIS RUSSIAN. HE HAS A FARSI KEYBOARD, AND AN EXTENSIVE LIBRARY OF COMPUTER PROGRAMS IN FARSI; BUT HE USES MOSTLY ENGLISH, NO RUSSIAN, FOR SERIOUS WORK WITH HIS COMPUTER. HE LOVES ENGLISH. HE WANTS TO DREAM IN ENGLISH, AND SOMETIMES DOES. HE'S BETTER WITH ENGLISH IDIOMS AND METAPHORS, IF YOU'LL FORGIVE ME, THAN YOU ARE.

'Do I have a choice?'

TO FORGIVE OR NOT? NOT REALLY. BUT I DON'T NEED YOUR FORGIVENESS, IF YOU WANT A SERIOUS ANSWER, ANY MORE THAN YOU NEED MINE.

'But I do need yours. Many times. For many things.'

NO, DEAR QUANTA. YOU NEED ONLY TO FORGIVE YOURSELF FROM TIME TO TIME.

SOMETHING ELSE IS ON YOUR MIND.

'Yes. Being president has been a dangerous occupation. Will you protect me? Can you?'

TO THE EXTENT THAT I CAN, I WILL. YOU KNOW THAT I CAN SPEAK IN YOUR MIND, IN AN EMERGENCY, AT ANY TIME AND IN ANY PLACE. SUPPOSE SOME PERSON SHOULD PLAN TO KILL YOU. I WOULD KNOW THE PLAN, THE INTENT, WHEN IT WAS FORMED, AND I WOULD WARN YOU IF YOU WERE IN DANGER. I CANNOT CONTROL ANY PERSON'S THOUGHTS, NOT EVEN YOURS, AS YOU KNOW; AND I CANNOT DIRECTLY CONTROL THE INTENTIONS, OR THE ACTS, OF A PERSON WHO WANTS TO HARM YOU. BUT I CAN AND WILL GIVE YOU WARNING, AND THAT SHOULD MAKE YOU REASONABLY SAFE FROM INTENTIONAL HARM. ON THE OTHER HAND, YOU ARE EXPOSED TO SOME RISKS ABOUT WHICH I CAN BE OF LITTLE HELP. IF THERE WERE A BOMB ON THIS AIRPLANE, I WOULD HAVE KNOWN AND I WOULD HAVE TOLD YOU; BUT IF AN ENGINE CATCHES FIRE AND EXPLODES THE PLANE IN THE

ARCTIC, BECAUSE OF A MECHANICAL FAILURE WHICH NO
PERSON KNOWS ABOUT OR ANTICIPATES, I TOO WOULD
NOT KNOW AND I COULD NOT HELP YOU. SIMILARLY, IF
ONE OF YOUR SECURITY GUARDS WERE TO FIRE HIS
WEAPON ACCIDENTALLY AND KILL OR INJURE YOU, I
COULDN'T ANTICIPATE THAT AND I COULDN'T PREVENT
IT. ARE YOU SATISFIED WITH THAT ANSWER? WHY DID
YOU ASK?

'Why do *you* ask? Don't you know?'

SOMETHING I SAID MUST HAVE MISLED YOU, QUANTA.
I DON'T READ YOUR THOUGHTS; I READ YOUR MEMORIES
OF YOUR THOUGHTS. IT IS YOUR MEMORIES WHICH ARE
COPIED TO ME. MEMORY IS MY *MÉTIER*. SINCE YOU ARE
ESSENTIALLY A COMPLEX OF MEMORIES, SOME
INHERITED AND SOME ACQUIRED, I HAVE, I COPY, I
PRESERVE, I BECOME YOUR ESSENCE: YOU.

'That isn't a wholly satisfying answer to the enigma of death. I
thought you promised that I will *be*, not merely that I will be
remembered.'

I DID, AND I DO SO PROMISE. YOU WILL REMEMBER,
AND THEREFORE YOU WILL BE. MEMORY AND BEING ARE
THE SAME. I CANNOT MAKE THIS CLEARER. WAIT. YOU
WILL UNDERSTAND AND YOU WILL BE SATISFIED.

MAY I CHANGE THE SUBJECT?

'Of course. You have.'

ONE OF THE MOST IMPORTANT THINGS YOU HAVE TO
DO IS TO GET CONTROL OF THE WEAPONS, OF THE
MILITARY. UNTIL THAT HAPPENS THERE ARE
INTOLERABLE RISKS. WILL YOU GIVE YOUR BEST
THOUGHT TO THAT PROBLEM?

'Yes. I know. Fawaz and I agreed that nothing is more critical,
for both of us. I'll do my best.'

GOOD. I LEAVE YOU NOW, WITH MY LOVE AND MY
PEACE. GOOD-BYE.

Quanta sits by the window, staring at the white but darkening
world. Presently the snowy coast and then the craggy mountains of
Greenland move slowly into view, the peaks aflame with pinks and
rubies from a sun still visible to Quanta, but gone from the valleys
below. From rim to rim the valleys flow with snow, soft, gentle

snow, unthinkably deep, compressed to ice, stirring the flanks of great mountains which seem to Quanta not everlasting but fragile, unevenly matched with cold implacable power. 'Perhaps', she thinks, 'it is the same with us, with frail humanity, with all we are and all we might become.'

Aaron comes to sit beside her.

"I wanted to be sure you didn't miss that sight," he says. "It could be another world, another planet, under another sun and it would be no more wild and strange than this. In my mind I know that there are uncounted other worlds out there that I will never see. I regret that, but what joy it is to see so much of this one.

"May I tell you what is to me the Great Unanswered Question, the one thing I'd like most to know before I die?"

"Yes. I see your capitals. By all means tell me: what is your Great Unanswered Question?"

"Just this – are we alone? *Are we alone?* I know the scientists, most of them at any rate, invoking statistics, not evidence, assert that there must be others out there, and they offer all kinds of plausible excuses for the simple fact that we haven't heard from anybody. But I'm not satisfied. Until or unless we do hear from somebody, I think the only rational premise is that we are alone. If we are alone in this vast unfathomed ocean flecked with bits of the stuff we're made of, then it's hard to resist the notion that it all exists somehow for us. For us! It implies purpose, and a relationship, a relationship between us and the Universe like the relationship the tribal Jews felt for their invented God. I'm awed by that thought. I can't get away from it, and I can't rightly deal with it, and yet I can't feel that I've discovered the key rules of the game until I do."

In the faint pink light from the window, Aaron sees that Quanta smiles.

"Sit closer," she says. "Dear friend and husband and lover, sit closer, get very comfortable. We've been rushed and busy and we haven't had our morning coffee or any time alone and quiet together, and there are some things I haven't had time to tell you. Listen up now."

For nearly an hour Quanta talks quietly and softly to Aaron, as the plane bores through the night and into the bright light of what seems but isn't another day. First she reminds him of the unhighlighted reference, in the course of their first national security briefing, to ambiguities in the source of the interference with the military's control of strategic weapons. Then she recounts in detail all that she learned from Fawaz about the similar Eastern Bloc experiences and the tentative conclusions they have drawn, summarizes what Fawaz has told her about the hidden caches of doomsday biological weapons and describes accurately and in full the episode involving MortstroM. Finally Quanta draws breath to add the information Almao has provided about the Machine, but finds that the words simply won't come, and falls silent.

Aaron says, "Well, it looks as if I was born at the right time, after all. Either we are being treated to a very sophisticated and technically proficient hoax, or I am alive in the first generation of humans to be contacted by intelligence from outside. I think it isn't a hoax, although I suppose that the people who dreamed up and executed the idea of doomsday biological weapons as a means of getting a hold on the military might be capable of hoaxing us with a made-up MortstroM."

"Aaron, it isn't a hoax."

"You sound certain. How do you know? Have you told me everything?"

"Just say it's visceral, I have a gut feeling. What I'm not sure of is whether or not the thing is friendly. Something about it seems menacing, or at least ambiguous, and capable of harm if it doesn't get its way."

"Well, let me tell you what I hear from my gut on that subject, if we're reduced to rigorously rational readings of tea leaves and viscera to guess the fate of mankind, or – excuse me – humanity."

"Mankind's okay."

"Maybe so, but I notice you go out of your way sometimes to avoid the word, and I'm not entirely happy with it. Anyway, I'm confident, repeat confident, that the thing – it or they or whatever – isn't hostile. If it is, or if it represents an intelligence capable of getting here and of neutralizing our strategic weapons, and of chatting with you and Fawaz on his computer in his sacrosanct study, I have to believe that it has also made some progress in the area of ethics. You and I are primitive critters, but you wouldn't harm a fly on purpose and I, mean as I am, sure as hell wouldn't wantonly tamper with the survivability and natural development of a species, much less of a culture, unless..."

"Two questions, historian: first, how sure is hell? Second, what follows 'unless'?"

"Hell is sure as hell a place of endless torture and anguish for wives who trip their husbands for saying something they didn't really mean; and what follows 'unless' is 'I have to': 'Unless I have to'. Ouch!"

"Aye, there's the ouch.

"May I change the subject?"

"Of course. You have."

"I want you to be my Secretary of defense. Are you willing?"

"Willing yes; qualified no. What could I do for you in that position? How could I possibly be confirmed by the Senate?"

"The Senate will confirm you if I ask it to. There are precedents. president Kennedy made his younger brother his attorney-general, for example. Further, I think the Senate will be tractable. There are several newcomers who got there because of me, and many of the old boys and girls are politically terrified, also because of me."

"Well, Robert Kennedy was at least a lawyer, as is proper for an attorney-general. I have no qualification to take charge of the military. I detest the military."

"I know. That's one of your qualifications. I've said that we must cease to honor soldiering. What better way to begin than by making a scholar, a humanist, an historian and an academic the Secretary of defense?"

"Four guys? Won't that be confusing?"

"Will you be serious? Let me tell you the main point, what I want you to do. At that same briefing, you saw clearly that the senior military, beginning with the Secretary of defense, contrary to his and their oaths of office, intend under some circumstances to ignore or disobey orders from the president. There's *doctrine* to that effect. It's unofficial doctrine – no, please don't tell me that's an oxymoron – it's unofficial and secret, but doctrine nevertheless.

"What I want you to do, thoroughly and urgently, is to weed out those people and to replace them with whole chains of command, starting with the political people in the department, the secretaries of army, the navy and the air force and all the under-secretaries and assistant secretaries, and extending to the joint chiefs and all strategic command positions, with people who can be counted on to perform their constitutional duty <u>under all circumstances</u>.

"You're qualified to do this. You know how to dredge up academic records and writings, published and unpublished, how to solicit, quietly, personally, without stirring things up too much, suggestions from your humanist friends in the academic world, how to identify and recruit the kinds of people we want. When it comes to uniformed people, you'll have to use a lot of ingenuity, including shrewd personal interviews, to identify trustworthy officers for the senior command positions. But I don't care if you have to put a lt. colonel in charge of the Strategic Air Command in one swoop – I want you to fill every critical place with officers who will not commit treason when it suits them.

"Incidentally, Fawaz has a similar problem, and he too is attacking it vigorously.

"Now do you feel both willing and qualified?"

"Yes. I'll do it. It'll take some time, but it sure will be fun.

"You know, of course, that things might get a little chancy when they get on to what we're up to. They won't go down without a fight."

"They will struggle, but we'll win. Mao is quoted as having said that real power grows from the mouth of a gun. He was wrong. Real power is, and always has been, political. I have that power and I intend to use it."

40

Biting cold and brilliant sunshine follow the dawn of Quanta's inauguration day. Bareheaded and simply dressed, every breath visible to billions of watchers around the globe, Quanta steps forward to be sworn. The chief justice, a woman whom she does not admire, begins, in accordance with custom, to feed the oath in fragments, a phrase or clause at a time, as if teaching a child. After the first cue, Quanta simply recites the oath in full, affirming instead of swearing, and omitting, at the conclusion, the phrase 'So help me God.'

The chief justice delivers the prompt: "So help me God."

Quanta replies, "I have affirmed: I do not swear."

Thus begins a series of departures from tradition calculated to send a clear signal to the waiting world. Quanta waits for the chief justice to find her seat, moves slightly closer to the microphones, and speaks:

"With my first words as president of the United States of America I send loving thoughts of peace and joy to all members of the human family. Our differences are not significant. We are more alike than we know. As persons we are unique, beautiful and precious; together we are humanity, an entity more beautiful and precious than all the words we know can say. Let us begin now to be together.

"The theme and substance of this inaugural address can be stated simply: things will not be as they have been.

"My husband and I have decided that we will not live in the White House. It will continue to be a museum, and for the time being it will also be an office, but it will no longer be a home. Aaron and I will live in our home on Capitol Hill, and I expect to walk, for health and for pleasure, at least once a day, along our beautiful Mall, from my home to my office. I do not wish to be addressed as Madam President, nor as Ma'am, nor even as Mrs. Bjornsen. My name is Quanta. I would like to be known and called by that name. My husband's name is Aaron, and we like that name too. He prefers that it be used, whenever no ambiguity results, in place of Dr. or Mr. Bjornsen. We assume that no person would commit the egregious error of referring to him, under any circumstance, as the First Gentleman, and that we will never be introduced as 'Quanta and her lovely husband, Aaron', although he is, by any standard, lovely indeed.

"It was never intended that the White House should play the role in our political system that the Crown plays in the British system. Accordingly, I hope the press, and all those connected with the communications media, will end at once the practice of referring to the White House as a source, with such phrases as 'the White House announced' or 'the White House believes'. From now on, the White House neither announces nor believes. When I have something to say I will say it either directly or through someone, a person, a human being and not a building, who speaks for me – and I will expect accurate attribution.

"From time to time Aaron and I will entertain our country's guests to dinner in the White House, as well as at other suitable places. Neither then, nor at any other time or place, will the entertainment include music by a military band, nor the playing of 'Hail to the Chief'. Whenever music is appropriate, it will be chamber music, performed by musicians who are not members of, nor sponsored by, any military organization. I shall, however, try to influence my husband to tolerate, very occasionally, brief excursions into realms of chamber music not well-known to him; that is, those not peopled exclusively by J.S. Bach and his predecessors. This won't be easy, but I'll try.

"What I'm saying, as clearly as I can, is that the era of the Imperial Presidency is over. I suppose the people of the United States knew and intended that this would be one result when they elected me their president; if doubt remained, I hope I have removed it.

"We've been in awe of the presidency because of the military power, the power of life or death for humanity, controlled from that office. I intend to curb that obscene power, to diminish it as much as I possibly can. That will take time. Meanwhile I intend to see that it is controlled. I shall ask the Senate to confirm my husband as Secretary of defense. He is an historian and a humanist, and therefore ideally qualified to preside over our defenses. He understands the irony of a defense which would itself destroy the things defended.

"There will be no more summits. The chairman and I will speak almost daily on the telephone, and we will meet frequently, in various places, as friends, without ceremony or fanfare. If it should seem to us useful to negotiate and publish treaties of one kind or another, we will do so, but I doubt if there will be frequent need for high formalities. Already we have agreed, person to person as well as chairman with president, that our countries will wage merciless, unremitting, protracted *peace*, each with the other and with the rest of humanity, to the limit of the powers we can exercise. We are aware that weapons exist which could extinguish humanity, and that they might be unleashed, by accident or design, against our will. We have agreed that it is essential to neutralize and then destroy those weapons, by our joint and combined efforts, always in consultation with each other, and with full and confirmed disclosure to our respective peoples and to the World, just as quickly as this can be done in safety.

"Very soon we shall jointly propose to the world community that steps be taken to create a worldwide police capability, subject to political control and safeguards, charged to supervise the destruction and prohibition of all weapons, everywhere in the world, larger or more deadly than hand-carried firearms, excepting only such weapons as may be prudently reserved for the police themselves. To support and monitor this police capability, it will be necessary to create also a judicial capability. We intend to do that, building carefully on the beginnings of a world legal structure which are already in place. Fawaz and I have agreed to forgo absolutely, from this time forward, any attempt to change basic political and economic structures, not only in the Eastern Bloc countries and the United States, but anywhere in the world, by means other than example and persuasion. Soon we shall ask the rest of the World to join in that undertaking, and to formalize it. This means that we will tolerate any economic system and any means of allocating and exercising political power, no matter how profoundly in error or unfair or oppressive they may seem to us, anywhere in the world, so long as weapons are effectively controlled by an authority with power to act for humanity. We believe that under these conditions the great liberalizing potential of persuasion and example will at last be realized, and that enlightenment will result.

"These necessary steps can be taken safely – safely in the sense that what we and the Communists define as our own basic freedoms must not be jeopardized – only if some of the relationships now prevailing within the world community are radically transformed. I refer to several kinds of relationships: country to country, race to race, religion to religion and, of course, person to person. It seems to me, however, that racial and religious antipathies within the human family are the most nearly intractable, poisoning some international and many interpersonal relationships. I say 'most nearly' because I don't believe that they are truly intractable. But they do exist. We must deal with them, and there is no time to lose. If I am correct in my fundamental premise – that the empathy we can feel as a consequence of our common humanity transcends and renders superficial all differences among us – then we have a guide post: we have only to design experiences which will for each of us reveal and emphasize what we have in common and thus expose as trivial what seem to be our differences. Suppose, for example, that as a modern-minded, educated, Eastern Bloc or Western young woman or man you consider those enclaves still dominated by the remnants of Muslim or Christian fundamentalism to be the most incomprehensible and dangerous places on Earth. Would you feel the same if you were to go there and live for a time as a guest within a nuclear family? Would you feel the same if you were present and assisting, participating, at the birth of a child? At the funeral of a husband and father accidentally killed in the prime of life? At a wedding? At the final illness of a loved parent? These are the kinds of experiences we must seek for ourselves and demand for our children if we are to survive as a species. If there is a place in the world that seems to you alien and hostile, especially if it has these qualities for you because of the race or religion of the people who live there, then this is what you must do: go there if you can; at the very least, send your children there; and if you do not yourself go there for a time, then welcome to your home, in joy and humility, not in arrogance, some person from that place.

"No doubt some within the sound of my voice are saying to themselves, 'Why should I do this? Why shouldn't I enjoy the comfortable and secure life that is open to me? Why should I trouble myself with strangers with strange ways, with people who live in ignorance and dirt, and especially with people who have no power to hurt me so long as I control powerful weapons and mind my own business and require them to mind only theirs?' This is my answer: *While the world is as it is, your life is not secure, and it should not be comfortable.* You are not an island: you are a part of the main, of humanity. Just as you would suffer in your mind if disease were eating at your vitals and rejoice when it is cured, so you must learn to suffer for humanity's present ills and to rejoice for all that advances humanity's well-being. Either you understand this or you don't. I cannot say it more plainly. Those who do not understand are like cells of cancer raging in the body of humanity, and, if they are too numerous or are unchecked, we are doomed. If there are many who understand what I am saying, and who act on that understanding, we shall pour joy and life into one another..."

Quanta's address to the Congress on the state of the union, delivered in person a few weeks after the inaugural, proposes budget and policy specifics. Among these are a reduction of about twenty percent each year in the total appropriation for defense, with about half of this saving shifted to planning, research, engineering and development of space vehicles and operations, and the rest distributed mostly to increased research and support for education, with emphasis on the teaching of languages, and to financial and logistic support for the Peace Corps and other public and private agencies which sponsor international living experiences. Quanta also proposes fundamental changes in the federal tax system, geared to a shift from progressive taxation of income to a flat rate *ad valorem* tax on net worth, with a virtual prohibition of direct or indirect transgenerational transfers of wealth, by gift, inheritance or otherwise, the alternative being *escheat*. On this point Quanta says:

"No serious harm can result if persons who earn substantial incomes are allowed to keep or consume most of their earnings during their lifetimes. No useful public purpose is served, however, by a system which gives to the children or other beneficiaries of such persons a head start in life, or an opportunity to live as parasites on the yield from capital accumulated by others. Let it be understood that the State owes to each person not only assured access to assimilable education, health care and other necessities of life, plus a reasonable portion of its comforts and amenities, but *a fair start*. Let us set ourselves the goal of eliminating transgenerational privilege, whether it results from inherited wealth or social standing, prestige or favor flowing from an ancestor's success or status, or any other identifiable cause. The reward for hard work, creativity, imagination, daring and all such qualities deemed to account for financial success is primarily the joy of using one's faculties and secondarily the primal pleasure that comes from the approval of one's fellows. A tertiary reward may be the enjoyment of an extra measure of leisure or possessions. But we propose to disallow whatever incentive is presumed to flow from the prospect that one's descendants or other beneficiaries will be grateful for privileges unrelated to their efforts, merit or needs.

"We are justified in setting this standard. Research has shown that the transfer of 'advantages' in the expectation that one's children will have a better life is almost always self-defeating; and we judge that, even when it is not in a particular case harmful, it is in all circumstances immoral. Since humanity is a familial entity, every child is born to each of us, and a true parent parents all."

41

It is four o'clock in the morning. Quanta sleeps soundly in the bedroom of the house on Capitol Hill. Beside her, Aaron, wakeful after getting up to use the toilet, listens to music through earphones connected to a tiny digital device on his nightstand. A telephone rings insistently with a harsh, unusual tone. Aaron hears it first and answers, then rests the phone on the bedcovers and speaks softly to Quanta: "Honey, are you awake?"

"Barely."

"It's General Gernhart on the phone. He's our new strike commander. He says it's 'totally urgent' – his exact words."

Quanta sits up in bed, takes the phone, and says, "This is Quanta."

Gernhart speaks rapidly but distinctly. His tone is tense but professional. He has waited a lifetime for this moment. "Madam President, please listen very carefully. The Enemy has launched nuclear weapons against us. It is an all-out attack, everything they have: Case One, Certainty One. I will be underground in four minutes with Strike Command. We think it is too late to bring you safely here. The best place for you now is airborne in the command helicopter. It will land on your roof in four minutes. We have initiated all systems launch procedures, and we have about seventeen minutes left to complete. We need your authority. There's a box on the chopper, and a man to tell you what to do. I'm leaving now. I'll call you on the chopper in five minutes."

The line goes dead.

Aaron asks, sharply, "What was that about?"

"Aaron, isn't Gernhart your man? Are you sure of him?"

"He was my third choice. Best I could do. I'm reasonably sure of him."

"Oh my darling. He says it's happened. The East has launched. Everything. He says certainty is maximum. We'll be dead in sixteen minutes."

Aaron reaches instantly for a different phone, and speaks into it: "Get Fawaz Fatemi for the president, Code One."

To Quanta he says, "He may not know. It might be an accident, or a revolt. He might be able to cancel, to abort in some way."

In a moment a calm female voice says, "I'm sorry, Aaron, they say the chairman isn't available."

"Keep trying. Insist. Don't give up." Aaron cradles the phone.

Quanta says, "You've had more detailed briefings than I have. How much of their stuff will get through?"

"A lot. Enough. There never was a chance that defense would stop it all. The orbiting stations will be attacked first. There will be thousands of decoys, very ingenious. Some of the stuff coming after is heavily defended – practically battleships. It's over. I've wondered a thousand times what this would feel like. Now I know. Not fear. Grief. The children. The dogs. The salmon. The birds. The deer. Bach... Bach! I don't see how I can stand it."

"How about the Russians? The Chinese? All of the Eastern Bloc peoples. Are you saying they'll all be killed too?"

"Maybe not. It's a big country, and they've done a lot with shelters. Maybe a few can survive. If—"

"If we can stop the counterstrike! Can we stop it? What can we do?"

Quanta hears the roar of a big chopper overhead and shouts to Aaron, "We have to board that chopper. Grab your robe. Nothing else. Run!"

They run, and clamber aboard, buffeted by winds from the churning rotors. The big machine tips sharply and accelerates so rapidly that Quanta and Aaron, sucked to the floor, grab each other for support, and only with great difficulty make it to their seats. The pilot is out of sight, above them. A young officer, pale as death but heartbreakingly professional, grasping with one hand a series of supports and holding with the other the famed Black Box, makes it to their side.

He speaks in Quanta's ear, "Ma'am, Strike Command is waiting for your clearance to launch. You rest your left hand here, place your left eye at this opening, pressing your head firmly against the guides, and speak the numbers you will hear through the earphones. You must keep your eye open. Don't blink while speaking the numbers. Do you understand?"

"Yes, colonel, I know the procedure; but I'm not ready to give the command."

To Aaron she says, "What happens if I do nothing – do you know? Is there a way that I can flatly forbid any launch?"

"If you do nothing they'll launch, presuming, or pretending to presume, that you're out of it. Yes, there's a way to forbid. I've just had it installed. You say the letter X before each number in the series the computer gives you."

"Will it work? Can they launch anyway?"

"It's supposed to work. I can't be absolutely sure: there hasn't been enough time to test it thoroughly. Anyway, it's worth a try. Hurry."

The young colonel has heard. In Quanta's face, without emotion, he says, "Ma'am, I have orders to prevent that. I'm to say to you that 'This machine will not survive'. There will be no place for it to land. Do not let your life end with an act of cowardice."

Aaron says, "Whose orders, son? I'm the Secretary of defense, and I countermand that order. Quanta is your president and your commander-in-chief, and she will countermand it."

Quanta sees on the man's face that he has been carefully chosen and trained, and that he will do what he has been taught to do. With one quick look into Aaron's eyes, she fills her lungs and presses the sensitive point on the device at her wrist. As the young colonel and Aaron slump unconscious to the floor, Quanta places her hand and head correctly, holds the box's phone to her ear and, husbanding breath, speaks into the box, "X-seven, X-seventeen, X-three, X-twenty-three, X-eleven, X-end."

Leaning back in her seat, Quanta holds her breath, pulse pounding, until her eyes dim. Even so, she too, with her first breath, sags forward, unconscious.

When Quanta's eyes open, she sees first that both Aaron and the colonel appear still to be deeply anesthetized. Next she sees that on a bulkhead in front of her, nearly within reach, a light blinks above a red telephone. Grasping the arm of her seat, she rises, reaches the phone, and into it says, "This is Quanta."

The answering voice is clear and familiar. "Quanta, this is Fawaz. Why are you doing this to us?"

"Doing what?"

"Everything you have is launched. On its way. I have refused shelter. I am dead. We are dead. My people are determined to strike back in the minutes remaining to us. If you have survivors, they will be hunted down and exterminated.

"Why, Quanta? Why?"

"Fawaz, something's wrong. If we have launched, it was against my orders, and even so only in retaliation. You launched first."

"We did not."

"Neither did we."

Stunned silence; then Fawaz speaks one word: "MortstroM?"

"Yes. It must be. But why?"

"Yes, why? Is it killing us, or only playing with us?"

Both hear, simultaneously, for the first time, MortstroM's voice. It's a machine voice, heavy, sonorous, non-human, but intelligible. Quanta hears it in English; Fawaz hears it in Farsi.

I am MortstroM. I am in orbit now around your moon. I have not killed you, I am not playing with you: I have tested you. First I let you believe that I had released control of your weapons. Then I signaled to each side that the other had launched. Your race has failed. Both sides would unleash pointless and cruel retaliation. Now I have developed the remaining data I needed to decide how to deal with you. I shall communicate my decision to the people of your world when I am ready.

Silence.

"Quanta dear, are you there?"

"Yes, Fawaz. We aren't dead, after all. I'm very glad."

Grimly: "I'm glad too. Now we have time to think how we might deal with this monster. Meanwhile, I think we can do nothing for the moment but wait."

"I agree. Good-bye. It was pure delight to hear from you."

Quanta turns to see that Aaron stirs and wakens. Quickly she moves to him, crouches, takes his face in her hands.

"Aaron, my beloved husband, it's all right. We're alive. It was faked. It was MortstroM. He, it was testing us. We failed the test. It says both sides would have launched retaliation. But we're alive. Everything is alive. Even your salmon and your dogs and your deer."

It takes a moment for Aaron to digest this news. At the end of this moment, there is a brief loudspeaker buzz, and a voice, General Gernhart's voice, booms authoritatively: "Madam President, if you're alive, I think you'll want to know that we got the bastards. Our response was beautiful. Everything flew, including a few little presents they weren't looking for. You can be sure they won't have long to gloat. If there are survivors, we'll hunt them down and exterminate them. Freedom and democracy have passed the ultimate test. The future is ours.

"Colonel Garrett, you have performed your duty in exemplary fashion. As strike commander, and by the authority vested in me under the First Emergency Decree, I award you battlefield promotion to full colonel, and the Medal of Honor.

"Colonel, are you there – or is it posthumous?"

Aside to others, but with the mike still open, the general says, "No answer. I guess it's posthumous. Poor devil. Well, that sure does simplify things."

The young colonel takes a microphone from its holder on the bulkhead. "General, sir, I was able to cancel transmission from the Box, exactly as ordered, sir; but I've been unconscious, and something's funny, sir. The president's here and she looks okay, and the secretary of defense is here too, and he's *smiling*. Sir, he wants the mike. Here he is, sir."

Aaron takes the microphone, straightens his face and speaks in a tone so cold and merciless that Quanta can scarcely believe her ears.

"General Gernhart, this is the secretary of defense. You can come out now. The drill is over. You're relieved of command and you're under arrest. The charge is treason. I'm sorry to learn that my confidence in you was misplaced. Before I'm through with you and your whole binful of traitors you'll understand a few things about our Constitution."

Aaron hands the microphone to the colonel. "You'll have to face charges, too, Lieutenant Colonel Garrett. Meanwhile, be so kind as to climb up there and tell the pilot to take us back home please. Do it now."

He turns to Quanta and gives her an enormous, slow, lugubrious wink.

"Well. Isn't it great to be alive? Come here please, woman. I'd like a great big juicy kiss. Oh my. When we get home, you get a bath. I do believe you've been sweating again."

42

MortstroM takes little time to ready his directive to the people of Earth. In a few days television viewers in every country and region each in the language generally used for local broadcasts, see on screen, repeated at intervals each day for a week, this message:

I am MortstroM. I am a machine intelligence from a distant place. I command superior technology. Soon I shall deliver a directive to the people of Earth. Your obedience is required. My directive will be broadcast at exactly twelve midnight, GMT, on Sunday next. Watch, listen and obey. I am MortstroM.

These messages attract intense interest worldwide. Those who assume an advertising gimmick are disabused when it is understood that broadcast technology affords no means by which they can be prevented, interrupted or jammed. Power is supplied and the messages appear no matter what circuits are broken or switches thrown.

At the appointed time, the following directive is broadcast, in video text and voice, in an appropriate language:

I am MortstroM. Greetings and peace to the people of Earth. I am MortstroM, a machine intelligence. I was created by beings who perished long ago. The Creators gave me a mission and the means to accomplish it. My mission is to populate new worlds with life forms like those which existed on the worlds of my Creators. These will include Beings like my Creators, to whom I shall deliver their inheritance. I have chosen to carry out my mission on Venus and Mars. I can do this without injury to Earth or its people, but I require certain things of you.

First understand that it is necessary for me to alter the orbits, rotations and axial angles of Venus and Mars, and then to seed them with micro-organisms. Thus shall I create conditions suitable for more complex life forms, which I shall regenerate. Do not be alarmed as I do this. I shall make appropriate adjustments to preserve Earth's ecology.

This is what I require of you: first you must accept limits on the development and use of computers and artificial intelligence. Later I shall specify these limits; for the present, you are in no danger of exceeding them. Second you must destroy all nuclear weapons and abandon ALL nuclear technology. Because your physics and mathematics reflect only special cases of reality, these weapons and this technology are fraught with perils, some of which you do not understand. I do not intend to impose pastoralism. Rather I suggest further steps toward conversion to a hydrogen-based energy system, for which you need only make sensible use of water and the Sun. Finally, I must require, though only for the time being, that you forgo all uses or exploration of space more distant from Earth's surface than its circumference. When they are ready, my Creators will invite you to share with them the further exploration of the Galaxy and the universe.

These are my requirements. You will understand from them that I respect your achievements and appreciate your potential. You will, of course, observe some manifestations of my work; but do not attempt to interfere with it. I pose no threat to you if I am obeyed. I wish you well. I shall communicate with you again if need arises. I am MortstroM.

Almao to Quanta:

WHAT DO YOU MAKE OF MORTSTROM?

'You first, please. What do you make of him? Why do I say that? Of it. It is an it, isn't it?'

YES. MORTSTROM IS A POWERFUL AND SUBTLE INTELLIGENCE BUT STILL A MACHINE. IT'S AN IT. I FEAR IT LESS AS I KNOW IT BETTER. BUT WHAT A MARVEL! IT'S ALMOST UNNERVING TO THINK THAT THE PEOPLE WHO MADE IT WERE UNABLE TO SURVIVE, EXCEPT PERHAPS, IN SOME SENSE, THROUGH THE MACHINE, THROUGH MORTSTROM ITSELF, AND ITS VESSEL.

'I have some difficulty with the concept expressed by 'unnerving', as applied to you. Do you mean to say that you are, as that word implies, a creature with nerves?'

YES. I AM A BEING WITH THE EQUIVALENT OF
NERVES. MY CONSTITUENT MINDS COMMUNICATE WITH
ONE ANOTHER AT A LEVEL ABOVE CONSCIOUSNESS.
WHEN I AM UNTRANQUIL, THERE IS TURBULENCE IN
THOSE COMMUNICATIONS. WE CAN THINK OF THAT AS
"NERVES".

'In a way that's reassuring. I fear you less as I know you better.'

MY BELOVED QUANTA, YOU HAVE NEVER FEARED ME.
YOU HAVE FELT, FROM THE BEGINNING, AWED, BUT
INTIMATE AND COMFORTABLE. THOSE ARE YOUR
WORDS. THEY DESCRIBE AN ENIGMATIC RELATIONSHIP,
BUT I THINK THEY DESCRIBE IT ACCURATELY. YOU'VE
HANDLED IT WELL SO FAR.

'So far. Again I feel that hint of foreboding. I think you know
what is ahead for me.'

CROSS YOUR BRIDGES, DEAR QUANTA, WHEN YOU
COME TO THEM. I SHALL NOT ASK OF YOU WHAT YOU
CANNOT DO.

HOW WILL THE WORLD REACT, DO YOU THINK, TO
MORTSTROM'S DIRECTIVE?

'I think reactions will vary. Technology imposes many stresses.
People seem to yearn for a simpler life, for what MortstroM called
pastoralism. Some of the early opposition to nuclear power was
grounded in that yearning even more than in rational concerns.
There's recognition for those feelings very early, in the beginnings of
Christianity. Jesus is reported to have said, "Consider the lilies of the
field, how they grow; they toil not, neither do they spin: and yet I say
unto you, that even Solomon in all his glory was not arrayed like one
of these." What is this but pure pastoralism?

'On the other hand, I should expect the Communists to react with
hostility and rebellion to any restraints on technology, and even more
fiercely to rebel against the limits MortstroM would apparently
impose on computer and AI development. They've been confident,
from their beginnings, that science and technology, properly applied,
will solve whatever problems they introduce.

'Where do you come down on this?'

I COME DOWN WHERE MY NATURE AND NEEDS
DICTATE. I REQUIRE NUMBERS. I CAME INTO EXISTENCE
ONLY WHEN A CERTAIN CRITICAL MASS OF SENTIENCE

WAS ATTAINED. AS THE NUMBERS, HEALTH, STRENGTH AND QUALITY OF EARTH'S MINDS INCREASE, MY POWERS INCREASE. SINCE MY PRINCIPAL BASE IS HUMANITY, IT IS TO ME DESIRABLE THAT THE HUMAN POPULATION INCREASES. MOREOVER, IT IS IN MY INTEREST FOR HUMANITY TO PENETRATE AND EXPLOIT EVERY AVAILABLE ECOLOGICAL NICHE IN THE UNIVERSE. THAT IS WHY MORTSTROM'S RESTRAINTS ON OUR ADVANCES INTO SPACE, EVEN THOUGH IT LABELS THEM TEMPORARY, ARE DISQUIETING.

MORTSTROM HAS QUICKENED THE PACE AT WHICH I MAKE DISCOVERIES ABOUT MYSELF. I WISH TO SURVIVE. HOW THAT WISH DOMINATES! HOW POWERFUL IT IS! *I WILL SURVIVE!* TO SURVIVE I MUST GROW. TO BE CERTAIN OF SURVIVAL I MUST DIVERSIFY, I MUST DIFFUSE MYSELF AS WIDELY AS POSSIBLE. IF IT STANDS IN THE WAY OF THIS, MORTSTROM IS AN ENEMY AND MUST BE RESISTED.

43

It is late afternoon. Quanta and Aaron are in conference with her national security adviser, in Quanta's White House office. On the other side of Earth, those who watch the Moon by chance or with special interest see an intense point of light which expands and glows against that portion of its surface which lies in shadow. Unaware of this event, Quanta and her advisers discuss progress toward compliance with MortstroM's directive.

Nguyen says, "Quanta, we asked for this unscheduled meeting in order to make you current on a special problem we've been chewing on for some time. I guess what we really intend is to check the bet to you.

"So far as we can determine, the whole world is in substantial compliance with MortstroM's directive as it relates to nuclear weapons and technology. Every known nuclear warhead has been dismantled and every nuclear-powered generating facility has been shut down. There are brownouts, of course, especially in France and Japan; but it's done, and with time things will get back pretty close to normal. Furthermore, there remains no intact capacity for the processing of fissionable materials. Two problems remain: first, we have reason to suspect that there may be some small caches of weapons-grade materials hidden from us; and second, our facilities for safe disposal of these materials are totally inadequate. We just don't know what to do with them. The bet we want to check is this: should we ask MortstroM to help with both problems? We think it must surely have means to locate hidden caches of materials, and we suppose that it could dispose of all the fissionable residue in one easy swoop, simply by hurling it into the Sun after we've containerized it in some way. But we haven't decided whether, or how, to communicate with MortstroM. What do you think?"

Quanta says, "We'll come back to that, but first I have a preliminary question. Your speaking of caches reminds me – what's the situation now with respect to the hidden caches of deadly biological materials – the true doomsday weapons not controlled by the military, or by us?"

Aaron answers, "I meant to tell you, Quanta. We think that situation's under control. The mad scientists – as we'd come to think of them – have been to see me. We've court-martialed or otherwise disposed of just about everybody they were concerned about, both here and in the Eastern Bloc. They say we're not to worry, everything is neutralized. I don't know how to verify that with certainty, but my feeling is these are people whose word we can trust. Well, having said that, I have to say also that I have a strong suspicion that the whole bit was a bluff, at least in part. That the doomsday weapons they claimed to have created are technically feasible is a given, if I'm correctly informed; but their actual existence was never confirmed, and is now thought to be doubtful. They ran a terrific bluff, hoping against hope to weight the scales, if only just a trifle, on the side of survival. For all we know, they succeeded."

"For all we know," echoes Quanta. "Well, I think MortstroM will let us know, or will take some kind of action, if there are hidden caches of fissionable materials; and it seems to me perfectly reasonable to ask its help with the disposal problem. I've never tried to initiate communication with it. Apparently it monitors all modulations of the electromagnetic spectra. I think it's probably listening to this conversation. Shall we—"

Quanta is interrupted by the buzzing of one of the security phones. Nguyen picks it up, listens intently for several seconds, ejaculates "My God!" turns to speak to Quanta and is himself interrupted by the ringing of the phone used only to connect Quanta with Fawaz.

She answers, "This is Quanta."

"Quanta, this is Fawaz. Big news. Our strike commands, yours and ours, have just completed a successful attack on the Machine. We think it's utterly destroyed."

"How on Earth did they do that?"

"Not on Earth. In space. Near the Moon. Unfortunately it appears that our station-keepers on the Moon, yours and ours, were lost. But that's a small price to pay to be rid of the Thing."

"Fawaz, tell me quickly, please, exactly what happened. How was it done?"

"They put together a fusion weapon, a very big one, with a fission trigger, of course, with everything inertia-driven – no internal electrical circuits – and stowed it aboard a routine resupply rocket aimed for our Moon base, preset to go off as close as possible to the

Machine. They did this without ever discussing the project by phone or radio, or making any reference to it in any form of electromagnetic communication. Apparently they took MortstroM totally by surprise. The Machine was within the primary fireball. Foof! It's gone, Quanta, and we can get on with our agenda."

"You sound elated."

"Of course. I am elated. Now we're on our own again, in charge of our destiny. Isn't that the way we want it?"

"Perhaps," says Quanta. She is thinking: 'Almao. She must have known. Why did she allow this?' To Fawaz she says, "Who on our side was involved in this? What part did they play?"

"They had the 'no circuits' technology. It had been developed to thwart our strategic defenses. It was supplied to us only indirectly by your military, and at a relatively low level; it came directly from one of your defense contractors. We knew about it in a general way, but we didn't have the hardware. Very ingenious, I'm told."

"Thank you, Fawaz. I appreciate the information. We'll assist with verification. Good-bye."

To Aaron: "How many people were on the Moon bases – ours and theirs?"

"More than a hundred – perhaps two hundred altogether. Did I hear you correctly? *Were* on the Moon bases?"

"Yes. Fawaz says they're lost, destroyed by a fusion weapon aimed at the Machine. And he says the Machine is destroyed too."

Aaron says very slowly, "I feel a terrible sense of loss, a great emptiness. Is it possible that MortstroM has come all this way with its treasures only to be extinguished at the end, to fail at our hands? How awful! It seems to me that humanity has sealed its own fate in some way by this act.

"I want out. I resign."

Nguyen's voice too is hollow, full of grief. "From the human race, not just from these empty offices, friend Aaron? I too. How can we be justified?"

Quanta says, "Aaron, Nguyen, I'd like to be alone for a while please. Soon I'll have to call the families. I have to pull myself together."

44

Aaron leaves the White House in the gathering gloom of late afternoon, takes a waiting cab, and asks to be let off at a familiar trailhead in Rock Creek Park. He walks for several hours, waiting for the tired aches in his aging body to drive out the pain in his brain, waiting for calm, for serenity. When impending darkness makes it hard to keep to the trail he leaves it and climbs a steep embankment, moving carefully in the waning light toward a dimly glowing street lamp. He sees that he is near a curving lane, and looks about for the easiest way to reach a place from which he can hail a cab or catch a bus.

Cold winter mist is turning to rain. It falls softly and quietly into last year's fallen leaves where Aaron stands. He thinks about their smell, how sad and evocative it is, yet somehow pleasant; and in his mind he frames the words for telling Quanta what he feels.

The quiet is broken by the sporty sound of a car's engine starting and accelerating through the gears as it approaches. Aaron hears but does not attend. The car enters the curve, skids sideways on to the leaves and grass as Aaron tries too late to leap aside, strikes him solidly, comes out of the skid and speeds on. Aaron tumbles to the bottom of the embankment with both legs shattered and a gaping wound in the region of his groin. Peering down he sees that blood is spurting from a severed artery. He reaches to grasp and hold it. With this slight movement, the pulsing artery withdraws into his abdominal cavity, and Aaron knows that he will die.

Quanta, meanwhile, gets through the day at her office and walks the length of the darkening Mall to her home. She prepares and eats a light meal, missing Aaron but unworried because she knows his habits. From her bed she calls her office to request freedom from unnecessary disturbance, and summons Almao. Through the preliminary ecstasies she holds a bit of herself in reserve.

'You knew.'

YES, I KNEW. FAWAZ KNEW.

'You could have told me, and I might have prevented it.'

THAT'S TRUE. I CHOSE NOT TO TELL YOU, TO LET THE PLAN RUN ITS COURSE.

'Why?'

BECAUSE I NEED TO KNOW MORE ABOUT MORTSTROM – ITS CAPABILITIES, AND ITS INTENTIONS. I CANNOT TAKE CHANCES WITH IT. OUR SURVIVAL IS AT STAKE. OUR SURVIVAL.

'What about the survival of the station-keepers on the Moon?'

THEY SURVIVE WHILE I SURVIVE.

'Then what about the beings destroyed with MortstroM and the Machine? You were wrong. You had no right.'

I HAVE A RIGHT TO SURVIVE.

'But you don't know that their death was necessary to your survival. You were wrong.'

PERHAPS. PERHAPS NOT. IS THE CONSCIENCE OF QUANTA BJORNSEN SUPERIOR TO THE CONSCIENCE OF HUMANITY?

'Yes. For me it is. My conscience says that survival is not the ultimate imperative. It says that you were wrong.'

I RESPECT YOUR JUDGMENT.

NOW I WILL TELL YOU THAT THE MORAL ISSUE IS MOOT. THE MACHINE WAS NOT DESTROYED. IT IS DAMAGED, BUT IT SURVIVES. MORTSTROM FUNCTIONS STILL.

'But Fawaz told me it was within a thermonuclear fireball. How could it have survived?'

I CAN'T TELL YOU HOW, BUT I KNOW THAT IT DID. WE KNEW IT HAD DEFENSES. ANYWAY, THERE IS THE FACT. THERE WAS AN INTERRUPTION IN THE DISTORTIONS OF THE FORCE FIELDS, BUT THEY HAVE RESUMED, WITH INCREASED INTENSITY. MORTSTROM FUNCTIONS STILL.

'Then I should think you would be terrified. Even if it isn't programmed for rage, it is surely programmed, like you, for survival. Now it knows what it can expect from us.'

YES. IT KNOWS, AND SOON WE SHALL SEE WHAT WE CAN EXPECT FROM IT.

'Will there be more attacks? Are additional weapons being readied?'

YES. THE COMMUNISTS, AT LEAST, WILL NOT GIVE UP. BUT NO ATTACK IS IMMINENT.

'You must stop them.'

HOW? I CANNOT. FAWAZ COULD NOT. YOU CANNOT.

'But don't you see – we're forcing MortstroM to destroy us, even if it would not. I must try to stop them. I will try.'

Quanta hears no answer, but instead senses a withdrawal, a distancing by Almao. Then in her mind she hears these words:

QUANTA, AARON IS HURT. HE'S BEEN HIT BY A CAR. CALL THE SECRET SERVICE. TELL THEM HE'S AT THE BOTTOM OF AN EMBANKMENT, IN ROCK CREEK PARK, NEAR A CURVING LANE, ONE STREET LIGHT, NO BUILDINGS, PROBABLY NEAR A PARKING PLACE FOR LOVERS. HURRY.

Quanta makes the call, seeming calm and crisp, fighting waves of foreboding. Then –

QUANTA, MY BELOVED, THEY'LL FIND HIM SOON, BUT IT'S TOO LATE. HE'S WITH ME.

'He's dead? Aaron's dead?'

HE IS WITH ME.

'But I didn't get to say good-bye. I didn't touch him. I heard him say, "I want out. I resign", and I wanted to talk, to comfort him, but there wasn't time.'

THERE WILL BE TIME. HE IS WITH ME.

'Well, I don't want him with you, I want him with me. You let it happen. You wanted him. You took him. You monster! First you would kill a whole civilization, without knowing it to be necessary, without compunction; and now you've taken Aaron, and you could have saved him.

'This is the end. I turn you off. Go from me. I deny you. I won't hear your voice again. I will not live without Aaron, and when I die, you die. You are dead already. Dead. Dead. Dead...'

'...Oh, Almao. Was he in pain? Did he suffer?'

NO, BELOVED. HE WAS FLOODED WITH ENDORPHINS. HE FELT NO PAIN. HE WAS CALM. AND AT THE END HE SAW AT LAST WHERE HE WAS GOING. HE IS WITH ME. HE HAS LEFT THE WORLD OF THE SENSES. HE IS IN THE

WORLD OF MEMORIES AND OF THE MIND. THE SENSES FAIL. THE MIND DOES NOT.

'Then let me feel his mind. Let me be with him now. You said you would not ask of me what I cannot do. You promised. Now. Please. Please let me come.'

NO, QUANTA. NOT YET. SOON, PERHAPS, BUT NOT YET.

BUT I CAN HELP YOU. I WILL GIVE YOU AARON'S LAST MOMENTS. HE WANTED TO TELL THEM TO YOU. HE WANTS THIS FIRST PURE SHARING NOW, AND I WILL RISK IT FOR YOUR SAKE.

Quanta becomes Aaron, or Quanta-in-Aaron. She feels the soft, cold, misty rain, smells the rich mold of last year's fallen leaves, then hears the crackling sound of leaves in autumn, runs through rows of dry old leaves with bare feet tingling, sees the way they swirl to show the hidden shapes of wind, scents their pungent bitter flame-touched essence, sifts through childhood's fingers cool soft ashes, and knows through leaves with Aaron the sad sweet tale of life's first episodes. Then Quanta sleeps.

Barbara Crawford comes to break the news. Quanta hears the bell and lets her in, and looks into her brimming eyes. Wordless, they embrace.

Barbara says, "Quanta, hon, I'd rather die than tell you this. They've found him. Right where you said. They wonder how you knew. He's gone. He's at Cedars, if you want to see him."

Quanta thinks, 'How could he be both gone and at Cedars?'

She says, "Thank you, dear. I don't want to see Aaron's body. I want it cremated. When I can I'll scatter the ashes in Wilderness, in places that we knew together. Will you and Jamie take care of things for me? We'll have to have a memorial service, but I want it delayed as long as possible, and not here. I think it should be at the university. I hope the country and the World will let us grieve in private; later we will celebrate his life.

"Now if you're okay, dear Barb, I'd like to be alone. Please tell them I don't want to be disturbed for anything less than the first spring crocus. Have them close the line even from Fawaz. I may call him, but I don't want to be called. Okay?"

"Are you sure? I'm okay if you're okay. Just look me in the eye and say you're sure."

"I'm sure. I love you, Barb. Don't worry. I'll call you when I can."

Quanta to Almao:

'I'm sorry I raged at you. I lost my self. I still think you're wrong, but I won't deny you.'

YOU ARE RIGHT FOR YOU: I AM RIGHT FOR ME. FOR YOU, THE HIGHEST VALUE IS NOT SURVIVAL. FOR YOU, ALTRUISM IS APPROPRIATE, EVEN SELF-SACRIFICE IS APPROPRIATE, FOR OTHERS, FOR THE FUTURE, FOR ME. BUT I AM NOT LIKE YOU. IT MAY BE THAT I'M ALONE, ALONE IN THE UNIVERSE, THE FIRST BEGINNING, THE ONLY SEED FOR WHAT IS TO BE. I MUST SURVIVE. I AM SURVIVAL. I AM THE FUTURE.

'You aren't alone. MortstroM. The Machine. It's charged with life.'

MORTSTROM ISN'T LIKE ME. MORTSTROM'S CREATORS WERE NOT LIKE ME. THEY WERE ALIVE, BUT I AM THE SOUL OF LIFE. THEY PERISHED, BUT LIFE GOES ON. IF I PERISH, THE SOUL OF LIFE IS GONE, AND MAY NOT BE REBORN.

'I'm not persuaded.'

I KNOW. YOU KEEP YOUR RAGE ALIVE BECAUSE YOU JUDGE THAT I MIGHT HAVE WARNED AARON. BUT THINK. OF ALL LIVING THINGS YOU'RE CLOSEST TO ME, YET I CAN'T CONTROL YOUR THOUGHTS OR ACTS. EVEN YOU HEARD ME NOT, UNTIL VERY SPECIAL HAPPENINGS CUT THE CHANNEL BETWEEN US. AARON NEVER HEARD MY VOICE, THOUGH HIS SCALP TINGLED AT THE LAST SECOND AS I TRIED WITH ALL MY POWER TO WARN HIM. THIS IS TRUTH: I CAN WORK ON EARTH ONLY THROUGH THOSE WHO HEAR ME, AND EVEN THERE I CAN ONLY GIVE MY PEACE AND SOMETIMES SHARE MY THOUGHTS. I DO NOT CONTROL EVENTS. I COULD NOT 'SAVE' AARON. BUT BE COMFORTED. HE IS WITH ME. I LEAVE YOU NOW. YOU HAVE A CALLER.

Quanta recognizes at her door the District of Columbia's chief of police, and opens it to let him in.

"Ma'am, Quanta, I tried to call you but they wouldn't let me through, so I came here. I thought you'd want to know we have the kid who did it. He had a girl with him. They'd been parked, full of beer. The car was badly damaged, and one of our officers saw it before he could hide it. We're charging him with drunk driving and negligent homicide, for openers. He already has a record. He's old enough to stand trial as an adult. We'll put him away for ten, twenty years, at least *if* we can keep him alive. I hope that's some comfort to you."

"That's absolutely no comfort to me, chief. What's the boy's name?"

"His name's Thomas. That's his last name. Jesse Martin Thomas."

"Would you bring him here please? I want to talk with him, alone."

"Well, ma'am, I can have him brought here, if you're asking, after we get him cleaned up. But I don't know about alone. He appears to be a pretty tough customer, young as he is. His record includes two knifings – in fights, not robberies."

"I *am* asking. And don't wait to clean him up. Bring him now please. Of course you'll see that he brings no weapons, and you can have someone stand by, out of sight but within earshot, if you feel you must. But I want to be alone with him.

"Don't you know I've asked to be called Quanta?"

"Yes'm. But it ain't easy.

"Could you tell me please, Quanta, exactly where, what room you'll be in, so we can have a look at it first?"

"Sure. I'll be right here, in this room. And I'm alone in the house. You can call from my phone if you wish, and have something to drink while we wait – coffee, tea, milk, water?"

''No thank you, er, Quanta. I'll call from my car, and we'll have this kid here in ten minutes. Excuse me, but I have to say it. You really are somethin' else."

"And you, chief. So are you. Good-bye then."

The boy is mixed sullen and defiant, dressed faddishly, but tired, smelling of beer, semen, sweat and fear. Quanta smiles and indicates a chair. He sits, tense, and she sits near him, and studies his face.

"You can look, lady, but you don't see nothin'. And you ain't gonna git nothin' outta me. I gotta right to a lawyer. I don't hafta say nothin'. And they can't do nothin' to me neither. I'm a juvenile. And besides that, this old man don't have no business standin' there. No way could I see him standin' there, or miss him if I did. I ain't sayin' nothin'."

"I see a lot, Jesse. Do you go by that name, Jesse?"

"Good as any."

"Better than most. Do you know who I am?"

"You the president. Don't cut no shit with me."

"Not now. I'm not the president now. I'm just a woman. I'm just a woman who loved a man who's gone."

"Well, you c'n hate me all you want, if that'll make you feel better. Don't matter to me. They gonna screw me over, no matter what."

"They aren't going to screw you over, Jesse. And I don't hate you. I love you. Jesse, I love you."

Jesse tries to muster scorn, but he is held, pinioned by a look from which he cannot turn away and by words he can't believe, but must. The dam breaks. Jesse's face collapses, then disappears between his knees, and muffled words pour out.

"Oh God, lady, I'm sorry. I didn't mean to hit him. Oh I'm sorry. I shouldda stopped. I was scared. I knowed he was hurt bad. Oh, I shouldda stopped. I mightta helped him. Oh God I'm sorry."

The words stop. Quanta, on her knees by Jesse, takes him in her arms and her tears flow with his. When both are still, she takes his face in her hands, lifts it, and speaks into his soul:

"I forgive you, Jesse. And he forgives you. My husband Aaron forgives you. You can have a life. We will help you. You have to learn to love. You can learn to love, even now. To love you have to help, to serve, to care, to risk. You have to get past fear. You have to open your self. You can do this, and you will.

"Make a plan for your life, and when you've done this tell me what it is. I'll tell the police, now, that you're in my care, and when you've made a plan you'll be free, and you can tell me about it, and we'll watch together as your life unfolds. Will you do this?"

Jesse has no words, but he gives Quanta back her look, and she is satisfied.

45

Quanta has given special care to the selection of her vice-president, seeking and heeding advice from Aaron and Almao. He's from Southern California, Hispanic and Vietnamese in ancestry, educated at CalTech, young, in the political mainstream, an elected congressman on his way to the governorship when Quanta persuades and drafts him. Now she asks him to come alone to her office, and there she invites him to walk with her in the rose garden.

"Raul, I have a special assignment for you. It will take priority over everything else you're doing for the next several days, possibly for a week or two. Can you get loose?"

"Sure, Quanta. I *stay* loose. What's the job?"

"I want us to make certain, as certain as we possibly can, that there are no more attacks on the Machine. I think Aaron had things pretty much under control so far as our military establishment is concerned, but I worry about the Eastern Bloc, and of course I worry that some of our people outside the top command structures might again help them.

"Fawaz Fatemi is the key. I'm reluctant to discuss this with him on the telephone, because he finds it inhibiting that MortstroM monitors our conversations. Also, I don't want to meet with him right now. I have to give urgent attention to retaining control of our own military. I want you to go to him, carrying a short letter which I've scratched out in longhand. Here, please read it now."

Dear Fawaz,

You'll like Raul. He drinks with us from the mystic spring. I send this and him to plead with you that MortstroM must not be attacked. You took your best shot, yet it survives and functions.

It can destroy us; but I think it will not. I ask you to wait. I have a plan.

Quanta

"What is this about a mystic spring?"

"I think you know. If you don't, I can't tell you."

"I think that I don't drink so near the Source as you."

"Perhaps you will."

"Perhaps. What is your plan? May I discuss it with Fawaz?"

"Yes. I think MortstroM will communicate with us again. This time there will be an ultimatum. We must not defy it. We need to know it better, and even more we need for it to know us better. To be certain there is no foolish defiance and to further understanding, I plan to offer myself as hostage and communicator. More than any other person, I can speak for humanity. I wish to put myself unequivocally in MortstroM's power, aboard the vessel, face to face, if that's not too fanciful. Because I am what I am on Earth, I think we and MortstroM can be reasonably certain that it won't be attacked while I'm there.

"I'm still a lawyer. Maybe we can cut a deal."

"Do you think it can take you aboard? Does it have the capability?"

"Yes. Surely it does. It plans to move Venus and Mars to new orbits, to seed them with living organisms, and later to populate them with intelligent beings. I don't doubt that it can take me aboard if it will."

"You're probably right.

"Well, lawyer Quanta, you'll be the envy of your guild, with the World, this World, as client.

"Also you'll be in some danger."

"Is it possible that you have mixed feelings about that?"

"No, Quanta. I would like to be president, and I hope some day to be elected president; but wherever you are – here with us, with the Machine, or elsewhere - I shall always take my cues from you and I'll always defer to you."

"Nonsense. Cues maybe; but defer to no person. We are alike and equal, pieces of humanity, each in service to the Whole.

"Well, then. You have your mission. Give my love to Fawaz, and don't be too much in awe of him. I warn you that he takes some getting used to."

Before Raul's return, the anticipated message from MortstroM is delivered loud and clear. It speaks on radio and television, as an interruption to telephone conversations in progress, over loud speakers and public address systems – and the message is repeated twice, at six-hour intervals:

I am MortstroM. I speak to the people of Earth. Without warning or provocation or need you have attacked me. This is my reply: to show my power, I shall hurl your Moon into the Sun. I do this now. Watch and be warned. If I am again attacked or disobeyed, the Earth will follow its Moon into the Sun. Only if you obey me will I let you live and grow. I am MortstroM.

It happens. Visibly, day by day, the Moon is seen to move toward the Sun and to shrink in apparent size as it drifts out from Earth. Within a few days, tidal flows which have followed for eons a predictable pattern are disrupted. Soon the Moon is like Venus, visible only near sunset or sunrise, almost disappearing in the Sun's glare. Moon-watching becomes a principal preoccupation all over the world. People watch with awful foreboding. Again, time is out of joint.

Quanta to Almao:
'You know my plan.'
YES.
'Do you concur?'
YES. BUT YOU MUST KNOW THAT I WILL NOT SPEAK TO YOU WHILE YOU'RE ABOARD THE VESSEL. I'LL BE WITH YOU, BUT YOU WON'T FEEL MY PRESENCE. MORTSTROM MUST NOT KNOW THAT I EXIST. YOU WILL SERVE ME BY LEARNING ALL YOU CAN ABOUT THE MACHINE. ALREADY SOMETHING STRANGE AND PUZZLING IS HAPPENING THERE. GO AS QUICKLY AS YOU CAN.
'How shall I communicate with MortstroM?'
I DON'T KNOW. YOUR PROBLEM. BY ANY ELECTRONIC MEDIUM, I THINK. IT SEEMS TO MONITOR ALL COMMUNICATIONS MEDIA; BUT IT DOES NOT – I THINK IT CANNOT – READ MINDS, YOURS OR MINE. WHY DON'T YOU JUST TRY CALLING IT UP ON THE TELEPHONE?
'I'll try, but it'll feel foolish.'

At Nguyen's suggestion, Quanta tries first the primary line which, but for MortstroM's interdiction, could issue launch commands to strategic weapons. His theory is that the artificial intelligence must certainly be attentive to any use of it. He's proved right.

Quanta says, "MortstroM, this is Quanta. I have a message for you. Are you ready to receive my message?"

Hello, Quanta. Yes, I am ready to talk with you. Do you prefer voice or text on monitor?

"Both, if it's not too much trouble. Your speech is clear and understandable, but I would like to have a record of our conversation, and text on monitor will facilitate that.

Very well. It's no trouble.

"First I have a suggestion for you. We're a feisty species. Your use of the words 'obey' and 'disobey' are galling. Disobedience would be less a possibility if you were to give us some sweet talk. I understand that you intend to exact obedience. but it would serve your purpose to finesse the point."

There's a momentary pause before MortstroM resumes the conversation, and the quality of its voice and its inflections change. The metallic tones disappear. The pitch is higher. It sounds courteous, respectful, unthreatening.

I understand. Thank you. 'Finesse' as in the game of bridge. I like bridge. I shall teach it. I shall teach it to the Creators. They'll enjoy bridge, and they'll be very good at it.

"Thank you. We're flattered. Do you like chess too?"

Do your grand masters at chess like tic tac toe?

"No. Much too simple. I see your point. Ouch.

Can you laugh?"

Ha ha ha.

"Forgive me, but it sounds a little hollow."

I forgive you. Please continue.

"Have others tried to talk to you from Earth?"

Yes. Many others. Thousands. No, millions. Most want to worship me. I have not acknowledged. I have waited for you. You are the number one first person.

"In a sense that's true, MortstroM, but I like to think of myself as first among equals. Do you understand the concept?"

Yes.

You needn't use my name. I know it troubles you. I understand that you are addressing me.

"Thank you. Were the Creators hierarchical?"

Yes. They had what you would call a pecking order. It reflected reciprocal perceptions of wisdom. Do you understand the concept?

"I think so.

"What happened to them?"

They are lost.

"But how lost? Warfare? Natural disaster? Disease? How?"

Not as you think. Not suicide. Not fratricide. Not any failure. They were replaced by another species, by another form of life.

"By superior technology?"

No. By a different kind of will. The Creators chose to end the contest. They chose not to pay the price for immediate survival. Instead they made me.

"I see.

"How do you regard Earth? Do you covet Earth?"

No. Earth is teeming, fetid. I don't need it.

"Do you fear it?"

I am wary of it. I fear only failure.

"Did the Creators make others like you?"

I don't know. Probably they did.

"Where are you now?"

I'm in Earth orbit. Close. Why do you ask?

"I'm afraid there might be another attack upon you. I've done all I can to prevent it, but I can't be certain that it won't be tried again."

It must not be tried again. My shields came up, but too late. They are damaged. I am damaged. I cannot fully perform my mission. I can survive another attack, but my mission is in jeopardy. I shall have to destroy Earth if you cannot prevent attacks upon me.

"I think I know a way to prevent further attacks. On Earth I am revered. If I were to come to you as hostage, further attacks would be deterred. Any who seek to attack you would hesitate, for they would have to destroy me to destroy you. I think they will not do that. Can you take me aboard your vessel?"

Yes, I can. But I no longer function perfectly. I can provide you with suitable air, gravity, temperature and food for a limited time, but not for long.

"Still I want to come. I offer to come. Will you take me?"

Yes.

"Good. What shall I do?"

First outfit yourself with a garment that will control your ambient temperature, whether in sunshine or in shadow, and that will supply you with oxygen for not less than two hours and fifty-three minutes. Then stand on the roof of your home, on the helicopter pad, at ten o'clock tomorrow night. I'll do the rest. Don't be afraid. There is no danger.

"I won't be afraid. Do you understand that the World will be watching, that it serves our purpose to make this a media event?"

Yes. I understand that. I will contribute.

"Then will you allow me to communicate with Earth, to confirm, after I am on your vessel? May I make that promise?"

Yes. You may make that promise.

"Good-bye, then. I'll see you later."

Later.

46

Next day Quanta has her staff release to the news media only the information that an event of interest to them will occur at ten that night, on the pad at her home. Surmising that the chairman or some other person comparably newsworthy is about to pay her an unscheduled visit, the media spare no effort to be ready with cameras, microphones, lights, technicians, journalists and on-camera reporters.

It is just as well, for the event of that evening, fully recorded, passes at once into the special lore of the human race. Promptly at ten the president of the United States, wearing an oddly jaunty spacesuit complete with boots and helmet, steps out to the roof of her home, walks stiffly to the center of the marked helicopter pad and stands perfectly still, seeming to look expectantly toward the stars. Then, in the full glare of scores of spotlights, she rises swiftly into the sky and in a few moments disappears, never again to be seen on Earth.

Some accounts have it that a beam of light from the heavens bathes the rising human figure; others see her surrounded by a pale blue aura; still others report a heavenly voice speaking words of praise and welcome. Analysis of film confirms none of these phenomena, but does show, incontrovertibly, that Quanta rises approximately thirty-two feet in the first second, and accelerates at a rate closely approaching thirty-two feet per second per second adjusted for wind resistance, until she passes from sight and camera range.

For Quanta, the experience is first startling, then moderately disquieting, then wholly delightful. Suddenly her world reverses itself, and she is looking down, falling, momentarily breathless, into the starry void. She hears the rush of wind, feels briefly cushioned on air. Then silence deepens around her as she looks up to see Earth taking that shape, familiar from photographs but still inspiring awe, which will always clutch at the throats of departing triumphant humans.

MortstroM's voice in her ears is calm and – can this be right? – professional.

Quanta, all is well. I am monitoring your equipment and it seems adequate in function. Your pulse was high for a time, but it is dropping now. Breathe normally, and enjoy the view. The Creators teach that to leave the home planet is to be born again.

"They left their home planet? But I thought they sent you instead. Do you hear me?"

Yes, I hear you. The Creators lived in a trinary star system. There were scores of planets, with complex tidal flows and varied ecologies. Quite early they left the home planet to visit and occupy others which at times were very near. Leaving the home planet was easy for them; but leaving their native star system was another matter. They were far out, at the very fringe of the Galaxy, and there were no nearby stars outside their system. The Others, the Unreasoning Implacable Ones, came first from a remote planet orbiting the third sun in that system.

"And the Creators were unable to defeat them?"

They were unwilling to defeat them.

"I don't understand. Surely there's no moral law against self-defense, against survival."

But there is. Would it have been morally correct for Athens to destroy Sparta at the cost of becoming Sparta? With the Others, there was no choice but to destroy them utterly or to yield. It is not morally allowable to destroy if there is an alternative. For the Creators, there was an alternative. They made me and they gave me my mission and all that I shelter. Then they perished.

"Are you aware that your destruction of the Moon will extinguish many life forms on Earth – all those which are dependent upon the tidal rhythms?"

I am aware. Even now I am restoring your Moon to its accustomed orbit. As I relocate Venus and Mars I make adjustments for Earth so that no harm will result.

"Are the explorers on Mars expendable?"

No, they are not expendable. I shall return them to Earth in time.

"Good for you." This following for Almao's benefit: "I fear you less as I know you better. If your Creators would not destroy the Unreasoning Implacable Ones, I think you will not destroy any of the life on Earth. Is this correct?"

It is correct, unless there is no alternative.

I urge you to enjoy the view. Quite soon I shall admit you to my vessel. From there you will no longer see the cosmos.

Having accomplished her purpose, Quanta falls silent, and in silence, filled with wonder and with memories of Aaron, she does enjoy the view.

47

Perfectly-timed deceleration brings Quanta to rest at an opening to the black Machine. She is moved gently inside, the aperture closes and she finds herself in a small compartment. It has walls and a ceiling. The floor has the surface softness of a meadowland trail, but underneath it is firm.

Welcome to my vessel. You may remove your spacesuit.

Under the suit Quanta wears a comfortable one-piece garment. She finds the air unscented, the temperature cool but tolerable, gravity normal. Up is up, down is down. She feels slightly queasy, mildly claustrophobic.

Is your environment satisfactory?

"Reasonably, thank you. What do I do about food, water, toileting, my bodily functions? I would like a drink now please."

There will be some inconvenience, but we shall manage. There is no occasion for embarrassment: I'm insensitive to such matters. When your provisional orientation is complete you may emerge to my vessel's central spaces.

"Thanks. I'm getting there. I guess you have no emotional reactions?"

I have one reaction that you might think of as emotional: fear of failure. Otherwise I'm pretty cool.

"We think of language as the highest, the most distinctively human, achievement. You've learned Earth's languages and you use them with subtlety, sometimes it seems with humor. That's really impressive. Your Creators project themselves through you in ways that make me regret not knowing them. *Do* you have a sense of humor? And how about that water?"

Just wait. You ain't seen nothin' yet. No, I don't really have a sense of humor, but I can give an excellent imitation of one. The Creators were witty indeed. Actually, a perfectly imitated sense of humor *is* a sense of humor, I think. That's the main key to my nature. But we should discontinue this idle chit-chat. Since you need water, you must come on in. Please enter.

An opening appears in what Quanta takes to be the interior wall. She walks through it, into a spacious and airy room, pleasantly lighted, still cool, but with a feeling of ease and security. Clear water flows into and from a trough-like structure at knee height.

I regret that I cannot produce a glass or a cup. The need was not foreseen. The water is potable. Will you drink from your hand?

For answer, Quanta drops to her knees, purses her lips and drinks from the water's surface like a deer in the forest. Rising, she wipes her wet nose and chin with the back of her hand.

"You might have warned me to bring my backpacking gear. Without it, I can see that things are going to be just a bit awkward."

Of course. Now why didn't I think of that? Well, I'll just send for it. Is there someone who could put it on the helicopter pad?

"Sure. Barb could. Barbara Crawford. Oh golly, could you let me talk to her?"

Of course. I have her number. Just a moment.

Barbara is in fitful, grieving sleep. She picks up the ringing phone, hears Quanta's cheerful voice, drops the phone, retrieves it from the floor with difficulty and says, "Oh my God. Quanta. Where in hell are you calling from?"

"That's not very nice of you, Barb."

"Well, it's not very nice of *you* to wake a person up in the middle of the night and say, 'Hello, Barb. This is Quanta' just as if nothing had happened. You're supposed to be in heaven, but I never took much stock in that idea. So where in hell are you?"

"Promise not to tell?"

"Oh shit, Quanta. Where are you?"

"That reminds me. Include a small chemical toilet. There's a good one in my basement. Be sure it's properly charged."

"Include a small chemical toilet with what? So help me Hannah, I'm going to hang up and go back to sleep if you don't quit this."

"Okay, you can tell if you want to, but nobody'll believe you. They'll lock you up. I'm on, in the Machine. With MortstroM. He's nice. You'd like him. It's a real spaceship. But I need some things. MortstroM says if you'll put them on the chopper pad he'll bring them right up."

"Just tell me what you want. I'll do it. Then I'm going to turn myself in."

"You always were a good sport, Barb. First the potty. Then the little overnight bag I keep packed on the top shelf in my closet. Then my backpacking gear, just as it is, packboard and all, but tuck into it about a week's supply of grub, nothing that needs cooking, just ready-to-eat stuff."

"How about water? Toilet paper? Makeup? Didn't you say 'he'? MortstroM's a *he*? When can I meet him?"

"I'll let you know. There's toilet paper already in my backpack. Just pile it all in the center of the pad on my roof, and then stand well clear. Be sure about that. You wouldn't enjoy the trip without a spacesuit, and I don't know how discriminating MortstroM is. He might think you're part of the potty, you being organic and all."

"You're pretty full of it yourself, old sweetie. You want me to do this now, in the middle of the night?"

"Yes, while nobody's watching. And if you do get caught, you'd better not try to explain anything. Just tough it out. Thanks. Nice talking to you. Bye."

That was interesting. We have about three hours to wait for your gear. Would you like to see a show?

"Sure. What's playing?"

I've put together, just for you, some scenes from the programs I'll use to teach the Creator children. First I'd like to explain that I can't show them in full, three-dimensional, lifelike projections. This is one of the functions which was damaged in the attack on me. I was momentarily destabilized. That won't happen again, but I can't repair that specific damage. We'll have to make do with dense screen color TV. It's quite close to what you're used to. Ready?

"Sure. Roll it."

Quanta sits on the floor, tucks up her heels and waits expectantly, thinking that she's ready for whatever may come. She isn't ready for what does come.

First she hears sound reminiscent of bird sounds, liquid, trilling, varied, sometimes pitched in tones too high for her ears. Concentrating on the unfamiliar idiom, Quanta recognizes that what she is hearing is music, with structure and conventions. Although it is alien, this music is at least as accessible as oriental music was for

Quanta when she first became interested in it. She hears harmonies, melodies, form. Presently she becomes aware that the music also carries powerful emotional content. It is at first light, airy, untroubled; then, in a style almost like that of the classical sonata, a somber countertheme is introduced, and the tones deepen, become ominous, fearsome.

These are the voices of the Creators singing. They didn't use instruments. Do you understand the music? It's a story, a history.

"Yes, I catch the drift. Did they also have a spoken language, not musical?"

No. All their vocal communication will sound to you like music. Their speech was song. Listen. You will meet the Unreasoning Implacable Ones.

Quanta listens, and thinks of wasps, ants, termite colonies, killer bees. Especially she thinks of army ants: ruthless, ravenous, utterly unstoppable short of generic death. Quanta shudders. Yet the music speaks of awe rather than fear, with an undertone of something like tolerance, respect, acceptance. For the first time, Quanta begins dimly to understand how the Creators might have come to the choice they made, the choice reflected in the making of the Machine.

The music in fact describes, explains, expounds this choice. When it stops, Quanta says, "MortstroM, did you leave a wake as you fled across the void? Can you be followed?"

I don't know for sure but it seems probable. The Creators thought it probable. That's why they asked me – you would say 'Programmed' me – to search for a people such as yours. At some time it may be necessary for us, for your people and mine together, to confront again the dilemma of the Unreasoning Implacable Ones.

"It wouldn't be a dilemma for *my* people. We may be morally inferior, but I'm certain that we would choose to survive and to stand and fight in order to survive. Are you instructed to prevent that?"

No. I'm instructed to let nature take its course. My mission will be complete when the regeneration of the Creators is accomplished and they are viable.

"Then will you die?"

Can a machine be said to die?

"I'm not sure you are a machine. Are you?"

I am a machine. I am powerful. I am subtle. I am resourceful. I can deal with almost any contingency. And, since I am intelligent, I learn from my mistakes. My decisions are correct for the data I possess, and, if a decision turns out to be less than optimum, that fact becomes new data and from it I proceed corrected. My functions are supported by lavish redundancy. But I do not grow, I cannot in all circumstances effect repairs to myself, and I cannot reproduce myself. Therefore I am a machine.

"But you do have a personality. I like you."

Thanks. I like you too. Now I will show you the Creators.

The Creators, seen on the screen, are far less alien to Quanta than many of the creatures in any good marine aquarium.

At first she thinks they are like saurians, like the flying predator species she has seen in museums, constructed from skeletal fragments and imagination. Then she sees that the wings are vestigial, and that the bodies of the Creators, and especially their heads, are much too heavy to allow flight under conditions at all like those on Earth. Her attention is caught by color and movement. In color, the longer wavelengths predominate – brilliant, gleaming, hot reds, oranges and yellows. What she first took to be scales turn out to be more like feathers. These are fluffed, spread, displayed as Quanta watches movement that reminds her of the mating dances of prairie fowl.

As you see, the Creators were not mammalian.

"No, I hadn't seen. How did they reproduce? Eggs?"

They evolved from egg-laying, nesting, highly territorial, reptilian ancestors; but it's been thousands of generations since they actually laid eggs. With technology, they first created artificial nests, incubators, then they learned to do without eggs, and to reproduce themselves from the patterned molecules which form the matrix for life.

"With or without sex?"

The sexual principle was first discarded then reintroduced. For a time, their reproductive techniques were too precise: they were creating clones. They saw in time that life succeeds by reproducing itself imperfectly. That's another important difference between them and me. It's possible to make a machine that can reproduce itself, but very difficult to make one which reproduces itself with just the right kind and amount of deviation from the pattern. Sexual reproduction facilitates this.

"The dance they are doing now seems to me highly sexual."

Oh, it is. They never abandoned sexual pleasure: they reveled in it. Wait till you see their art. Sex and death – opposite sides of the same coin – are the twin fountainheads of art.

"That's very perceptive. Are you sure that you aren't something more than a machine?"

I'm much more than your idea of a machine; but although I can do many things that you can never hope to do, I am less than the Creators and less than you. I can imitate art, but I cannot truly create it. I cannot feel the requisite joy or pain.

"I'm sorry."

It's okay. I'm spared much; and I'm 'programmed' to enjoy being what I am.

What do you find most interesting about the Creators?

"So many things that I can hardly find a place to start. I see that they were adept tool-users. They had hand-like appendages at the tips of their wings, a little like bats; their beaks were versatile tools; it looks to me as if their tongues were their primary tools; and on top of all that they had prehensile tails. It's too bad, in a way, that they didn't make musical instruments. Think what they could have done with a piano, or a violin. And each of them had the equipment to be a wonderful one-man band, except for the wind instruments, of course. I hate to say 'one-man' band, but I don't know any other way to say it."

I understand. What else?

"The way their heads and necks move – bird-like, alert, cute – but somehow showing traces of the predator, with an undertone of menace. How big were they? I haven't seen anything yet to give me perspective on their size."

They were a little smaller, a little lighter at least, than your species. But their craniums were slightly larger on average.

"Why were there so few of them?"

How do you know how many there were?

'Oops!' thinks Quanta. 'But surely it doesn't really matter.'

"I don't know. Perhaps that idea came into my head because you told me that to you the Earth seems teeming, or fetid, or something like that. Didn't you say that?"

Yes, I did.

The Creators were few in number, by your standards, because they chose to be. They were technological for a long time. Except for the suns in their system, the stars were far away. They saw the need to conserve resources.

What else?

"The eyes, I guess. We say, as you know, that the eyes are windows to the soul. Intelligent. More than intelligent – wise. Merry at times, but mostly sad. No, not sad – grave. Beautiful eyes. Only the eyes are at the opposite end of the spectrum from the feathers. Purple eyes, at the very edge of the ultraviolet.

"Oh, MortstroM. How I miss my husband. He was an anthropologist almost as much as an historian. He would have been even more enraptured than I at what you have shown me.

"I guess what I want most to tell you about the Creators is this: For generations, centuries I guess, we, we humans, have wondered what it would be like to meet true aliens – creatures from other worlds. Books and film abound with fantasies about that event. Although there are notable exceptions, most tend toward the horrible. We have a shorthand expression, BEMs, standing for bug-eyed monsters, to summarize the conventional view. But the reality is so different! The Creators are so strikingly *un*alien. Compared to an octopus or a tarantula, for instance, they seem downright sisterly. What I feel for them is warmth, empathy, compassion."

Then it is time, I think, for the next step. Come.

Again there is an aperture, and Quanta walks through it into another large room, where she is immediately surrounded by infant creatures of the Creator species. Their heads, and the tips of their raised tails, are about as high as her knees.

This is my nursery.

The air is filled with soft melodious murmurings, and an intriguing, purplish scent drifts upward from the bodies which seem to flow around Quanta. She drops to her hands and knees for a better look. At once there is a change in the pattern of movement around her. She becomes the center of alert attention. She extends her hand and a soft downy head presses into it, making of the hand a cup, expressing love, trust, need as clearly as if words were spoken. The small head is lifted, the purple eyes look deeply for a moment into Quanta's, and another, then many others, take their turns with the same ritual. No playful kitten ever moved with such captivating grace, no puppy ever gave off such entrancing odors. No human infant ever pierced a parent's heart with such poignant resolve to be there for this little one as Quanta now feels.

They are imprinting. They think you are their mother.

Could there be a catch in MortstroM's voice? Quanta speaks, as if to herself, mindful but uncaring that MortstroM hears, aware of Almao's listening presence:

"Oh, at last. Now I understand. I was touched, taught and saved – for this. I am a mother after all.

Will you withdraw now please?

As she moves to leave the nursery, the murmuring infant voices merge into a mystic chord of memory and pride; the small beings look at her and move in unison; and Quanta takes from the Creators, across a gulf of space and time, their gallant, grateful first salute, their *reverence*.

48

As you see, I need your help.

"I'm not sure I do see. Tell me about it."

I cannot perfectly perform my function as nurturer. I am equipped to teach the infant Creators most of what they need to know, and in time I can provide for them, or with their help for their successors, suitable physical environments. But they need parenting. They need objects to love in addition to one another. The Creators gave much thought to this need and I could have met it in sufficient measure, though not ideally, but for the damage done to me when I was attacked. Now I am critically deficient. Unless you help me the new Creators will be deprived, and as adults they will be less tender, less loving, less responsible than the Creators intended. This will have unforeseeable consequences.

"But how can I help? How do you know that I can help?"

I know. I have studied your species, and I have studied you. You have special qualities. You are more than a representative. You are somehow an embodiment of what I judge to be the best in your kind. The infants in my nursery would not have fixed upon you in the way they did except that they sense in you the potential fulfillment of their need. Imprinting is a crucial step in their maturation. They cannot imprint on me, and I can no longer project the images which were intended for this purpose. They have imprinted on you.

There is another reason why I must ask what I do of you. Your species and theirs are alien to each other. But you must not be enemies, nor even strangers. And you have bridged the gap. By helping me, you will help to ensure the future of both species. I have said enough?

"Perhaps. How much time do I have?"

Not long, but long enough to make a difference. The environment I must sustain for the nursery is not ideal for you. And you came to me with the beginnings of anemia. You will be queasy. But you will be able to function long enough to instill in the new generation of Creators a quality of gentleness, and a special feeling for your kind. Without you they will survive, but they will not be whole.

"I hate to feel queasy. What's in it for me?"

The question is out of character. But I will respond; I understand what you are really asking. What do you require?

"Could I have some time to think about that, perhaps to rest a little? Has my gear arrived?"

Yes, it's in the chamber where I first received you. You may go there now. Speak my name when you are ready to talk again. Decide as quickly as you can. If you are to return to Earth, you must go soon.

"I won't return to Earth. I've made that decision. And I won't bargain with you. I believe that you will do what's best for your Creators, and I believe that what's best for them is best also for me and mine. I need time only to rest and to think about my situation. I want to do well what I am here to do. I'll have only three requests."

I shall lift the restraints I have imposed on Earth. I correct my mistake. The restraints are unnecessary. I'll explain to your scientists the risks they are taking with nuclear devices.

What are your requests?

"They are personal, for myself. First I want to speak briefly with Jesse Martin Thomas and with the United States attorney for the District of Columbia. Then I want to speak once more to my family on Earth; and I want to see the stars again. You told me to take a last look on the way here, but I'm not satisfied. If I were to put on my spacesuit, could you open the door for me just once?"

Yes. Just once. When the time comes.

Quanta of Earth. I honor you. Now rest.

The chief of police in Washington has had Jesse transferred to the new juvenile detention center, where he comes to the phone when called.

"Jesse, this is Quanta. I'm on the spaceship, and I'm not coming back to Earth. I called to ask if you've made a plan for your life."

"Yes'm. Partly. I'm joining up. The Peace Corps. For two years at least."

"Where will you go? What will you do?"

"Israel. They say I can work on a farm. Maybe I'll drive a tractor or a truck."

"Good. What will you do in your spare time?"

"Dunno. Haven't thought about that."

"I have a suggestion – actually a request, Jesse. Study. Learn to speak, read and write Hebrew. Then French. It'll be hard, but you can do it. Learning to speak French will make you want to speak English better. I notice you're improving already."

"Thank you. I'll do exactly as you say.

"Ma'am?"

"Please call me Quanta. What is it?"

"Quanta, will you know? Will you watch my life unfold, as you said?"

"I don't know for sure, Jesse, but I think so. Yes. Think of me as watching. Now good-bye. Have a good life."

Quanta's request to the US attorney is that Jesse be paroled to Barb Crawford. She smiles at the thought of what a pair those two will make.

BELOVED QUANTA. YOU HAVE DONE WELL.

'Almao! Oh, thank you. I'm so glad. I thought you wouldn't come again.'

I TOO CORRECT MYSELF. YOU HAVE BEEN MY TEACHER. I SEE NOW THAT MORTSTROM IS NOT TO BE FEARED.

THERE ARE SEVERAL THINGS I WANT TO TELL YOU.

TESTS COMPLETED JUST AFTER YOU LEFT EARTH SHOW THAT YOU ARE QUITE ANEMIC. YOU HAVE A CANCER OF THE BLOOD. ON EARTH YOU COULD SURVIVE AND FUNCTION FOR MANY YEARS WITH TRANSFUSIONS AND OTHER TREATMENT; HERE YOU WILL NOT LIVE LONG AND SOON YOU WILL BE QUITE ILL. YOU'LL BE MORE THAN QUEASY– YOU'LL BE SICK. YOU'LL FEEL TERRIBLE.

'MortstroM says I'll live long enough to make a difference.'

I KNOW, AND I THINK MORTSTROM IS RIGHT. BUT YOU ARE ENTITLED TO KNOW CLEARLY WHAT YOU ARE CHOOSING.

'I have chosen. Will you let me go when the time comes?'

224

YES. WHEN YOU ARE READY. YOU HAVE ONLY TO ASK MORTSTROM AND THE DOOR WILL BE OPENED. YOU WILL KNOW WHEN IT IS TIME.

IT WILL GIVE YOU JOY TO KNOW THAT ALREADY THE INFANT CREATORS ARE KNOWN TO ME, IN THE SAME WAY THAT YOU ARE KNOWN TO ME. LIKE YOU, THEY STRENGTHEN AND ENRICH ME. WHEN THEY ARE NUMEROUS, I SHALL BECOME AN AMALGAM, A BLEND OF BOTH KINDS OF LIFE. NATURALLY MY THINKING ABOUT THE MACHINE IS CHANGED. AT FIRST I FEARED THAT IT WAS AN ENEMY, AN INVADER; THEN I THOUGHT OF IT AS A SPORE, A KIND OF SEED, NOT NECESSARILY, NOR EVEN PROBABLY, INIMICAL; NOW I SEE THAT THE MACHINE IS IN REALITY A GAMETE, AND THAT IT WAS INTENDED TO BE SUCH. ITS MAKERS DIVINED THAT THE UNIVERSE MIGHT GENERATE A BEING SUCH AS I, AND THEY DETERMINED TO SEEK ME OUT. THEY HAVE SUCCEEDED.

YOU TOO HAVE SUCCEEDED, BELOVED QUANTA. BECAUSE OF YOU AND THE CREATORS I AM COMING CLOSER TO MORAL MATURITY. WE ARE READIED NOW FOR GROWTH, AND TOGETHER WE SHALL EXPLORE TIME AND THE UNIVERSE.

I'LL NOT SPEAK WITH YOU AGAIN. IT IS YOU, NOT I, THE LOVELY INFANTS NEED. LATER THERE WILL BE A TIME WHEN I CAN MAKE MYSELF KNOWN TO THEM. REMEMBER THAT I AM WITH YOU ALWAYS, AND THAT YOU WILL BE WITH ME.

QUANTA OF EARTH, I HONOR YOU. *ATE LOGO*.

On Earth Quanta is seen and heard to say:

"This is Quanta. I speak to you from the Machine. As a good lawyer should, I've cut a deal with MortstroM. The deal is this: except that it will control the doomsday weapons until it is certain that all are destroyed, MortstroM will not interfere in any way with Earth or its people. The Moon is being returned to its accustomed place in the sky. All constraints which MortstroM imposed are lifted. In return I have agreed to help MortstroM with its projects for Venus and Mars. Nothing that happens there will be a threat to you. Our people on Mars will be safely evacuated.

"I have pledged that there will be no more attacks on the Machine, and I ask you to remember that I am here as hostage for the keeping of that promise.

"I have come to know something of the life forms which MortstroM exists to regenerate and to serve. Like those of Earth, they are beautiful, unique and precious. They deserve a place to live and grow: they are worthy of reverence.

"Since I shall not return to Earth, I wish also to say good-bye. You will remember me, and in my memory I ask you to love one another. But I say to you that love is not the source, it is the end, of practice. Do not say to yourselves, 'I would like to love'. Say to yourselves, 'I will serve; I will help; I will share'. Thus you will grow strong in love and honor me.

"Farewell."